THE GLASS GOD

THE GLASS TRILOGY
BOOK 1

FORREST BEZOTTE

For Grandpa David
The one who told me a long time ago it was time to lift my
'creative lid'

PART ONE

PROLOGUE

HEAVY RAIN BEAT the concrete and swept the glowing blood from the body and into the sewer grate. The yellow and blue beaming from the fluorescent neon sign above the alley illuminated the white hair of a tall young man. His hair matched the white of his high-collared jacket—the shoulders accented with chromed padding. His arm was outstretched, gun in hand, the barrel still smoking.

The man studied the corpse in disbelief. He hadn't shot just anybody. The twisted body on the ground was Chase, a member of an underground crime syndicate called the Jacks. Above ground, they were the pop band Paragon.

Chase's golden eyes were glassed over. His jaw drooped in a state of permanent shock and his silver hair was soaked in rain and blood. Around his neck was a strand of black and white pearls.

Someone would find him. Everyone, under and above ground, will learn he's dead, and his murderer will never hear the end of it. To him, it was a test to see if he had the willingness to kill. Not only that, it was a way to knock the most powerful gang in the City down a peg for the chance to rise above their level, then prop them back up himself, taking the credit with it. His father wouldn't have approved of the murder, but Daniel Kostov, known to most people only as Captain, wanted to get a taste of his newfound freedom, now that his father was dead.

So far, that freedom was gratifying.

He checked his surroundings. He was alone, but he knew it wouldn't be for long. The Jacks were nearly inseparable. Pursuing this powerful target required following Chase around for a while, but he managed to catch him alone, using the alleys and back roads to avoid crowds. The young man got a brief glimpse of Captain before the crime lord put a bullet between his eyes. Born into privilege in this great City with a reputation that was assumed to be eternal, Chase's legacy ended in a dead end alley.

After the deed, Captain expected to feel something, maybe at least a smidge of regret. Instead, nothing.

He wrestled the pearl necklace from Chase's neck and stuffed it in his pocket. He ascended a flight of stairs onto the roof of the building next to him and got halfway across it before he heard a scream followed by a long wheeze of grief. His walk careened into a sprint, stomping up puddles and feeling the soggy wind lash his face. He got far enough away from there, and merged into the tangled fabric of the glorious borough within the city that had forgotten its name —Glass.

The next couple months should be interesting, he thought with an insidious smirk.

RIPLEY

ONE YEAR After Chase's Murder...

THWACK.

If it wasn't for the fence between them, Trevor would have likely knocked his brother, Ripley, out. Ripley watched Trevor tussle with two shirtless men in the middle of a makeshift fighting ring surrounded by a crooked fence. A crowd of people pushed and cheered around Ripley.

Standing proud next to Ripley was the leader of the Amon Tribe, Amon himself. His fiery red wool jacket with a mandarin collar and a lapel pin resembling a golden hydra affixed to it made him stand out like a cherry moon in the early morning sky. His grass-green hair was slicked back and doused in stilling gel. Resting between his teeth was a cigarette.

In the ring, Trevor recovered from his blow against the fence. Before his opponents could corner him there, he delivered his fist into the face of one of the attackers as he advanced towards him. A tooth or two snapped loose and the shirtless man struck the ground. Trevor shot his other arm out at the second man and the opponent's nose ruptured upon impact. He gripped it and wailed in pain.

Trevor was a large man, chocolate eyeshadow complementing the dark skin he shared with Ripley, whose own skin was marred by the narrow scar over the bridge of his nose. Ripley had on a deep charcoal suit jacket with a white dress shirt underneath. Pierced in his earlobe was an aquamarine stud earring.

Ripley often fidgeted with his earring, having never gotten used to it being there.

"So," Amon said, blowing a smoke train into the musty air. "Let Amon get this straight. Your Captain wants to make deals with Amon without being here himself?"

Ripley nodded, the flesh behind his ears perspiring. "Captain is a busy man."

The man with the bleeding nose managed to strike Trevor's gut, but it wasn't enough to faze him. Trevor snatched the man's arm and twisted it until bone splintered, forcing the opponent onto his knees. Trevor used his free arm to get several blows in to the man's face, then let go and watched him crumple to the floor in agony.

Amon gripped the fence and snickered. "He's no *Chi No Akuma* in strength, but Amon thinks he'd make a better leader than your Captain."

I don't even want *to ask what that is.*

"Captain *will* negotiate with you. He's just trying to be careful for now. Whatever terms are on your mind, we'll tell him," Ripley said.

Amon wagged his finger at Ripley. "Amon doesn't negotiate with faceless men. Men of *honor* negotiate with Amon face-to-face."

"There's nothing I can take back to him from you?" Ripley asked.

Amon grinned and Ripley regretted the question. He braced himself for whatever was coming next.

"You can go back to Captain and tell him he's a *pussy* for sending his lackeys instead of coming himself, like an honorable man." Amon dropped his cigarette on the ground and stomped on it. "You can quote Amon."

About as bad as I expected.

"I—will do that," Ripley replied.

"You better," the syndicate leader said. He spat on the floor and disappeared into the crowd. Defeated, Ripley joined Trevor at the gate's doorway.

"*Malas noticias?*" Trevor asked in Spanish between heavy breaths. He shoved his shirt back on.

"*Más o menos,*" Ripley replied in the same language. "I don't think Captain and Amon are going to be friends."

3
CAPTAIN

CAPTAIN'S EYES flew open from the same restless dream he'd experienced more times than he could count, as vivid as a memory.

He turned under the covers and noticed his wife, Joan, was missing, with the covers on her side whisked over. The scent of cooking eggs was in the bedroom.

Oh, I better get up.

Today was supposed to be a good day. At least, that's what he mandated for himself after a screaming match the night before with one of his father's old friends and colleagues, Simon. His father, Lazarus, was gone, but not some of his friends, who were responsible for sustaining the family fortune. Captain didn't have full control over the fortune yet, and after a year he was beginning to think the council his father put together wasn't ever going to relinquish it. Simon was the primary handler of the Kostov bank account, and Captain was ready to take that responsibility from him.

Captain's white-dyed hair dangled over his eyes when he sat up. Today, he was expecting to meet a few new potential recruits for his gang, now little more than a seed of what his father's empire once was. Most people didn't stay after he died, as if there was no successor. Just some older men who wanted to cling to the wealth left behind. Finding new people to build Captain's own empire was a necessity. He didn't want to work with his father's people. He wanted his own.

Something caught his eye and he jumped when he saw his best friend, Damien standing at the door. In his hand, he held a tablet.

"Can I help you?!" Captain asked.

Out of all of Captain's associates, Damien was the biggest showoff, with boots that glowed blue and golden lights weaved into the seams of his leather jacket.

"Buddy, you know what time it is?" Damien asked.

Captain's chest did a flip and he retrieved his phone. It was just after nine in the morning, and he had multiple missed messages and calls—all from Trevor, Damien, and Carmilla.

Damien continued, "Ripley and Trevor talked to Amon last night."

"And?"

"You're a pussy."

"Excuse me?"

Damien, with a toothy grin, put up his hands. "Amon's words, not mine."

"Care to elaborate?" Captain asked slowly, unable to hide his irritation.

"The Amon Tribe won't negotiate unless they get to see you face-to-face."

A lump formed in Captain's throat. "Trevor and Ripley couldn't do *anything* to convince them?"

"Apparently, there was no getting through to Amon. He's made of tough stuff."

"I'll figure something out. Have Trevor and Ripley come back."

"Can do. And finally, Carmilla found your hopefuls. Two guys: one named Benji, the other named Sparks."

"What do we know about them?" Captain eased back against his pillow stack.

"Benji is from Central. He applied for the military but was not accepted. As for Sparks...there's almost nothing, actually."

"I'm in love already. You'll be responsible for leading them to my office," Captain said.

"You got it, boss," Damien replied.

"Great, now *leave*," Captain ordered with a smile.

Damien winked and left. Once he was up, Captain brushed his hand through the lineup of suits in the bedroom closet before finally settling on one he liked. His white jacket, one of the few gifts left by his mother. Next, he browsed his lineup of pistols and found one to hold on to throughout the day. An RE-47, a silver double-action revolver; a gift from Damien.

Captain found Joan in the kitchen, which was enveloped by tiny robots spraying and disinfecting the counters and the stove. Captain noticed two eggs broken on the floor with shells littered in all directions, which the robots got to almost as quickly as he saw it. The robots then scattered, hiding back where they belonged until they'd be called again. On the sleek, white counter that separated Captain and Joan from each other, Captain's breakfast waited for him: a combination of eggs and several strips of bacon. Captain stared back up at Joan, smitten by her yet again.

She was pale, as if most of the blood had drained from her body, and she wore a dark pink suit, with her curly hair matching it. Thin scars fractured her otherwise delicate hands.

Captain's attention returned to his breakfast. "Hmm," he ruminated.

Joan groaned. "No, Daniel, don't do this to me again."

Captain raised a halting finger. "Just one minute, hold on...ah!"

He had found what he was looking for. A single, insignificant piece of eggshell wedged between the scrambled eggs. As if he was trying to diffuse a bomb, Captain pinched the shard between his thumb and index finger, removed it, then flicked it away. Neither of them saw where it landed.

"You ass!" Joan cried between laughs, smacking Captain's arm.

"*Now* it's perfect," Captain said with a grand gesture.

"Some day I'll make the perfect egg," Joan claimed.

To Captain's surprise, Joan stuck a small candle in the middle of the eggs, wiggling it around to seep it in. Then, she lit it.

"Anyway...happy birthday," she said.

Captain shrugged. "Why did I tell you my birthday again? It's not like I'm ever going to die."

"Sorry. Old habit," Joan replied with her own shrug.

"Well, it's not a *bad* one," Captain said. He blew the candle out, leaned forward, and his and Joan's lips met, staying locked together until Captain's stomach protested being shoved up against the side of the counter.

A drone hovered over to them and poured coffee into a waiting mug before retreating.

"That's for you. I still can't drink that crap," Joan said,

sliding the mug over to Captain. With a wink, he took it and started crossing the room.

"I heard about how negotiations went with Amon last night," Joan said as she made her own plate.

Captain sipped his coffee. "Great stuff, right?"

"You're not gonna like this..." Joan started.

Captain stopped walking. "Out with it."

"But Amon isn't completely wrong," Joan walked around the counter with her own plate and sat at the dining table.

"You don't think I'm a pussy too, do you?" Captain asked. There was a flutter of anger at remembering Amon's insult. Insults weren't easy for him to scrape off.

"Of *course* not, love," Joan said with a wicked grin before biting into bacon. "I agree that you need to show your face if you want to make deals with people like him, and that goes for the other syndicates too."

Captain sipped from his coffee again. "I guess I just wasn't ready for that kind of intimacy. My father was a good negotiator, and respected. I'm just the poor guy that got left behind while some old people are the ones managing *my* fortune."

"You're not going to get very far if you don't embrace the fact that you're more than that, love," Joan said.

The compliment made Captain's cheeks burn, but his face stayed neutral. "Hmm," he grunted. "V, open the windows," he commanded his service AI.

"As you wish, Daniel," V chimed over a speaker in the ceiling.

In the back of the room that served as both the kitchen and the living room, there was a glass wall, tinted almost black top to bottom, blurring the City outside.

The shade over the wall dissipated and the neon lighting in the living room retreated as well, putting the City in focus. Captain and Joan were so high up in the penthouse it was nearly impossible to see the streets below. If Captain had the window partly opened, he'd be able to hear all the noise outside. Glass had an eternal union of sounds that everyone in the City was numb to. Inside, however, Captain's windows were noise-proof. It was one of Joan's first requests when she moved in, and Captain was getting used to it.

The City itself was a marvel to see. A successful and exuberant evolution of humanity itself that Captain was privileged enough to be a part of. Some of the buildings were made completely of glass walls, exposing all the people, rooms, business, and parties. Crisscrossing through the City, connecting a majority of the buildings, were long bridges and walkways, causing the City to appear as a convoluted maze. Some of the bridges allowed cars to ascend to higher levels of the City where most residential areas could be found.

Captain slowly sipped from his mug, shutting his eyes and reminiscing over the coffee's warmth and bitterness. He opened his eyes and watched the City sway and vibrate. He was in love again. He wasn't sure anyone loved Glass as much as he did. Most people simply loved Glass for the pleasures, but Captain loved it for the freedom it promised him. With his father gone, nothing stood between him and that freedom now.

The City called to him every day. All he had to do was look outside to see why. There was nothing outside of Glass worth seeing nor pursuing. He would build his empire and his eternity here.

"I should get started reaching out to all of them then.

The Delanos, the Garks...the Jacks. Even the Purpletells," Captain said.

Joan joined her husband at the window. "Just figure out what they'd want, and make sure you can give it to them."

Captain nodded. "That's what I'm afraid of. I don't know what they'll want."

And what if I can't give it to them?

4

CAPTAIN

"HEY, did Damien tell you Amon called you a pussy?" Trevor asked.

"No, Trevor, he didn't! Thanks for telling me!" Captain shot back.

"Oh good, he did, just wanted to make sure," Trevor smirked.

One of Captain's first acts after his father died was breathe life into his old office. Neon blue lights were installed in the ceiling, wrapping the room in a luminous coat. A device in the ground made the floor look like a bobbing ocean floor, giving the illusion that anyone who walked on the floor was walking on water.

It was over the top, and everything that Captain wanted for the room where he felt his best, despite its past. Sitting behind his curved cream desk, with Joan perched cross-legged on the end, Captain felt at the top of his game, ready to take on anything and anyone. He exhaled a smoke ring, a large cigar positioned between his fingers. To his right, Trevor and Ripley sat on couches that formed an L, and a

TV screen fixed to the wall played soft music sung by a nameless woman.

The door slid open and a young man no older than twenty-five with his hands clasped behind his back stepped in with Damien trailing behind. In his right eye was an implant that glowed crimson. Once he reached the desk, he straightened his shoulders. Damien stayed a few paces behind.

"Apologies for my tardiness. My mom has been sick," he said.

Captain stared up at the man, but didn't say anything at first. He liked to keep newcomers on their toes.

This one was just vexing him. He was acting too calm for someone who was late, even if he did apologize.

Captain picked up his stylus and made a mark on the tablet in front of him.

"Excuses earn you a point," he said.

"Again, my apologies," the man replied, still no regret or remorse visible.

Captain frowned, but continued. "Benji, right?"

"Yes, sir."

"And what kind of an excuse for parents gave you *that* name?"

Captain didn't much care about the name, he just wanted to see how far Benji could be pushed.

"Ones who were mostly absent, sir. I go see my mother at her bedside regardless."

"Oh yeah? What's wrong with mommy?"

"Cancer, sir."

"It's 'Captain'."

"Cancer, Captain."

Captain sat back, chewing his bottom lip with his cigar alone in his hand. Benji's approach felt forced, and Captain needed him to drop the reserved facade and start showing his true colors. Insincerity irritated him.

"Benji, I'm starting to think you're trying to piss me off," Captain said.

"Captain?" Benji's face was unchanged besides the hint of a frown.

"No one gets cancer unless...did your mother ever take Bathory?"

"No, Captain. She refused to take it. She always wanted to live a life with an ending."

"And you still give her the time of day." Captain set his tablet down and leaned forward with both hands on his desk. "So why should I take you in, Benji?"

"I believe being within this underground framework will give me the tools I need to live a good life."

"You're joking. You think this is the only thing you could possibly do to have a good life?"

Benji hesitated this time, which Captain appreciated.

"Correct," Benji replied.

"Literally nothing else?"

"Yes."

So formal with his words. Gross.

"No other job? Not even the strip club down the street? Sure, you're not that good looking, but you can at least wield a mop when they close up shop."

Benji's steel wall still worked, in spite of Captain's best efforts.

"I don't want a regular job. These nine-to-fives are not exactly what I have in mind for my life."

"You and I both. Have you ever been with another syndicate before? Don't lie to me now."

Captain wasn't as tense as before, but he wasn't done. Benji's eyes turned distant.

"My older brother Jade took me out at night from time to time to shadow him at one of his...meetups," he said.

"Did any of those...*meetups*...ever get messy?"

"It did once, yes."

"So you've had experience trading punches with another gang then. Which gang was this?"

"The Amon Tribe."

Captain stiffened, as if a lightning bolt tore through him. He even noticed Damien's face change, as surprised as him.

Could I...actually use *this?*

Captain forced himself to settle down, adjusting himself in his seat. "Well, those guys are pussies." That got a laugh from his associates. "Did you have a weapon on you?"

"A knife Jade gave me."

"Did you kill anyone with it?"

"Yes."

"How many? Do you remember?" Captain drew from his cigar.

"I think it was twelve."

So this guy has Amon blood on his hands. Excellent, excellent...

Captain popped the cigar out of his mouth. "Wonderful," he said, spilling smoke over his desk. "That means there's hope for you yet."

Benji kept his chest puffed up and his arms behind his back, but he was opening up gradually like curtains on a stage. Soon Captain would see the play.

"So what happened?" He asked.

Benji cleared his throat, his eyes ping-ponging everywhere. "Jade failed to secure something of importance to the Tribe and got into an argument with them. It led to violence."

"Most of these things do, I hope you know that."

"I do."

"What happened to Jade?"

"He...passed," Benji said without a change in tone.

"Hm, my condolences then," Captain said dismissively. "Was that when you lost your eye?" Captain gestured towards his own eye.

"Yes, but not during the fight. The police got to the scene just as I made it out and fired a few shots at me and I turned just as one of their bullets ricocheted off the concrete wall. The debris caught my eye."

That's some damn accurate debris, but nothing about him says he's lying.

Captain pulled out the RE-47 from his holster, set it on the table, and gently pushed it towards Benji.

"Are you familiar with shooting something like this?"

He noticed Trevor and Ripley sit up straight, silently questioning Captain's motives. Even Damien was puzzled.

"Captain?" He asked.

Captain raised his hand to silence him.

Benji eyed the gun like it was a viper behind bars.

Captain put his hand down. "It won't bite. I mean, unless you do something stupid and point it at yourself. If you can't do this, we can't have you. You want to be part of our happy, little family?"

"Yes, Captain."

"Good. Then pick it up."

Benji picked up the gun, quicker than Captain was comfortable with, but he stayed silent. Benji turned the gun over in his hand as if he had never seen one before.

"Quit eyeballing it and show off your aim. Point it at me..."

Captain stuck his thumb in his chest.

"...Then Trevor there, and then Ripley there."

He pointed at them both without looking at them. With a deep breath, Benji aimed the gun at Captain, held it for several seconds, then did the same with Trevor and Ripley.

"You're not afraid I'll shoot any of you?" He asked.

Captain cracked a smug grin and shrugged, "Should we be?"

"You don't know me."

"I *do* know you, you're stupid. You think I'd give you a loaded gun?"

Benji pointed the gun away from the gang and aimed it at the TV instead. Without hesitation, he fired three rounds. The bullets fractured the screen, and sparks popped. Benji pulled the trigger a fourth time but it clicked.

Trevor and Ripley were on their feet, and Damien had a gun in hand, the barrel lined up perfectly with the back of Benji's head.

Captain gave him a disapproving hand. "Put it away, Damien. You won't need it." He continued with Benji. "I like you, man. You've got passion, obvious drive, you weren't afraid of coming in here when you were late, you know whether or not a gun is loaded, and managing to kill at least twelve of Amon's men on your own? Well..." Captain inhaled from his cigar and blew a smoke train with a satisfied sigh, his eyes giddy. "I think we're going to be good friends."

"Thank you, sir. This means the world to me, seriously," Benji replied. He didn't smile, but Captain could tell he was relieved by the way his shoulders rested.

"What did I say? Call me 'Captain,'" Captain replied, not unfriendly.

"Yes, sorry, Captain."

"Go see if the next guy is here," Captain said to Damien, who nodded and left the office.

Now that I have something the Amon Tribe wants, negotiating a relationship with them just got a lot easier.

The door slid open again. Standing there was a dark-haired, scrawny man with green, bright eyes. Behind him was Damien, carrying a duffel bag that looked like it was dragging him down.

Maybe I can be friends with this one. Let's really have some fun.

"OH, good, you brought your own bodybag. I was afraid I'd have to use one of mine," Captain said.

Damien plopped the bag down on the desk beside Joan, and Captain unzipped it to peer inside. A tense silence captured the room as everyone waited to know what was inside. Out of the corner of his eye, Captain noticed Joan leaned in to look.

The bag was full of different kinds of guns. Glocks, semi-automatic rifles, and even a sniper rifle. Tucked in one side were boxes of attachments and ammo.

Captain loved the gesture, but he didn't want to make that clear. He wanted to keep the stranger on his toes and see what happens.

"What the hell is this?" Captain asked.

"He insists they're a gift," Damien replied.

"Let's hear it from the statue here." Captain refocused on the stranger. "Is that right?"

"Yeah," the stranger replied in a deep, raspy voice.

Light the match.

"Well, now I just have the urge to kill you," Captain said.

The stranger's face didn't change. "That's not going to happen," he replied.

Okay...the match is out.

Everyone except Captain turned taut. Trevor and Ripley moved to side with Damien, just in case.

Captain leaned forward, still managing to hang on to his cigar.

"Are...are you telling me what I can and can't do?"

"I think he is," Damien said.

"No. Just that killing me isn't an option," the stranger said with spite.

Captain eyed the bag again, as if there were explosives primed to go off inside.

"You've got balls, but no respect. Take Benji here," Captain gestured to Benji, who had moved beside him, "*He* knows respect. Do you know respect, Benji?"

Benji cleared his throat. "Um, yes, I know respect."

"See?"

The stranger's eyes dwindled to slits and appeared ready to fire off an insult of his own. His next words came slowly, as if meditating on each of them first.

"Respect is earned. You respect me, I'll respect you."

The only sound in the room was the fake water rolling across the floor. Captain remembered what Amon called him. He latched on to the stranger's words. His chair screeched across the floor. He catapulted himself off of it with his hand out and grabbed the back of the stranger's head. Before the man could react, Captain smashed his face down on the desk. When he lifted it, there was a deep gash on the side of the stranger's nose. It pleased him to see. He wanted to see this man hurt.

Nothing is going to change until I make it clear to people that it has to.

"You're right! Respect *is* earned, but it's not like *you* earned it! Take a good look at my people here. They all earned respect and have a place with me. Would you like to know how?" Captain hauled the stranger's face closer to his, wanting the man to say something else, but he didn't.

"Really, *now* you have nothing?" Captain lowered his voice. "Smart. The magic answer is, 'they weren't an asshole to me'."

Captain shoved him away, and the sad, lanky man crumbled to the floor.

"Damn waste of my time. *Get out*," Captain bellowed.

The stranger picked himself up off the floor and started reaching for the duffel bag.

"Hate the man, love what he provides."

Captain remembered hearing those words from his father once. Though he didn't want to apply most of his father's influence to his work, this was a rare exception.

Keeping the guns would *be nice.*

"Uh uh, what are you doing? I'm keeping the guns. They were a gift to me, right?" Captain said.

The stranger didn't argue. He just stared at Captain with his bright eyes.

Who is this guy? He had one bold thing to say and now nothing?

"Sorry. I shouldn't have said what I said," the stranger muttered, dusting off his clothes. "But you'd be making a mistake turning me away."

Captain's mouth twitched. "Yeah no, I don't think so. And clean your face off after you go, you're a mess."

The stranger went for the door, holding on to his still

bleeding nose, then stopped. "In case you change your mind, you know my name."

Sparks. I don't think I'll forget that.

Captain didn't watch Sparks go. He was tuned in to what was going on his mind, biting his lip as he thought and thought. An idea blossomed in his head.

I'm not letting him go. What if he goes to another gang and they take him in? He can compromise my ability to turn those people into my friends. He can say whatever he wants about me and everyone he talks to can believe him. He has to be mine.

Trevor cursed at the door in Spanish just as the door slid shut.

"I'm sorry, Captain," Damien said. "I didn't know about the bag until—."

Captain cut him off. "We'll see him again."

6
RIPLEY

RIPLEY DIDN'T CUSS at Sparks when he left like his brother did, but he wanted to. The stranger, Sparks, made him feel like a dirty film was stuck to him all over.

When Benji came in, the most infuriating part about him was how unreadable he was, even if his intentions were pure. With Sparks, there was a wild light in his eyes that made him uneasy.

Another thing that stuck out to Ripley was that Sparks's blood didn't glow.

So he doesn't take Bathory. Interesting.

He looked older than Captain and his crew, and his blood explained why. Taking Bathory every day made people's blood glow. A side effect the manufacturers assured was just the Bathory 'at work', and posed no health risks.

"We'll see him again," Captain said.

Ripley frowned, as he and his brother exchanged glances.

"Are you sure?" Trevor asked.

"We'll talk about it." Captain turned to Benji. "Why

don't you go get settled in your room? We'll celebrate your baptism into our little family later."

"Family?" Benji asked with an eyebrow raised.

"Yep, we're family," Captain said. "Joan will take you to your room now."

"Oh, really?" Joan asked with a teasing grin. "Is there something *I* can't hear either? No secrets, remember?"

"No secrets, but I promise I'll tell you everything before the end of the day," Captain said.

Ripley didn't have to ask Captain what his ulterior motives with Benji were. When Benji admitted that he had killed men from the Amon Tribe, Captain's acceptance of him wasn't because of who he was, but what he had done. Captain could use it in his negotiations with Amon. No matter how good it must have felt for Benji to be one of them, he was part of Captain's game.

Damien spoke up first after Joan and Benji left.

"I've seen that guy before," Damien said.

Ripley's throat caught.

"Where? *When?* Details, man!" Captain urged.

"*The Raise.* I think he's a dishwasher there."

"We can use this," Captain said.

"Yeah, I meant to ask you about the part when you said we'd see him again," Damien replied.

Captain steepled his fingers and a grin expanded across his face.

"We find out everything he has, and we take it all away. Then I let him into our family and everything he gets then will come from me, so he'll have no choice but to serve me. He'll learn who's in charge of this city. And then I'll kick him to the curb once the time is right."

Is Sparks really worth that much? Is Captain really that desperate to make a point?

Trevor tried debating with Captain. "I know it hasn't been easy to connect with the other gangs, but bullying *escoria* like him when he's not a threat to you feels..."

"What, Trevor? What does it feel like?" Captain asked, though not impatiently.

"...It feels...unproductive, Captain."

Captain didn't answer right away.

"With all due respect," Trevor said hurriedly.

"Being called a pussy by Amon is one thing. But that man," Captain pointed at the door, "is a nobody. No one will care what I do with him, so what's the risk?" Captain asked.

Trevor didn't have a counterargument, but Ripley knew he was full of them. He just knew when to shut his mouth around Captain. Ripley kept his mouth shut all the time. It made life with Captain easier.

Captain got up from his desk, holding his phone. "I think I have a plan to get started. Damien, you're the first step..."

His voice trailed off when something on his phone caught his eye. He continued staring down at his phone, his shock morphing into quiet outrage.

"What?" He muttered.

"What is it?" Damien asked.

Captain's eyes widened like cave mouths. The corners of his lips twitched.

"I just got robbed by my dad's friends."

7

BENJI

THE DOOR to Benji's new bedroom slid open and Benji was hypnotized for a moment. There was a king-sized bed, a door that led into a private bathroom with a jacuzzi, and a glass wall with a view of the City.

He set the suitcase by the bed and peered out at the City sprawled out ahead of him: a collection of buildings, bridges, and towers. There were also holograms advertising goods and services. Beyond that was Central, a city that still had enough to boast, but no towers and no pretty colors. After that was the Labyrinth that eventually led to the Web, a dark splotch where the lights were out and the suffering of the people went unnoticed.

"Pretty sweet, huh?"

The young, pink-haired woman, Joan, was leaning against the doorway. In her hands was a stack of blankets and towels. She was beautiful, he couldn't deny that. The ring on her finger, however, sent the message she was taken.

"'Elegant' is more or less the term I would use," Benji said, clasping his hands behind him.

Joan smirked. "Sure, why not? I'm not one for using big words."

"Ah."

Joan invited herself in and placed the blankets and towels on the edge of the bed. "Captain figured you could use these."

Benji cleared his throat. "I'm Benji."

"I know," Joan chuckled. "I was in Captain's office when you told him."

"Ah, yes. I take it you know Captain's real name?"

"I should hope so! I'm his wife."

"I...figured that. I wasn't sure if he shared his real name with anybody."

"Only with the people he trusts most. AKA me."

No secrets, Benji remembered.

Joan narrowed her eyes. "But now it's *my* turn to ask questions. What's with your eyes? They're flying around everywhere except looking at me."

"They are?"

"Yeah, it's like they can't do eye contact, like, at all."

Oh. She noticed.

"I've never noticed."

"It's not a problem, it's just funny," Joan said, chuckling. "You said you came from Central, right?"

"Yes."

"Okay, at ease soldier! You're not in the military."

Benji dropped his arms, eased his shoulders, and took a deep breath.

"Sorry. That was kind of an asshole thing to say. I heard they turned you away," Joan said.

Benji nodded. "They deemed me not...mentally fit enough." It felt good to tell the truth about something. "They took issue with my inability to understand certain processes correctly, but my initial enlistment granted me the ID needed to enter Glass."

Getting that ID was the single greatest moment of Benji's life. Both he and his brother became desperate to leave Central, a modest but depressing box of housing, restaurants, grocery stores, clubs, and bars. It was also tense just beneath its bland surface.

If family budgets began to deplete with no sign of getting back on track, police knocked on people's doors and escorted them to the Labyrinth to be left wondering what to do next. The measure was decided after an organized protest full of people with diminishing savings turned violent at the border. Dozens of citizens trying to force their way into Glass were killed by Glass police and dozens more were rounded up and arrested.

"What assholes," Joan said, snapping Benji back to alertness.

Benji's failure to make it in the military wasn't really a subject he wanted to dwell on.

"You came from the Web, didn't you?" Benji asked.

Joan flinched but kept her smile. "Dang, do I make it *that* obvious?"

"I've met others with those kinds of marks on their hands. They all came from either the Web or the Labyrinth."

Joan rubbed her hands together and her face fell.

Jade warned you about prying into people's private business. Stop it, Benji.

"I apologize if I'm prying," Benji squeaked.

"It's whatever," Joan replied with a dismissive wave, then looked up, a brash grin lighting her face. "Want to see something cool?"

Benji allowed the smallest of smiles. "Sure."

"V, darken the room and turn on the screen," Joan commanded to an unseen presence.

"As you wish, Joan Kostov," an electronic voice said from the ceiling.

Benji glanced around, trying to find the source, but saw nothing. The glass wall darkened, cloaking the City, and the wall opposite to the bed brightened.

"Play 'Glass'," Joan ordered, and the screen started playing a montage of images all about Glass. It was slow and reflective, with victorious music swelling in the background. Above the music was a woman's voice.

"Glass. The place that always has been and always will be. In Glass is life, and in life is our transcendence to greatness."

The images transitioned from wide views of the City's skyscraper to the City streets, highlighting the people that went about their daily business. The many clubs, restaurants, hotels, and shops that served as the lifeblood of the City's economy were brought to life. Not one person in the picture looked like they were down on their luck.

Benji sat on the edge of the bed, fascinated by the wall screen. Though the montage only consisted of pictures, the colors swirled and danced like purple fire.

It's beautiful.

Though Benji had been in the City for a while already, he was only just now believing he was there. Though he didn't show it, he was happy.

This...this is where my life can really start. Jade would be happy. Just as long as Captain never finds out I lied to him...

"Yeah, I know. I thought it was a lot at first too," Joan said, a smile in her voice. Benji didn't look away from the screen when Joan's phone buzzed.

"It's Captain," Joan said. "We're supposed to meet up with him. I hope you can shoot people as well as you shot that TV."

SIMON

"APPOINTMENT OR WALK-IN, DARLING?"

Simon, the handler of the Kostov fortune, cleared his throat and answered the woman in black lingerie. "Walk-in."

Simon kept scanning the club, hoping that no one he knew was there. It wasn't a place he wanted others to know he went, and not just because of what he came for. The last time he had had a conversation with Captain, it didn't go well, and it wouldn't be long before Captain discovered that something was off about the family bank account, if he hadn't discovered it already.

When Simon first knew Captain's father, Lazarus, the two of them were only teenagers. They witnessed the construction of Glass' towers, both smitten *and* disturbed. Every time they thought the towers wouldn't rise any higher, they did, until they began to block out the sun's light. They laid the groundwork for Lazarus's criminal empire, built upon the business of selling drugs, weapons, and Lazarus's own breakthrough tech, SpeakWare, a chip that gave people without a voice a way to speak again. Their unending and uncompromised friendship formed significant trust between each other. Simon became Lazarus's most valuable advisor and eventually even his money handler. It seemed like nothing could snap their bond, and thanks to the godlike power of Bathory, Simon believed for a long time that it was eternal. A friendship that would last longer than the history of the world before Glass. Lazarus's empire was the first link in the chain that created the vast network of the underworld.

Simon believed it was his duty to keep Lazarus's wealth from his unhinged, immature son. It had been a rough year without Lazarus, and after transferring seven hundred million dollars, Simon knew he was going to be looking over his shoulder for a long time. He even turned off his phone so that he couldn't see if Captain calls him.

Standing behind a desk, the lingerie girl grinned at Simon. Over her ear, a small patch of her skin glowed an eerie blue.

"We *should* have a room available still. Follow me," she replied, stepping around the desk.

Not wanting to appear too excited or greedy, he stayed relaxed as he followed the girl down a narrow hallway, holding his mustard colored coat close to him. The air was misted with a thin stream of smoke leaking from an unknown source in the floor, which faded the further back they went. Finally, the girl stopped and opened a door with a key card.

"After you, babe," she invited, gesturing inside.

"Thank you," Simon replied. The bed inside the room was massive, enough to hold four people. On the ceiling above the bed was a large oval mirror. There were no windows, and the walls radiated a comforting pink. Simon's heart was still racing, his mind unable to shake off thoughts of Captain.

"Just make yourself comfortable and start thinking about what you'd like. Do you have any preferences I should know about before I get someone?" Lingerie girl asked.

"Um, no, not really. Just someone in her early twenties," Simon requested.

"Of course, love. Be back soon."

Simon sank into the edge of the bed, removed his coat, and let himself settle backwards. The mattress felt like it could swallow him whole. Sleep was leading him away, which he didn't want. He didn't want his girl to find him that way.

He heard the door whoosh open, and he blinked the sleep out of his eyes. Before he could sit up, Captain's face emerged over him.

"Hello, Simon," he mused.

Simon felt two sets of rough hands grab his shoulders, yank him off the bed, and force him onto his feet. Captain stood in front of him with his closest friend Damien. Simon also recognized the two men holding him, Trevor and Ripley.

"I'm disappointed, Simon. You steal from me?" Captain asked.

"It was the right thing to do," Simon groaned.

"You were dad's closest friend. Why steal from his son?"

"Oh, why do you care so much about that money? You still have *plenty*!"

"Very true, but what's your point?"

"Your father was a good man, unlike you. I can't *stand* the thought of you destroying his legacy!"

Captain touched Simon's shoulder. A snarl formed. "He destroyed it himself."

To Simon, it was bizarre to see Captain this way. He had known him all seventy-eight years of Captain's life, seen him as a small child staying close to his father, and watched him grow into an entitled young man, despite Lazarus's wishes for him to be better. His smile used to be full of awe for the world, pride for his father, and love for his mother. All of that had withered away into this crooked, bitter snarl fueled by zealous pride. Simon wasn't sure when this started. Maybe when his mother Stella left and took on the life of a prostitute, or maybe when Lazarus died behind his desk. Either way, there was no force great enough in the world to stop him now.

Simon knew he was dead already, but after hundreds of years of life, he wasn't going to die a coward.

"Your father regretted what he did with his life. If you had known as much as *I* do, you wouldn't be doing this."

Captain's expression remained unchanged. "Take him to the bedside table."

Simon's knees skidded along the ground and his head was rammed into wood. Pain reverberated through his ear.

"Daniel, stop!" He cried.

He felt something metal crack against the back of his head, presumably dealt by Captain. More pain split his skull.

"It's 'Captain', Simon, get it right. Now if you can please give me the password to the bank..."

"What? No, *wait*..."

"*Now*, Simon!" Captain's voice rose higher, untethered,

uncontrollable. Try as Captain might to sound scary, Simon knew he was just a whiny child who wasn't getting his way.

"That money doesn't belong to you. It belonged to your father!" Simon cried.

"Don't know if you've noticed, but he's not really here anymore!"

The barrel of Captain's gun leaned hard against Simon's head.

"Password. Now!" Captain roared.

"Go to hell! You *and* your new 'family'!"

The gun came down on him again, this time thrashing his back between shoulder blades. He screamed and tears streamed down his face, his mind scrambled, feeling sanity begin to leave him.

Captain lowered his voice to a deadly whisper. "The password, or I start shooting random parts of your body and you won't like where I start."

Think of something!

"The money is not...in...my bank. I...I transferred it all."

Simon groaned as Captain clamped the back of his neck and squeezed.

"What. Are. You. *Saying*?" Every word tightened Captain's grip on Simon's neck.

"I sent...the money to...Samsara Financial...as a donation," Simon wheezed, gasping for air.

A lie, but a believable one.

"Seven hundred *million* dollars all at once...is now the property of Samsara Financial?" Captain said, removing his gun from Simon.

"You don't deserve it." Adrenaline gushed through Simon as he found the last bits of strength to stand up to Captain. He had nothing left to lose now.

He turned his head enough to look at Captain. "You

don't deserve that money. You're not your father, and you never will be."

Captain heaved a sigh. "You're right, I'm not. I'm *better* than him." He motioned to Damien. "I think we're done here."

Damien drilled the barrel of his gun into Simon's head.

Simon felt at peace when—after hundreds of years—death finally took him.

9
VIOLET

SOMETHING *about those eyes just don't sit right with me.*

Violet stared up at the shining green eyes that belonged to Sparks, her least favorite visitor at the nursing home.

"How has he been?" Sparks asked, his figure shadowing Violet. The nursing home assistant wanted desperately to take a step away from him, uneasiness nipping at her like a pest trying to burrow its way into her.

"He's…" Violet cleared her throat, "…he's fine."

"Hmm," Sparks grunted.

The tiny nursing home Violet worked in, which kept itself open thanks to donations by people that just wanted to keep old and dying people away, was like a portal to a time Violet had never gotten to live in or see. There were no neon lights, no smartphones, and no robots or AI. A flatscreen on the wall played a gameshow on the only channel the residents liked. Even then, most of them did crossword puzzles instead of watching it.

Violet's position as a caregiver was the easiest job she'd ever gotten. Most people didn't want to work there for reasons that she understood, yet she tolerated. It beat spending more time at home with her boyfriend.

She swiped strands of butterscotch hair out of her hazel eyes with nails painted sea blue and cleared her throat again. "He's been pretty content even."

Sparks arched an eyebrow while staying still as a statue. "Really?"

Without waiting for Violet's answer, Sparks moved past her and got a chair to place in front of his father, Charles, who was motionless at the sight of him. Since he couldn't speak, Violet had no idea what Charles was really feeling, but it looked nothing like happiness, joy, or relief. Nothing that her own father would've expressed upon seeing her.

The old man's jaw was rigid, and his eyes were ready to pop free from their sockets. Sparks leaned in to talk to him in a hushed tone that Violet couldn't hear. She was tempted to get closer, but didn't dare do it, afraid of what Sparks might do if he noticed.

She cared about Charles, and he cared about her. Despite her efforts to hide it, Violet's stress was etched into her face, easy for other people to read, including Charles. According to him, if Violet's job was to take care of him during his last years when he had nothing left to do, the least he could do was make sure Violet didn't feel constantly miserable. He couldn't speak, but he was a fast writer, passing along messages to Violet on a tablet.

Charles was older than the City liked, like the other dozen people housed with him. They chose at one point to go the rest of their lives without ever drinking Bathory again, usually calling the drink 'Satanic'. Violet wasn't sure if she agreed with them to that extreme, but she did dislike drinking it every day—doing it only for the sake of appeasing her boyfriend, who warned her she would be unattractive over time without it.

By the time Sparks stood up, Charles's face was sickly and gray. His hand was gripping his tablet to the point of whitening his knuckles. Whatever the conversation was, it didn't go well.

"He's all yours again," Sparks said, sounding defeated as he hurried past Violet.

Violet watched him turn the corner into the hallway and disappear. The icy hold Sparks had on the room shrank back, and she hurried to Charles to make sure he was intact.

"Are you okay?" She asked.

Charles looked away, as if ashamed to be seen. His hands strangled the armrests. Violet's heart fluttered when she spotted a thin tear forming in the corner of his eye.

"I can make sure he doesn't come in again," Violet said.

Charles took his tablet, typed something, and handed it to Violet.

There's no keeping him out, said the tablet.

"No, no, don't *say* that," Violet said, sitting in the chair Sparks had used. "I see the way you are around him, you're not *happy*."

Charles's face softened, and he gestured for the tablet back, which Violet gave him. Once he passed it back, it said:

I can't escape him, but you can escape your partner.

Violet looked up at Charles, tears blurring her vision. The old man sighed, one of the only sounds he was capable of, with a sad smile that said 'you know I'm right'.

"It's not that simple," Violet whispered.

It never is, was Charles's next sentence.

Violet got up, searching the room for anything to do that would get her out of the conversation.

"I'm sorry," was all she managed to say. It sounded

glacial and professional, like she was just a caretaker at a nursing home that kept herself emotionally distant from the people she looked after. Charles shook his head in disapproval, but Violet moved on before he could argue with her.

————

DAMIEN

Damien watched Sparks from his car as he left the nursing home. Once Sparks disappeared, he grinned and reached for his door.

10

DAMIEN

EVERY NIGHTCLUB in Glass was unique in its own right, but *The Raise* club prided itself for standing out as a blast from the past. It was the first nightclub that was built for the City, and its owner, Thorne, had no plans to change it or 'upgrade' it to match the City's standards.

The Raise, named after how the City's towers rose to the sky, threw a blanket of lush yellow light over its guests, the waitresses, and the jazz band onstage. Rows of booths were set up across the club's checkered floor, and there were a dozen round tables near the back for playing cards and gambling with coins that held no value.

The Raise was Damien's favorite club and a big part of his history with his father Isaac. Isaac used to take—or more accurately, drag—Damien with him to *The Raise* so he could watch him negotiate with other crime families and learn his ways. While Isaac wanted Damien to learn to be a leader in the underworld some day, Damien never believed he was leadership material—his short temper and constant, underlying paranoia over people being some of the reasons. He decided a long time ago, that being an associate for his best friend held enough meaning, and he felt no inferiority over it.

"You're *way* too humble for this line of work," Captain told him once.

Captain may have been right, but Damien took it as a compliment. He never wished for anything better. Besides, listening to the jazz band in *The Raise* was a better source of learning than his father's meetings ever were. During those meetings, most of the time, Damien just watched the band play instead, enamored by the sound that unraveled the tension in his chest he felt over his father's insistence on having him there. In fact, the music tended to transport him away from his father's world and dip his toes into a different one. One where he could imagine himself playing cards, meeting women, and laughing with other people. No gang politics, no potential for fights. It was a perfect world.

Damien's distaste for the political side of the criminal underworld propelled him to tell Captain, when he first agreed to work alongside him, that he wanted nothing to do with negotiations. He wanted to be Captain's muscle, which he believed was where he was at his best.

He looked at his "friends" with a lump in his stomach. As two common criminals, whose most impressive feats in Glass were stealing batteries out of electric cars and snagging jewelry wherever they could find some, Connor and Richard were as far away from the organized crime families in the City as lower-level criminals could be. Damien fanned the card set he had in his hand on the table with a pleased smile. Pride flashed in his eyes.

"Another straight win," he declared.

Connor, a man with an ugly lip piercing, groaned. "Damn it."

"Why do we keep doing this again?" Richard asked.

The synthetic blue tattoos on his cheeks made his face appear fragmented.

"Because it's fun," Damien said. He gathered up the valueless coins sitting in the middle of the table.

"Hey, I remember you," a scratchy voice said.

There was Sparks, a towel over his shoulder, and his long hair more frazzled than the last time he saw him. Unlike last time when he was in Captain's office, Sparks looked happy, appearing glad to see Damien.

Damien flashed his winning smile again. *Time to play ball.*

"And I remember you too!" He said.

"You know this guy?" Richard asked in disbelief.

Damien shut Richard up with a halting hand, maintaining his grin. "Hey, no hard feelings about earlier, right?" He asked Sparks.

Sparks squinted at Damien, as if he couldn't see him well. "None taken," he replied neutrally.

Damien guffawed, trying his damnedest to play along. Sparks was hard to read, but Damien had met many people like him.

"So, dishwasher, huh?" Damien asked.

"Yeah."

"You off the clock now?"

"As a matter of fact, I just got off."

Damien pointed to an empty chair at the table. "Then how about joining us for a round? You and I start over?"

Sparks frowned, his eyes cautious. "Really?"

"I won't tell Captain a word. It can be our little secret."

Sparks grunted, but then nodded, took the chair, and pushed himself forward.

"Good choice," Damien said, then gestured to his friends. "This is Connor and Richard, they'll be playing with us. Do you know how to play Odyssey?" Damien asked.

Sparks nodded. "My uncle taught me how to play. Haven't played much with other people though."

Damien's next words came slow. "Then why don't you repeat the rules back to me real quick, so that I know we're on the same page?" He still smiled, but it ached keeping it on.

Richard started passing cards around to everybody. Sparks took up each of his cards and formed a hand out of them.

"The goal is to get as many Odysseus cards as possible in your hand by the end of the round when the final timer goes off. You can trade a single card you *don't* want with another player and choose one of his," Sparks explained.

"Well said, but what about the 'Calypso'?" Damien asked.

"If by some...rare chance...you get five Calypsos, you can lay those out and you automatically win."

Damien nodded. "Getting those is almost impossible. I mean...not for me, of course...but still nearly impossible."

Sparks didn't answer. He was already engaged in the game. Heat pinched Damien's cheeks, but he regathered himself and cleared his throat.

"Let's get started then."

The jazz music continued swinging as the players studied their hands in silence. Damien was impressed by Sparks's unflappable face as he stared at his hand, his eyes exposing nothing, so Damien couldn't deduce if Sparks was looking at good cards or bad ones. In his own hand, Damien didn't have five Calypsos. Still, he *could* win by getting as many cards as possible by the end of the round...

Sparks spoke up. "*I'll* make a trade."

Damien's head jerked up. "For what?"

"Your far right card."

Damien blinked when he saw what his far right card was. A Calypso.

There's no way he could've known that!

Damien pricked his tongue with his teeth and granted himself a cheeky grin to keep playing it cool until he didn't have to anymore.

"Sure. What the hell?" Damien said, passing the Calypso to Sparks.

Sparks took it and gave Damien his trade. Nothing remarkable.

"M'kay, it's *my* turn to trade now," Richard said.

This went on for a little while, each player trading cards and studying their hands. Every time the timer went off, everyone had to draw a card from the stack in the middle, adding more and more to their hands. Damien noticed that Sparks was requesting the most trades and seemed to care very little about the new cards he drew. What exasperated him most was that he still couldn't read Sparks's face at all.

Is that on purpose or is that just his natural state?

Then Sparks spread his hand on the table.

"Calypso," he announced with a smile.

Everyone at the table gawked in disbelief. It was embarrassing for sure, and while Sparks's skills did catch Damien off guard, he had to see the plan to the end.

"How...is that possible?" Damien whispered, hoping he was putting on a convincing performance.

He's not stupid. He's better at this than I thought he would be.

"Because it is," Sparks replied, his voice frigid. He started to reach for the coins in the middle of the table.

Damien shot his hand out and snatched Sparks's wrist.

"Whoa, hold on there, buddy. That was just a practice round," he lied.

Sparks recoiled and his face darkened. "You and I both know that's not true," he said.

"It is because I said so," Damien said.

Sparks stood up and Damien felt his heart tear nearly out of his chest. His hand wasn't holding onto Sparks's anymore.

"So, even when I play the game right, it's still not enough," Sparks seethed, his voice venomous.

"Um, hey, man, we're just playing a game. The money's fake anyway," Connor said.

"Yeah, maybe that's part of the problem," Sparks suggested as he stepped around the table and hovered over Damien. "*Everything* about this is fake."

Damien's hand floated towards the knife under his shirt and rose to his feet, making sure to keep his hand out of sight.

"Captain was right about you. You're nothing but a loser who will wash dishes and wipe our asses until you die because you don't drink the red stuff."

Damien barely finished his words before a fist trapped his throat and lifted him off the ground with inhuman strength. That fist flipped him over onto the table. The table's legs cracked under the impact and he collapsed along with it. The back of his head struck wood. Despite the table collapsing under him, Sparks still had his grip on Damien's throat. Richard and Connor rushed to tackle him, but Sparks let go of Damien to smash his elbow against Richard's nose and twist Connor's arm until it popped.

Sparks's hand spidered around Damien's throat again, but Damien had enough strength back. Twisting and writhing his way out of Sparks's grip, his hand went back for the knife on his belt and stabbed it through Sparks's side. Sparks moaned in pain and attempted to get up, loosening his grip on Damien. Captain's best friend held onto the knife to keep Sparks down with him. Satisfied after a moment, Damien yanked the dagger out of Sparks's shredded flesh.

Sparks fell to the floor gasping for breath. Damien stayed lying on the floor while Sparks lost consciousness next to him. A coughing fit raked Damien's throat. He rolled over onto his side with a pained groan and spat a wad of blood on the floor.

Captain and I are definitely gonna have a talk.

11

CAPTAIN

"HE'S *DANGEROUS*, CAPTAIN!" Damien cried.

Captain leaned against the edge of his massive balcony overlooking downtown with a cigar in his hand, a glass of Syre beside him, and a dull pain throbbing in his forehead. Damien was back after his encounter with Sparks at *The Raise*, and he looked spooked. Captain had never seen him that way before.

Not even on the day when he received the news that his mother had been assassinated. In fact, he showed nothing when the news was broken to him. Captain acquainted that with strength.

Like Captain, Damien was the son of a crime family, and this family had deep ties to Captain's. They wanted Damien to one day lead the family business, but he was more interested in being Captain's friend. Their long lasting friendship led to Damien being the first person to join Captain after Lazarus died.

"I can see that, buddy," Captain replied, pointing out the red marks on his friend's neck. Humiliated, Damien rubbed at them.

"He could've killed me," Damien said.

Captain waved a hand. "He didn't though. Join me up here."

Damien took several heavy steps forward. "He broke my friends and held me down by the neck!"

Captain stuck the butt of his cigar against the balcony to put it out, driving it in deep so that it left a mark, along with the other ones that were there.

"You and I both know Connor and Richard aren't *really* your friends."

Damien glared at Captain, which motivated him to shift gears.

"He's in jail now, right or wrong?" Captain asked.

Damien sniffed. "Right."

"Then he's *exactly* where I want him. He'll lose his job. He'll need a new line of work. I'll have him brought right back to me," Captain said. He sighed as he reached for a match in his breast pocket to relight his cigar.

"He can't be worth *this* much time, man," Damien said, joining Captain at the edge of the balcony.

Captain exhaled a smoke trail and stared back out at the vibrating City.

"Do you remember the way my father's friends would look at me after he died?"

"Yeah," Damien snorted. "They obviously never wanted you around them."

"Not only that, but they didn't even want me to bring people together like you or the brothers...or Joan. They were afraid of what I might do...now that my father's gone."

"So, what does this have to do with Sparks?" Damien asked.

"Let me finish," Captain held up a finger. From his breast pocket, he removed a thin flask of Bathory. "Then I tried connecting with other crime families, and do you remember what Amon called me?"

"Pussy," Damien answered with a snicker.

Captain ignored him. "My father's old friends don't want me nor respect me. These other crime families in the City don't respect me. So when I saw that idiot, I saw an opportunity. Why let him join another crime family that won't respect me, especially after he tells them whatever he might tell them about me? It's obvious the city beneath the City isn't going to accept me with open arms if I don't show them strength, so Sparks can be the ultimate example to the underworld that I have that strength. That I have every right and every intention to be just as powerful as all of them...maybe more."

Captain popped the lid off of the flask and took a swig of the scarlet liquid. First came the burn in the back of his throat. Then his insides warmed and his cheeks vibrated. He sighed in contentment when all the little aches in his body dissolved and he felt like floating away.

Damien stroked his chin in thought, and his eyes glimmered.

"What if you tell everyone that *you* were the one who killed Chase?" Damien asked.

Captain twisted his head around searching as if there was a listening device or someone hiding.

"Damien, I love you, but that's a stupid idea. Chase was more valuable. He had status. Sparks is a complete *nobody*. I don't think anyone is going to come after me if I hurt him." Captain slipped the flask back in his breast pocket. "Besides, how bad would it make me look if I become known as the guy who killed a member of one of the crime families?"

Damien nodded as he understood.

Captain continued. "If I reveal what I did, the Jacks won't bend. They'll want war, and that's the *last* thing I want to start."

"Then shouldn't priority one be negotiating with some of the other families face to face instead of chasing after this seven hundred million dollars? That's pocket change compared to what you have," Damien said.

Captain blew out another trail of smoke. His voice turned monotone.

"Look at *you* suggesting politics," he remarked.

Damien shrugged. "Only going as far as presenting ideas."

"If I let this slide and word gets out about the missing money...well, people will think I'm vulnerable. The words 'Captain' and 'vulnerable' can *never* be allowed in the same sentence."

Captain inhaled from his cigar again and sighed out a trail.

"Every single thing I do has to be done *carefully*. If I fail to build those relationships my father had with the other crime families, I will never get far enough. I can't live with that. I called a meeting together with my father's council tomorrow afternoon at *Nine Circles*. I'm sure they're wondering where Simon disappeared to. I'll be honest with them. I'll take them out of the game, and get my money back from Samsara Financial," Captain said.

Damien raised an eyebrow. "You managed to make an appointment with Samsara?"

"After some...convincing...yeah," Captain answered, sucking in from his cigar.

In two days. Two days too long.

He was able to arrange a time to meet with Sylar Han,

the CEO of Samsara Financial himself. The woman he got to talk to on the phone promised they would prevent any investors within the bank from using the donations from the last several days in any way until the situation was resolved. The process of tracing transfers and poring over bank records wasn't something the receptionist had the power to do. It was a power that Sylar prided himself with. He didn't trust anybody else to do it. A private meeting with him was the only way anything was going to get done. Captain was lucky to get an answer from a living, breathing person at all.

"Get some sleep, pal. You look like you need it," Captain said.

"One more thing," Damien said, and reached into his pocket. He fished out a key card and handed it to Captain.

"I meant to give this to you sooner, but now's a better time than any," he said.

"What, to your place?" Captain asked.

"Yep."

"Okay...why?" Captain asked.

"My dad once told me 'building empires makes enemies'. It's not the most original thing, but he was right. You'll need a safe place you can turn to should you start seeing them pop up behind you."

Captain knew Damien was telling the truth but it still felt weird to hear it.

"Thanks," he said, pocketing the card.

"Good night," Damien said, and he left the balcony. Captain dropped his cigar in his glass of Syre and clutched the railing with both hands, hearing the cigar sizzling in the liquor. His heart was palpitating fast. Something thick and heavy was lodged in the back of his throat. To distract himself, he pulled himself forward a bit, as if he could get absorbed by the City and become one of its arcane colors. A warm tear stung his eye.

It's so beautiful. And it will know me soon, just like I know it.

12

JOAN

JOAN JOLTED awake from disturbing dreams. A conglomeration of memories, nightmares and fears, birthed from her time in the Web that still entangled themselves in the comfortable life she led now.

Joan yanked the covers closer to her naked body and she folded herself in a tight ball. Captain's snores—the reminder that she wasn't alone—was enough to calm her down. He was the only man she had slept with that ever made her feel safe, but she wasn't sure if it was the man or knowing where she was now.

No one ever truly felt safe in the Web. A winding maze of malnourished and bony peasants, shacks stacked like teetering wooden blocks, stitched together with duct tape and prayers, and enough scavengers and creeps that made you want to stay huddled in a corner inside. The Web was like Glass in that everything was permissible, but most people went about it like animals clawing away at the dirt—or other people—with wide, lifeless eyes absent of remorse or tolerance. Sometimes Joan saw people like these at night, their eyes seeming to glow in the blackness unsupported by any lights. She would have staring contests with these people until they slinked away, deciding not to take any risks.

Even after a year of being away from the Web, Joan still woke up seeing those eyes burned into her brain. She didn't want to think about what the creatures with these eyes were doing now, or if they were even still alive.

As quietly as she could, Joan got out of bed, tied her bathrobe around her, and started down the hallway. The tall windows displayed the flamboyant City outside, splashing an orgy of lights over Joan's form. After fetching a bottle of bourbon and two glasses from the kitchen, she reached Ripley's bedroom door and shamelessly but gently rapped on it.

Ripley and Trevor had rooms of their own in the penthouse like Benji, complimentary of their loyalty to Captain. Damien was the only one who didn't have his own room. An intentional choice by Captain, who was concerned that Damien's obsession for his protection would mean very little privacy for him and Joan. Even without his room, he still tended to come over unannounced. After a moment of silence that almost made Joan change her mind, the door hissed open and Ripley stood there blinking at her through blurred vision.

"I can't sleep," Joan said.

"Oh," Ripley replied, indifferently.

"Yeah."

Ripley's eyes darted up and down, taking in Joan's bathrobe.

"Well, what should we do?" He asked.

Joan sheepishly grinned, and in a moment, the two were seated outside in chairs surrounded by Joan's garden balcony, full glasses in their hands. Growing food was a luxury there nearly nobody in the Web had. Whatever did grow was stolen before the growers could collect.

Seeds were hard to come by, even in Glass. Very few people grew their own gardens, so there wasn't much demand, and therefore not much on shelves. The upside, however, was that Captain brought back seeds whenever and wherever he managed to find them, which was sometimes even the black market.

Despite Joan's best efforts, nothing had grown yet.

Ripley and Joan stared out at the vast City ahead of them, at a level where they could see Central just beyond Glass' borders, and then even patches of the Labyrinth and the Web. The lack of lights in those boroughs made it hard to see them.

"This is nice," Ripley said, taking a swig from his glass.

"Yes. Yes, it is."

"If it helps, *querido,* I wasn't sleeping great either."

Joan took the bottle that was resting between them and poured another glass.

"And *I* wasn't sleeping at *all*. You still having nightmares like me?"

"*Sí*. We're ex-Websters. It's like our curse or something."

Joan set the bottle down. "I think we're *all* cursed with something, Webster or not."

Ripley chortled and swirled his drink. "So when should I expect to see a bump?"

"A what?"

"You know..." Ripley circled a round shape around his stomach.

"Should I be weirded out that you want to know that badly?" Joan asked, laughing.

"You told me once that that's something you wanted!"

"I *told* you that?"

"*Si.*"

"I must've been drunk or something."

"You weren't."

Joan released a sigh and took another drink. "I don't think kids are on Daniel's radar right now."

Ripley frowned and leaned his head forward. "Aren't they on *yours?*"

"Even if it is, it doesn't matter. Daniel has other shit going on. All I can do is just...wait and see."

"Oh," Ripley shifted in his seat. "You haven't brought it up to him yet, have you?"

"Let's change the subject."

"*Lo siento*, I'm just trying to..."

"I know," Joan replied abruptly, "I know. You're sweet. I get it. Just not right now, okay?"

Ripley was the kindest man Joan had ever known. Sometimes she felt more comfortable talking to him than Captain. There were some things she just couldn't talk about with Captain. Either he didn't care enough or his attention was on something else. He was a laser-focused man. When his sights were set on something, there was very little room in his mind for anything else.

One of the things that struck Joan when she first came to Glass was that everything she had wanted so much in her life growing up finally felt possible. She wanted children, a family, and more than anything, simplicity. She was starting to wonder if these things weren't ambitious enough to Captain. More than once, she thought about suggesting children to Captain, but couldn't find the courage to bring it up, and Captain never brought it up himself. His mind was fixed on building his empire.

"May I ask a question though?" Ripley asked.

"Are you seriously asking for *permission*?"

"It's Daniel's obsession with this Sparks guy," Ripley said, his tone no longer light.

Damn, should've seen this *coming.*

Joan didn't know why, but hearing the name gave her goosebumps. She had tried to forget him, but it was impossible.

"What makes you think it's an obsession?" Joan asked.

She knew it was ridiculous to ask, because even *she* knew it was an obsession. That and the missing seven hundred million dollars. It exhausted Joan just thinking about it.

"*El jefe* made a *whole* plan with Damien to bring Sparks into our little...family, as he calls it, and I don't think he's worth the effort," Ripley said.

Joan lowered her glass to her lap. She hated how right Ripley was, but, like talking about the possibility of children to Captain, she didn't feel like her opinion mattered. The next best thing was to side with Captain to keep the peace. She thought back to the Sparks incident, attempting to draw from it anything she could use in Captain's defense.

"What if Daniel's right, though? I mean, you *saw* that guy. What if he tried coming back? And how'd he get all those guns? Did he seriously just buy them all to give them to Captain?" Joan said.

Ripley frowned, realizing Joan's point.

"And, if he can somehow get his hands on all those guns, what *else* is he capable of?" Joan asked.

Ripley didn't reply, which wasn't uncommon. He was a man of few words, unlike his brother. He still appeared unconvinced. He *hmm*'d instead.

Joan took the last sips from her glass and got up. "I should try sleeping again. *Buenas noches, el amor.*"

She turned, and came face to face with Benji's ghostly stare.

"Shit!" She screamed, dropping her glass, which shattered upon impact. Ripley shot up from his seat.

"What are you doing?!" He demanded.

"I like the view, I came out here to look at it," Benji answered. Joan and Ripley stared at him in disbelief.

"I-I'm sorry. I didn't mean to scare you," Benji said, his gaze down on the ground. Joan swathed her arms around herself to better cover herself up and stepped past Benji to get back inside.

"This house is getting *way* too crowded!"

Going back to bed, Joan didn't feel any less stressed or anxious than she did when she left it, and she was convinced she wasn't getting any more sleep that night.

Not with Sparks and a couple of uncertain dreams on the mind.

———

RIPLEY

Ripley bit his tongue and sat back down after Joan and Benji left. He pinched his eyes shut and shook his head.

He never told Joan what *el amor* really meant, but didn't bother to correct her.

He traced his finger down the narrow scar between his eyes. A parting gift from the Web during one of their last days there. A few guys who had a bone to pick with Trevor jumped them, one of them pinning Ripley to the ground and smashing his face into the dirt and fractured concrete. Within seconds, Ripley's attacker got a bullet through the side of the head from Trevor.

All of their attackers died, none of them killed by Ripley.

Joan was the first woman Ripley met in Glass, and he quickly found out that her rough exterior was misleading. Her eyes told a different story. One of the same trauma, terror, and fatigue most people in the Web had.

Ripley slapped himself across the face, a little harder than anticipated. An ache beat behind his cheek. He got his phone and speed dialed a number.

"Please wait while we transfer your call. This line will take additional time."

After two rings, someone answered.

"Ripley?"

"Hi, Mama."

13

CAPTAIN

CAPTAIN SMIRKED as the double sliding doors to the club, *Nine Circles*, swished open, inviting him and his whole gang inside.

He spread his arms. "Gentlemen—and lady—welcome to *Nine Circles*."

Inside, the club was made to look like they were in hell itself. Orange and red lights mounted on the wall swayed to make it look like everyone was walking through lava. Even the tables looked like they were carved out of molten rock.

"None of you are drowning, I promise," Captain assured his crew.

"Sure *feels* like I am," Joan said, drawing closer to Captain so that her side was touching his. Captain weaved his arm around her waist and held her.

"Then let me help you stay on your feet, love," he said.

"Where's the council?" Damien asked.

"Bottom floor," Captain said, and led his gang to the glass elevator in the center of the room.

As the elevator took them underground, they caught a glimpse of each of the nine levels. Every level was something different, from casinos and fighting rings to strip clubs and buffets, all in one building. The gang got to the bottom floor, which was hazy to the point where it was difficult to make people out. Along the walls were sheets of ice, with some stalagmites even hanging from the ceiling. The air was cool. Captain could see his breath when he exhaled.

Around a long table arranged like shadows were Lazarus's associates, speaking in hushed voices. As Captain drew closer to the shadows, ignoring the nippy air, there was a low ringing in his ears, and his anger was barely containable now. It had been hibernating deep in his gut, bearing down on his stomach for over a year. Now it was fully awake, rattling the fragile cage Captain had stuffed it in, thrashing and roaring as it starved for a swift, vengeful justice.

They were all there. Every man's face he remembered from his childhood, taking up space in his family's home, chasing his mother into the other room to drink herself into a frenzy.

Taking a chair from another table, Captain dragged it behind him and swung it around to a rest at the end of the council's table. At this point, the council had noticed him, and the fear was palpable. It was as if Captain could hear their heartbeats and taste their sweat. He sat in his chair, folded his hands, and gazed around at the five men. No one said a word. No one dared to.

"How nice is *this*?" Captain said.

His own associates formed a half-circle around him, their guns clasped visibly in front of them. He had control of the room, he had the backing of his own colleagues, and he was the only one willing to speak.

It's about damn time.

"It looks like I finally have your respect. *That* took a while," Captain continued.

The council stared at him stunned and unable to move, a few of them stealing glances at each other to see who had the courage to speak first.

The youngest in the group, Chen, cleared his throat. "Where's Simon?" He asked.

"You don't know?" Captain asked coyly.

"Daniel, we're asking..."

Captain shot his hand up to cut Chen off. "I prefer 'Captain', please."

"Captain..." Chen corrected, his voice in danger of breaking, his two cybernetic eyes blinking rapidly. "We had no idea what Simon was doing."

"*Really?* I find that hard to believe considering none of you wanted me to take what my father left behind."

Another from the council, Torrence, spoke up next. "Your father was a good friend, and a great leader, neither of which you are. Simon knew it, and so do we," he sneered.

Then it was Bradley's turn. "You never cared about picking up where your father left off! You have a street gang, not an empire. You're not a mob boss, you're a hoodlum!"

The words rolled off of Captain like drops of water. He expected this, and he was glad the council wasn't holding back either. It was all things he knew and needed to hear in order to justify what he was about to do. His father wasn't there to defend his friends this time.

Captain bent forward, keeping his hands folded. "What's wrong with being a bit of both?"

He waved at his gang behind him. "You see these guys? They've always been there for me, and they always will. All of *you*, on the other hand, have always *hated* me. One of you stole wealth he had no right to take, and I know *you* know he paid the price for it. You don't get to cling to the wealth that belongs to me anymore."

The sight of the council disgusted Captain. They were afraid for their lives, but there wasn't an ounce of regret visible on them. They only feared for their lives and their wealth.

How predictable.

"Oh, *I know*, it's *so* hard for you people to let the wealth go and let someone else have it, but it all belongs to *me*. So does the City. It's all mine, and *none* of you will be around to see what it becomes under me."

Captain steepled his hands and continued. "People have created amazing things all across history, but something I'm beginning to realize is that it had to take gods—not people—to build Glass. I don't believe in God, but I believe that *people* can be god, because *they* made something like Glass. The only thing Glass needs now to be perfect is a god like *me* to run it."

Torrence vaulted up from his seat with his palms splayed on the table. "You're insane!"

Captain flinched, the words cracking open some unwanted memories. The bars of the cage inside him were bending now, a dangerous gap widening between them.

"Torrence, sit down!" Bradley cried.

"No! He has to let us leave! He at least owes us *that*!" Torrence cried.

The cage bars stopped bending.

"What do you mean 'leave'?" Captain asked, his voice a flat note, entranced and numb.

No one was even breathing now.

Captain studied the table one final time and a great sigh sliced the air like a box cutter.

"You've all been talking about leaving the City...and taking my father's money with you."

Everyone was still. Then...

Every member of the council exploded from their seats, hands entwined with their guns. The enraged beast finally broke out of the cage, stumbling and flailing like a confused zombie famished for blood, and the roars were out of control inside Captain's head.

After a split second, the frosty air erupted with gunfire behind Captain. All of Lazarus's men collapsed back into their seats, their heads lolled back and their eyes glassed over. Captain remained sitting straight, his face expressionless, his eyes fixed in a straight line. A mist of glowing blood coated his cheek. Casually, he removed a white cloth from his breast pocket and slowly wiped it off.

The whole thing only lasted for a few seconds. The beast in Captain's head fell silent, and in its place was a faint bee's buzzing. No one in the room cared about the carnage. It wasn't the first time it happened on the bottom level, nor would it be the last.

"Holy shit," Joan said, her voice small and quiet, almost too quiet to be heard above the buzzing. A half smile sheared through Captain's face and he took a deep breath.

"Feels good to start over."

CAPTAIN

"OW! DAMN IT!" Daniel exclaimed as he lost his hold on the slide at the top of his gun. It shot forward after he yanked it back, the metal slicing the skin of his pinkie. A little blood dribbled from the cut.

Damien gently took the gun from him. "Easy there, partner."

Daniel pushed his dark brown—not yet dyed—hair back and folded his arms. The more time he spent in the shooting range with his best friend, the less confident he felt that his father was wrong. Lazarus refused to train him himself for reasons that he kept vague, so he went to the range under his father's nose with Damien, who was more than willing to help him. Daniel had been to the range so many times at this point that his movements now were repetitive and felt like muscle memory. The problem was that he still wasn't perfect. He was *far* from perfect.

This wasn't the first time he had cut skin at the range.

"I told you this thing'll bite if you don't treat her with care. How many times do you have to get cut to remember that?" Damien asked.

Daniel muttered another curse as Damien handed back the weapon. With extra caution, he slid the slide back again, slower this time and felt the weight of it as it protested. As he reloaded, his mind wandered away into his own private world. Damien tried talking to him, but he didn't hear a word that had been said.

Just last week, his father stopped taking Bathory, meaning he will die some day soon. Daniel swore he'd never do the same. It was the only thing that granted a life without an ending.

His animosity towards his father's decisions helped his muscle memory during his target practice. He hated him for giving up on Bathory, thus giving up on him, even after his mother left. He hated him for withholding his future as a criminal kingpin in Glass. His father made sure he knew everything else a dad would teach him, but nothing that had to do with his work. He even taught him the best ways to win over a woman, but teaching him how to use a gun was too close to the lifestyle he thrived on behind the doors of his empire.

Daniel slid the gun shut once it was reloaded, then switched the safety off to aim at his target. A sound like a tiny engine powering up pulsated through the gun and the lines on the sides glowed blue.

"Um, Daniel?" Damien said uneasily, but Daniel was already in the zone. He pulled the trigger multiple times, and bullets circled around the bullseye until, finally, one shot found Daniel's intended mark.

Proud of himself, Daniel checked the slide and saw no bullets. The final one caught the bullseye.

Now that's *progress.*

Turning to gloat at Damien, he froze when he saw his father standing at the doorway of the booth.

He was already showing signs of aging after giving up Bathory. His light brown hair was graying under his fedora. His silver eyes were losing the youth they'd radiated not too long ago.

"Gentlemen," Lazarus rasped, his voice sounding ill. After he had stopped drinking Bathory, he was bedridden for two days—too sick to move and could barely talk.

Daniel and Damien exchanged frightened glances, unsure of what to do and feeling cornered. Lazarus stepped into Daniel's shadow.

For a moment, Daniel found courage. "Oh so *now* you've found out? Right when I was getting good?"

Lazarus shook his head. "That wasn't 'good', son. You would've been dead before you landed that mark."

"Well, maybe I would've been better if you had already trained me," Daniel spat.

Lazarus took a deep breath. "That's not going to happen."

Heat licked Daniel's throat and he tried to say something, but he was at a loss for words.

I can't believe this...I can't believe he won't—

"Not ever?" He cracked.

"Not ever," was Lazarus's reply.

"You're insane," Daniel seethed. Damien's hand went to his shoulder, his touch firm and warning.

"I don't blame you for thinking that," Lazarus said, his voice now gentle.

Daniel humorlessly laughed. "Dad, you're *dying*. Do you understand that? How could you do this to me?"

Lazarus didn't answer right away, and Damien butted in.

"That's a pretty legit question, sir," Damien said.

Lazarus's eyes blazed. "*You* stay *out* of this!"

Damien shut up after that.

Even with his anger, it was as if every word of the conversation was aging Lazarus by another year. Maybe they were.

"Doesn't everything get passed down to *me* some day? Aren't I supposed to at least know *some* things?" Daniel asked.

His father heaved a heavy sigh and placed his hands on his hips, unable to make eye contact with his son.

"Daniel. You need to leave Glass. Right away."

Daniel's jaw fell.

What?

"What're you talking about? Why would I ever leave? Doesn't everything get passed down to *me* soon?" He asked, his voice cracking and nearly inaudible.

"Out there, you can be whatever you want. *Anything.* Glass only has room for one kind of person, and it's not the kind of person I want you to be," Lazarus said.

"What about Angel? Angel was—."

"And look what happened to him! That boy was left bleeding out in the streets. Is that where *you* want to be?" Lazarus protested, a new wild light in his eyes.

Hot tears surged in Daniel's eyes and the heat in his throat grew worse. "You just don't want me to succeed like *you* did! Why else would you tell me to leave? What other *possible* reason could it be?!"

"I've already told you," Lazarus replied, turning back to leave. "As long as you stay here, you can only be the kind of person I wish I never became."

Daniel took a heavy step forward, glaring at his father through blurry vision. Damien watched without saying a word but even Daniel could see out of the corner of his eye that he wasn't happy with Lazarus either.

Daniel wanted to scream at his father, shake him, and punch him in the face. Instead, he stayed still for a moment, pulling words together to throw at his father as he walked away.

"I'll *never* become what you are! I'm going to be something *better*! Something that people will *cheer* for and respect! No one will throw a parade for you after you're gone, but people will celebrate *me*!"

Daniel's passion didn't shake off the lingering reminder in the forefront of his mind. Lazarus wasn't immortal anymore, but Daniel was still powerless in his shadow.

LAZARUS

Sylar Han's meditation chamber was massive, drenched in neon scarlet with a high glass ceiling that displayed the sky in a violet haze. On both sides of the room were bubbling fountain pools, the scarlet reflecting off the water—blood-like. Accompanied by two bodyguards, Lazarus strode into the chamber, hampered by a sharp pain in the back of his knee.

Waiting at the other end of the room with a cigarette in one hand and a stress ball in the other was Sylar Han, the CEO of Samsara Financial. He was tan-skinned, with black hair dangling over almond shaped eyes. In his hand, he held a stress ball. Three other people stood with him.

Ratchet, Sylar's best assassin, was leaning against the

wall behind Sylar with his arms folded, watching Lazarus through a pair of large shades. Wrapped around him was a wine-colored leather trench coat that extended down and stopped at his knees. Strapped to his waist was a long scabbard that held a katana.

Sae, Sylar's closest associate and surrogate brother, sported the same shade of hair as Sylar's, had skin just a shade lighter, and the same almond eyes just slightly wider. He was sitting on one of the fountains, his gaze locked on Lazarus.

Finally, there was Arbor, whom Lazarus didn't know much about. The most he knew about him was that he brought Sylar his tea and pulled out his chair for him. Lazarus pitied him for it. He was the one lingering closest to Sylar with his hands clasped behind his back, peering at Lazarus with guarded brown eyes.

Sylar didn't know it yet, but Lazarus was free of him. It took willpower and weighing a lot of pros and cons, but Lazarus's desire to tear himself out of Sylar's arms overpowered the allure of eternal life through the Bathory. He got a clap on the back by Sylar for every dollar he earned—or took —but when his family came into the picture, Sylar acted like a jealous lover, insisting that Lazarus's wife and child were going to be the death of him.

Funny that he wasn't wrong now.

"I'll be damned! I didn't think you'd actually show," Sylar crowed with his arms spread out as he stepped forward. His smile was real but Lazarus had known Sylar long enough to recognize the caution in his eyes.

"I wouldn't have missed this meeting for the world," Lazarus replied with a wide grin.

Sylar raised an eyebrow, his grin stayed intact. "*You* were the one that set it up...for once. So, what's this about?"

Lazarus shut his eyes and rehearsed his first words to himself. He had been thinking about this conversation for a long time and what he was going to say.

"Hold up," Sylar got within less than six feet of Lazarus, squinting at him. "You don't look so good, Laz."

No turning back now.

"I'm done," Lazarus announced.

Sylar laughed. "Oh?"

Lazarus moved closer, and out of the corner of his eye, he saw Ratchet's hand stray to the hilt of his katana, his back remaining against the wall. Lazarus's bodyguards flinched for their own weapons just in case. Lazarus waved his hand at them to calm them down.

"Tell your lackey to stand down," Lazarus said to Sylar, quietly.

Sylar nodded at Ratchet. The assassin dropped his arm back to his side with a grunt.

"When was the last time you took Bathory?" Sylar asked Lazarus.

"At this point, three weeks. I'm done, and I mean *done*. I've entrusted all my wealth to Simon, and I've blocked all of Samsara Financial's accounts from transferring funds to mine."

Ratchet uncrossed his arms and straightened. Sylar shook his head in disbelief and squeezed his stress ball tighter. Lazarus could hear the ball straining against the CEO's grip.

"After everything I've done for you?" Sylar said.

Lazarus turned to Sylar for help a long time ago when his equally wealthy father, who hated him, threatened to keep his fortune from him and send it somewhere where he felt it'd be used responsibly. Desperate to obtain the fortune, Lazarus consulted Sylar for help, who roped him into the life of building the first criminal empire in Glass, setting him on the path that had been his life for over a hundred years. He grew even wealthier than his father ever did, but more than half of it was practically handed to him.

Having a son was Lazarus's single greatest offense to Sylar. Sylar saw the potential in Daniel to be a threat, for the same reasons that he told other crime leaders to avoid having children. Having children meant raising people who might one day desire their family fortunes and disturb the peace by prying them from their parents' hands without Sylar's approval.

"You can't just tell me you're done and not expect consequences, Laz. This is Glass. Power doesn't switch hands, it's predetermined," Sylar continued.

"You can't punish me any more than I've already punished myself," Lazarus laughed, motioning to his face and its fast evolving wrinkles. "Your threats mean nothing. I've learned that death is the only way to freedom in this godforsaken place, and if it means you lose an asset, then even better."

"There *is* no freedom outside Glass," Sylar remarked, his words like ice daggers. He was staring past Lazarus as he said it though, his eyes directed at Sae instead before flicking back to Lazarus.

"What about your son? What becomes of him when you die?" Sylar sneered.

Lazarus laughed. It was a thrill to see Sylar this upset.

"You hated the fact that I got *married*. Why do you care what happens to my boy?"

Sylar's fingers vibrated around the stress ball. Arbor took a few worried steps back, his hands now unclasped. He was the only one of Sylar's associates who was growing visibly apprehensive. The sight only strengthened Lazarus's resolve.

"My son might be *beyond* saving." Lazarus's voice cracked. "Unless...once I'm dead, he'll get to know what death is. He'll eventually grow to hate this place and find a life somewhere else. He still has time. I don't. What he does after I go will be *your* problem. I'd be careful though. My son is a relentless man."

"What if I *force* you to take Bathory?" Sylar said.

Lazarus laughed again. "Well, good luck. I've already taken the pill."

Sylar's eyes widened. "You..."

Sae spoke for the first time. "Damn."

Everyone knew what it meant when someone took the 'pill'. The pill was provided by the Suicide Watch Division in Glass, an organization designed to watch people who were contemplating suicide, and giving them the pill if it was clear they weren't going to change. Their patients were never provided with therapists or medication to help improve their mental health because it was viewed as a waste of time and resources. If it was clear beyond a shadow of a doubt that the patient was determined to die, the pill was provided so they could die quietly and alone, and the cause of their death would be ruled as a heart attack.

"It has at least another fourteen hours to do its work and then I'll be dead," Lazarus said.

Sylar dropped his stress ball. "You think this is how you win the game? This is a *coward's* way out."

"Then I'm a coward," Lazarus shrugged.

Sylar had no more words as Lazarus turned to leave, his bodyguards trailing behind him. Sae's head was down, no longer tracking Lazarus's every move. Behind Lazarus, Sylar called after him.

"Kostov! *Kostov!*"

———

Lazarus never allowed Daniel in his office, and he knew the risk he was leaving behind by dying. His son would come into his office. It might even become his, but he knew there was no stopping that possibility. Raising him in Glass was his mistake. The young man's mind was integrated with the cogs of the City, and once that happened, it was damn near impossible to sever it from them.

Life was draining from Lazarus's body as the sun's first light set the towers of the City on fire. He was on his knees now, his hands clinging to the end of his desk. The only upside was that it was a painless process, just as the Division promised. For a moment, as he lay sprawled out on the floor, he wondered how many people in the City took the pill.

What was it like for them? To embrace this thing we don't talk about anymore and very few experience now?

What he knew for certain was that anyone who did take the pill had reached a point where not even the wonders and opportunities of Glass were enough to convince people to stay alive.

Death is part of the game...and I'm long overdue for it.

As his vision blurred and the lights in the ceiling bled together, Lazarus whispered a silent prayer and his mouth stopped moving just before he could utter...

Daniel.

———

CAPTAIN

To Captain's surprise, his father's office door wasn't locked. It was always locked. He braced himself to pound on it, but it slid open on its own. Sunset blanketed the room in a fiery orange glow. He didn't see his father at first. He hadn't seen or heard his father since he'd vanished into the room hours ago, so he still had to be there.

"Dad?" Captain called, turning his head as his eyes swept the room. Then he saw them— a pair of shoes jutting out from behind Lazarus's desk. His walk broke into a sprint. He rounded the desk and froze. His father's body was sprawled on the floor, eyes sightless, jaw slack.

Captain's breath caught in his chest, and he waited for his throat to constrict and tears to sting his eyes. Nothing happened. He stayed still and hollow for a minute. He lowered himself against the desk, sliding down until he sat beside his father's corpse. He didn't look at it. Instead, he gazed out the window at the flying cars as they zipped past the penthouse in eternal lines. The sunset orange faded, and night cloaked Captain in shadow.

For half an hour, Captain stayed sitting in silence. Once, Lazarus's phone buzzed in his pocket, but Captain didn't move to retrieve it. He would have to tell everyone in his father's world that he was dead. Everyone in Lazarus's life knew he was going to die, but they didn't think it would happen this soon.

Once it was clear the tears weren't coming, Captain finally glanced back at his father's body, which was now just another shadow in the dark. Motionless, and already irrelevant.

A strange calm washed over him, like an old friend, quiet and familiar. There was an ease as though he was breathing freely for the first time. He sat still with it, his heart pounding, as if by moving he'd disturb that calm and it would kill him. Like Lazarus, his jaw was slack, but he was alive. It was as if he was discovering that for the first time. What was he to do with that?

Then two simple words struck a chord in his heart.

I'm free.

The calm went with him, even while he broke the news to Lazarus's associates.

RIPLEY HAD NEVER SPENT any time in jail—a fact that both relieved and surprised him.

Glass's prison was a tall narrow tower in its own sector, isolated from the rest of the City. Atop it was a bright, white light that circled around like a lighthouse, reminding Ripley of the Lighthouse Borough at the shores of the ocean. There was only one prison in the City, housing every kind of criminal from the pettiest of offenses to the cruelest, darkest depths of human depravity.

Having been picked by Captain to bail Sparks out, Ripley followed the officer that led him through the dark hallways of the prison. The glow of the shield walls that kept the prisoners contained in their cells was the only light provided. Armed guards lined the walls, staring straight ahead. Ripley recognized a few of them as robots.

As Ripley peered up the tower, he could see the dozens and dozens of floors and the countless number of cells. Echoing through the tower was a symphony of cackling, yelling, cussing, and screaming.

Captain believed sending Damien to retrieve Sparks

would've been a bad idea, but Ripley didn't understand why he didn't send Trevor or Benji. He was grateful that he didn't send Joan, and even if he did, Ripley would've wanted to go with her.

He wagged his head to get out of his thoughts, and he left his heart behind on the ground as he was taken up in a crude elevator with the officer. The elevator shuddered as it stopped on the right floor. Continuing, Ripley strived to keep from looking into any of the cells, but he knew some of the prisoners were watching him. Mercifully, the officer stopped at one of the cells, a distorted grin creeping across his face. With a silent gulp, Ripley peered into the cell himself. Behind the laser wall that protected him from the prisoner, sitting on the bench, was Sparks.

His head was bowed and his eyes were shut. His legs were folded and his hands cupped his knees. He was shirtless, revealing several broad, grotesque scars on his chest. There was a scar over one side of his forehead that appeared fresher. Ripley guessed it was from his face getting bashed into the desk by Captain.

The officer pressed and held a button on a console beside the cell. "Today's your lucky day, gorgeous. You've got a Good Samaritan here to bail you out."

Ripley had seen many despicable, dangerous men in the Web. All of whom threatened to shank him, shoot him, club him, or strip him of his clothes and bury him alive in a ravine. Only a few of those things had ever happened to him, but it was enough to make him shrink back at the sight of every ragged-looking man lurking on the side of the path.

Sparks looked like one of those men from the Web, gazing at Ripley with an unquenchable rage hidden beneath fatigued eyes. Ripley felt trapped with him, despite being on the other side of the cell.

Several other guards formed a line behind Ripley and the officer, and the cell wall was deactivated. Ripley's heart shot up and felt like it was lodged in his throat. He watched the man slowly stand up.

What is Captain thinking?

Will Joan get hurt if I bring him back?

What happens to Trevor and me if we don't get out in time?

JOAN—ONLY half engaged—watched Captain raise two glasses filled with the blood-red liquid, Bathory. He got them from Carmilla, a woman he trusted to point people in his direction for potential recruitment. Captain even asked her at one point if she wanted to be part of the gang. A generous offer that she ultimately turned down, but Captain insisted she have some role to play. She was willing enough to look out for people who'd be interested in coming into his growing family, even if she wasn't officially a member herself. She ran her own Bathory truck on the side of the road. Apart from that, Captain didn't really know much about her, and she wasn't an open book about it either.

In celebration of his most recent accomplishments, the Bathory had a bit of vodka mixed in. Captain was grinning like an ecstatic child, his eyes wide and eager like one too. Seeing the Bathory only made Joan remember the glowing blood all over the table where the council was sitting. Five men, all sprawled out on chairs with their unblinking eyes.

Joan wondered if Captain knew that she was the only one in the group who didn't fire her gun.

"Joan, you good?" Captain asked, forcing Joan out of her head.

"Uh, yeah. Sorry," Joan replied, taking her glass. Captain raised his.

"In Glass is life, and in life is our transcendence to greatness," he quoted.

Okay...what do you follow that up with?

Joan raised her own glass. "To...greatness, then?"

They clinked glasses as Captain chuckled. "Yeah, let's go with that."

Joan took a deep breath before plunging the contents of the glass down her throat, bracing for the burn she was going to feel in the back. The burn morphed into a dull warmth, losing its edge almost immediately. Her whole body tingled and she felt stiff and unable to move. Once she was able to move again, she gasped.

Carmilla, a taller woman than Joan, laughed as she watched her.

"Still not used to it? It's been a year," she chided.

Captain placed his empty glass down with a happy grimace. "She'll get there."

Something wet plinked off Joan's head, and she held her hand out to feel rain beginning to fall.

"Time to get back home," Captain announced. Carmilla rolled the window of the truck down, and Captain unfolded a large, white umbrella fit for two. He drew Joan in so that their sides were touching. Her head sank to his shoulder as she walked with him down the sidewalk. All around them, people were popping up their own umbrellas, a cascade of blue, red, purple, white, and black flowering from the sidewalks and roads, creating a stream of chaotic colors.

"So what's the plan now, genius?" Joan asked, trying to make herself heard over the rain.

"First, we go to Samsara Financial so I can get my money back. Then, I talk to the other syndicates in Glass... face to face. My father left behind a list of every major cartel and gang in the City, so it can be my map to figure out who to talk to, and where I can find them. The Purpletells, Delanos, Jacks, Garks, all of them among others I can talk to."

"Do you really think the Jacks would be willing to meet with you? They've been off the radar since Chase's...well, you know."

"I think they will. Once I come up with an offer they can't refuse," Captain replied.

The penthouse came into view through the steady rain. Joan couldn't wait to finally get inside. She was hesitant to talk, knowing her voice would come out chattering and incoherent, but something weighed down in her stomach. A nagging feeling that this was the best time to talk to Captain about...

"So, I've been thinking..."

"Hm?" Captain replied, shifting his head to see Joan.

"...Is it...I don't know...*possible* if we..."

...can talk about kids.

Her last words didn't make it out as a taxicab passed by them, shooting up a wave of water that showered Joan's and Captain's legs. Joan heard—and felt—growling rising in Captain's throat as he about cursed. The car pulled over on the side ahead of them. At that point, they were in front of the penthouse. The rain was still falling with no sign of abating. Though Captain got the worst of the splash, Joan's legs still shivered.

"Could be Ripley and hopefully..."

Captain stopped when the passenger side door swung open, and an umbrella ballooned in the air as someone stepped out. Standing under the light of countless neon signs was Ripley.

"Well? Were you able to..."

Captain's voice froze when another umbrella ballooned and a second man got out of the car.

Sparks.

A tiny, tiny part of Joan hoped against all doubt that maybe, just maybe, Captain wasn't going to bring Sparks back. It sickened her to find out how foolish she was to think that at all; sickened her to think she could have one moment to tell Captain what she really wanted.

Seeing Sparks killed that last ray of hope.

Ripley caught Joan's eye, whose face confirmed that they both had the same thought.

This was a mistake.

Sparks somehow managed to disturb Joan even more upon seeing him a second time. There was the ghost of a smile creeping through his face, and his green eyes glowed in the evening rainstorm. He wasn't here because he was forced to. He wasn't Captain's prey. He *wanted* to be here. His eyes told Joan that, somehow, he *needed* to be here. *He* was the one in control, and Joan had no idea how.

Joan was reminded of something her father told her, not long before she ran away from the Web.

"There's monsters everywhere, love. At least in the Web, they're easier to spot."

Joan had no trouble seeing what Sparks was. She wished her husband did too.

PART TWO

17

WILD

RAIN BEAT *and flooded the alley. Blood-diluted water rushed into the sewer grate nearby, consumed by the rainbow of dizzying colors that dominated the City. Standing above Chase's corpse was his brother Wild.*

Wild toppled to his knees and raked his hands over his brother's chest.

"No, no no, Chase! Come on, Chase, wake up! Wake up, Chase! Don't do this to me! Don't—."

Wild stopped between heavy, grief ravaged breaths when he noticed something unusual, and unnerving. Chase's black and white pearl necklace was absent around his neck.

There's no way he left it at home.

Which means...

Wild's despaired cries diverged into anger that rose above the rain, the wind, the whirring machines...

Wild woke up gasping, glistening head to toe in sweat. He laid there in bed for a moment, his breathing coarse and rapid until he remembered where he was. A sly cynicism slinked into his mind like an ominous rain cloud, as it always did. Hours of sleep and he still woke up feeling the same as he did when he first let sleep take him. The only way to escape it was to sleep, and even then, it waited patiently for him to emerge back into the land of the living.

With a sigh, Wild sat up, hanging his legs over the side of the bed, and wiped tears from his walnut-colored eyes. His shaggy hair stuck out in all directions. The sunlight coming through his tall pill-shaped window was colorless and it stung Wild's eyes. That didn't make sense. He normally kept the window tinted.

Dad.

Wild checked the time and groaned. It was almost noon. He woke up several times earlier, only to drift off back to sleep, hoping that the next time he wakes up, life would be different. He needed to know who killed Chase, and why. He wasn't even close to finding out, and any hope of getting answers was nearly gone thanks to the police shelving the case a long time ago. Probably for the best. The police could've come across truths about Chase and the rest of the Jacks that shouldn't be found.

Wild wanted to get up and use his remote to darken the window again, but he didn't even have the energy for *that*.

Maybe one of the boys can meet for coffee.

The thought disappeared as quickly as it started. Wild was glued to his bed as if it was the extension providing him life support.

The buzzer by his door chimed, and Wild heard his father's voice.

"Get up. We need to talk."

Wild stared up at the low, gray ceiling, his expression blank and his eyes in another world. His room was claustrophobic, but so were most of the others on this side of Glass in the Lower Housing District. It was a neighborhood designed for citizens that appreciated simplicity and possessed only the bare minimum, finding more space and enjoyment in whatever downtown offered and spent as little time at home as possible.

One of the reasons Wild and Chase were so eager to leave their parents was because they hated feeling boxed in. As members of the band Paragon, they wanted the freedom to move for dance practice, and that wasn't possible in their rooms. Their parents refused to move somewhere bigger.

Wild finally pressed the button beside his door, allowing it to slide open and he came out into the living room in his fur robe. His feet were silent as he crossed over to the dining table positioned against the wall. Everything was in one room. The living room, the kitchen, the dining area. The three bedrooms were side by side, which Wild hated. His parents were far from a sexless marriage, and most noise carried through the wall.

A large flatscreen on the wall played Glass's anthem, displaying the same tired montages of the City and its people. Sitting at the dining table were both of Wild's parents. His mother, Glenda, was thin, with the skin on her face stretched like dough. In her hands was a steaming cup of coffee. Wild's father Denarius was bigger than Glenda, with broader shoulders, a larger bald head, and a goatee that even impressed Wild. He had a transplant for an eye, after his real one was stabbed in a bar fight and his surviving eye was golden.

Golden like Chase's.

Sitting in the middle of the table was a cup of coffee, but it wasn't steaming. Wild didn't care. He sat down and reached for it, but Denarius took it and slid it towards himself.

"I adjusted that window two hours ago," he said.

Wild didn't reply. He was a man of few words these days.

Denarius frowned. His grip stayed on the cup.

"Sorry," Wild muttered without looking at him.

"What?"

"Sorry," Wild said again louder.

With a deep sigh, Denarius allowed Wild the cup.

Yep, cold.

"How long has it been now?" Denarius asked.

"Since what?"

"Don't toy with me, boy. You know what."

"You should know, he was *your* son," Wild remarked between sips, keeping his eyes downcast.

"Your mother and I said goodbye to him a long time ago. We get up early *every* morning and still live our lives, so why can't you do the same?"

Wild didn't answer, though he had about a dozen ideas of what he could say.

Because, unlike you, Chase dying meant something to me.

Glenda set her mug down and leaned forward. "Everything you've done so far in your life is more than we could've hoped for, Wild, but you're..."

"I'm *what*, mother?" Wild asked, his gaze still down. His mother never liked saying the uncomfortable parts out loud.

"Ruining all of it," Denarius finished.

Wild grunted with a roll of his eyes and sipped again.

"I've signed you up for a couple appointments at the Suicide Watch Division," Denarius said.

That got Wild's attention. Glass didn't have therapists since the concept of 'bad mental health' was so foreign to the City. Between the gift of eternity through a drink and opportunities everywhere one looked, how could anyone *consider* being miserable? Instead, there were police that monitored people's mental health if they showed troubling signs of degradation, and added their names to a watchlist. If things turned serious, they were sent to the Suicide Watch Division to decide what kind of medication they needed, of which most were advised to be taken with Bathory, believing that the combined effects of both could help sustain one's mind.

Wild's cheeks flared and his throat tightened the longer he sat on his father's words, but he swore never to look up. He was getting better at that part.

"I didn't realize grief was a punishable offense," Wild said.

"This isn't a punishment, this is a necessity. You can't live with this grief anymore, son. Grief is the ultimate thief of life. You need to go live again. That's not a request," Denarius replied, folding his arms.

Wild finally turned up his gaze, eyes trained on Glenda.

"Mother, do you have any objections?"

Glenda shook her head.

Wild continued, "Of course you don't. You agree with *everything* dad says, that's how the relationship works." He stood up, leaving his cup unfinished.

"By the way, if you two are going to do it while I'm gone, do it on *your* bed this time," he remarked.

"Where are you going?" Denarius asked.

"Out. Apparently, I'm not welcome in here," Wild replied. He left without saying goodbye or waiting for his parents to say anything. He figured he might as well leave the house and make the most out of the free time he had left.

18

CAPTAIN

THE LIMOUSINE DOOR slid shut behind Captain as he stepped out into the balmy morning air. He groaned as he stretched, feeling his body loosen.

"I'll be right back. Step outside, stretch your legs," Captain said to his gang. Everyone was there, including Sparks.

They were in Samsara Financial's courtyard. The building itself wasn't just another tower clustered with all the others in the City, but in its own private sector, dead center in a courtyard surrounded by trees and grassy lawns. The tower was shaped like a twisted DNA strand with the giant letters WF shining on the side. At the center of the courtyard, in front of the building, was an inky black fountain with water gushing out from beneath a statue of Sylar Han. His hands were spread apart as if eager to embrace someone and there was a stiff prideful grin stretched across his face.

That grin is going to be a frown when I show Sylar that someone else can be more powerful than him.

"Damn, is this all *real* grass, *real* trees?" Joan asked.

Captain shrugged, his gaze stuck to the front doors of the building. "When it comes to Sylar, what's really *real*?"

"Still," Joan said, kneeling down to stroke her fingers through the blades of grass.

"Definitely prettier than anything I've seen in the Web. Besides the stars," Ripley said.

"Alright, wish me luck," Captain announced.

He ascended the stairs leading up to the line of doors. It was time to get his money back and get started growing his influence.

Last night, when Ripley made it back to the penthouse with Sparks, Captain didn't waste any time to try putting the fear of God in Sparks.

Captain sat across from Sparks in his office. Rain pounded the glass behind him. The artificial pool in the floor cast shifting reflections that licked up Sparks's face, making his features seem less like a man's and more like something moving under a mask.

"Are you familiar with the pop band, Paragon?" Captain asked.

"Who isn't?" Sparks shrugged, mild in tone. His gaze drifted, then returned, as if nothing in the room could anchor him.

"Then you heard that one of the members, Chase, died."

"Yeah. Murdered."

"What if I told you *I* killed him?"

The confession was like a gunshot. Even Captain shuddered after the words rolled out. He couldn't pull them back in. They hung in the air. Yet, Sparks didn't even blink. He folded himself into the chair. His expression was half-reflection, half-mask.

"Why not turn me in?" Captain said. "You can go to the Jacks. Tell them it was me."

Sparks smiled without using his mouth. "No," he said, soft and certain.

So, even he *understands the risks.*

Captain leaned forward. "I'm glad we understand each other." He allowed a brief smile.

Sparks's stillness unsettled Captain. There was no fear there. Instead, his bright eyes glimmered something Captain couldn't name. He had to keep talking to keep control of the room.

"Paragon and the syndicate—the Jacks—are one and the same. They were *the* most powerful gang in the City. Not anymore. I didn't think I could do it at first, but I was inspired by the same guy who killed Angel. You heard about that too, right?"

"Yeah," Sparks said, slower, like he was tasting the word.

"The killer was never caught. If *he* could kill an untouchable celebrity, so could *I*. I can shake up the City a bit. Anyone with half a brain would've done the same thing. My father would've called it cheating. And speaking of fathers..."

Sparks's gaze sharpened and his face moved. The twitch of a cheek and the flaring of a nostril was all Captain needed.

"If you disrespect me again, in *any* way...I will go to the nursing home and kill your dad."

Sparks went rigid, still as a statue. The reflection in the floor trembled as if the fake water was reacting. Captain's stomach tightened, discontent with what Sparks gave him. Did his threat land at all?

Fine. I'll have to go further to make my point. He can't keep this up forever.

Captain watched Sparks go and the rain tapered off. The silence trapped him in his thoughts.

It's a little too late now to toss him back on the street.

————

Captain was greeted by passionate opera chirring from a machine on Sylar's desk, where a large disc was slowly rotating atop it. Sylar himself was relaxing at his desk with his feet up and his hand fondling a stress ball.

"My Captain, my Captain. Don't be shy now," Sylar said.

Captain hesitated at first, jarred by Sylar's superfluous demeanor, but sighed and crossed the room. The clouds outside masked the sunlight for a bit, cloaking Sylar in shadow and winking out the bloody lights in the ceiling.

"What do you think of this?" Sylar asked, holding out his tablet and pressing the play button on the screen.

"*What do you mean he can't talk?!*" Captain's voice exploded over the speaker.

"*Sir, he's in a meditation session, he will be willing to talk to you when—.*"

"*How is meditation reason enough to be busy?!*"

"*He takes it very seriously and—.*"

"*Do I sound like I give a shit?!*"

Captain smoothed his hands down his face, hoping to hide his embarrassment while an ache throbbed in the back of his head.

"We record every phone conversation for quality assurance," Sylar said.

Captain ignored Sylar, deciding to jump straight into his reason for being there. "Simon—an old friend of my father's—sent seven hundred million to Samsara Financial without my consent. He...*used* to manage the family finances."

Sylar tilted his head and his eyes sparkled. "He's dead now, isn't he?"

"What do *you* think?"

Sylar bit his bottom lip. "Well, let me do a little digging. I can trace the transaction and see where it ended up with us."

Captain blinked. "Wait, seriously? You wouldn't already know? A transfer of seven hundred million dollars doesn't just get overlooked. Can't you just give me seven hundred million and we can call it a day?"

Sylar's head jerked back to face Captain, eyes bright enough to light up a dark room. "I can't just give you seven hundred million dollars. I have to make sure this transfer was real."

"How could it not be real? Simon told me himself!" Captain argued.

Oh...

"That's what I thought," Sylar replied, seeming to notice what Captain realized.

"I mean, he was in excruciating pain and seconds away from death, it was kind of assumed he told the truth," Captain whimpered.

"Why bother telling the truth when you know you're already dead?" Sylar said.

He's not wrong but I'm not walking without answers! I don't care who this guy is. Sylar the Invisible, Sylar the Immortal, Sylar the Brave. I've heard it all! He's just a man!

"Where *is* it then?" Captain seethed.

Sylar stared at him blankly. All the playfulness and enthusiasm had been sapped away.

"Sit down," he ordered, his voice like dry ice.

Captain glanced around, expecting to see a chair that he overlooked, but there was nothing.

"Um, there's no..."

"Sit down," Sylar repeated with the same tone.

Captain sat down and folded his legs. Sylar towered over him, doused in the red lights.

The CEO touched his tablet screen. "Now, let's try this again. Can you think of *anyone* Simon was close to that he might be willing to share with?"

Captain never bothered to learn too much about Simon, nor most of the other council members. He was more focused on building the foundation of his own empire, not learning the nuances of his father's. He didn't know anyone that Simon could've been close to or had any relationships with besides his father.

"No," he finally answered, hating himself.

Sylar clicked his tongue and swiped over his screen, his eyes swerving left and right as he read. Suddenly, they stopped.

"You found something?" Captain asked, moving to get up, but Sylar gave him a finger, halting him.

"Interesting," he muttered.

"Who has my money? Can you get it back?"

Sylar gazed at Captain as if he forgot he was there, and a humored grin cracked across his face before laughing.

"No I can't 'get it back'! That's something even *I* can't do. I can trace transactions and transfers, thumb through someone's account history, but I can't take money from someone's account or freeze it. That requires a special request to Uncle Sam where he then calls the bank and gives the order—*if* he decides it's worth his time."

Captain sucked in a long breath and scraped his teeth against his tongue, welcoming the pain. "Why *wouldn't* it be worth his time?"

"Because the world doesn't revolve around you, Kotstov. Simon was your family's money handler, right? He had stake in it, so there's no way to prove this was nonconsensual, or theft. Your crocodile tears over *pocket change* means *nothing* to the government," Sylar explained.

Captain's eyes fell to his lap. "Where did Simon send the money?" He asked, his voice a near whisper, the tension from earlier missing.

"Don't ask me why, but he sent the money to Jiang Band. Paragon's dance coach."

Paragon.

Captain wrung his wrists to try and get the trembling in his hands to stop, but it was no use. There was a perfect opportunity to use this to get to the Jacks. He had never heard of Jiang, but his connection to the Jacks would serve Captain well.

Of course, there was the matter of figuring out how to get in contact with the Jacks. They weren't exactly a simple phone call away, and hardly anyone within the underworld had seen them face-to-face in the last year.

All because of Captain.

If I play my cards right—if—they can become great allies.

"Then I guess we're done here," Captain said, trying to stand again. This time, Sylar didn't stop him.

"I guess so," Sylar replied, returning to his desk.

Captain started to head back to the door, but Sylar wasn't finished.

"I know who you are, Daniel Kostov."

Captain stopped but didn't turn. Sylar continued.

"Your reputation precedes you...as in, you don't have one. Your father killed himself, and who knows where your mom is? Probably in some back alley doing...unsavory favors. So what does that make *you*?"

"*Better than you!*" Captain screamed, spinning around with his finger extended towards the banker.

As the words shot out, he knew too late that Sylar had set him up.

Mission accomplished.

"Huh." Sylar bit his lip again, and he took his stress ball. "You're *exactly* what you leave behind."

"What...do I leave behind?"

"Chaos. Everyone knows it was you that had that whole group of guys killed at *Nine Circles*. I even knew a few of them, longer than you've been alive. You carry a lot of anger, and you leave evidence of it wherever you go. Word of advice to the young and hopeful: keep your act clean, or that mess will catch up with you," Sylar said. He thumbed a button in the desk, and the doors behind Captain slid open.

"Get this guy out. We're done here. And don't be gentle," Sylar ordered the two men at the doorway.

The men snatched Captain's shoulders and roughly led him away before he could say anything else. He attempted to wrestle his way out of their grips, but they were like steel.

He's just a man! He's just a stupid man!

And yet, the stupid man was the one in control.

———

The front doors of Samsara Financial split open and Captain was tossed out. His body landed on the steps and rolled down, seized by gravity. Pain ripped at him and flesh tore as Captain fell down the staircase all the way to the bottom.

"Ow!" He cried.

I think I broke something.

"Daniel!" He heard Joan shout.

The first face he saw was Damien's, rushing to his rescue.

"Is it bad?" Captain asked, not daring to move a muscle.

"It's bad."

"Bathory, *now.*"

Damien removed a narrow vial from his breast pocket and held it to Captain's lips, tipping the liquid. The Bathory rushed down his throat and burned his stomach. A few coughs came hard and dry. Joan slipped her hand under Captain's head to support him.

"So, did you get your money back?" Benji asked, seemingly with no remorse for Captain's pain.

"Benji, not now," Joan scolded.

Captain was starting to feel his strength return already. It was a fast-acting remedy, and though the fire in his gut made for an uncomfortable experience, it was worth it. Inside, his body was healing. Bones that had been splintered reforged themselves, veins were restored, and fissured flesh closed up. His breathing, however, still came rapid, labored and haggard.

Captain sat up as the pain drifted away, turning his head to take in his whole crew, who had formed a circle around him.

"So, you good?" Damien asked.

"Yeah, I'm good. I learned what I needed to know. We need to talk to the Jacks."

19

SAE

SAE STEPPED on the elevator that only existed on the top floor of Samsara Financial, pressing the only button on the control panel that would take him down. He keyed in a code that only he and Sylar knew. As the doors started to close, Ratchet came up and stopped them.

Sae tapped the 'down' button again, hoping it would shut the doors on Ratchet's hand, but Ratchet's grip held up. Sae was stuck until Ratchet decided to let go.

"Leave me alone," Sae growled.

Instead, Ratchet pushed the doors further apart.

"You can't keep your secrets forever, you know. Not from the Children of Glass."

Before Sae could respond, Ratchet finally let go of the doors and leered at Sae until they shut in his face. Even as the elevator descended and Sae was clearly alone, he shivered.

Ratchet was one of Sylar's personal assassins and his contractor that was responsible for last resort crises. If Sylar needed someone dead within the hour, Ratchet was the man to do it. He would swoop in with a wide variety of weapons and explosives, oftentimes choosing a different method to kill each target. Repetition bored him. He also worshipped Sylar, though he tried not to make that clear in front of him, but Sylar knew.

The elevator halted, then veered left for a while before stopping. The doors opened, and Sae entered the library on the other side. An old, musty smell smacked Sae in the face, but he embraced it. It was familiar and homely. The ceilings were high, allowing the bookshelves to stand tall and imposing. Sae was allowed to scale them if he wanted to, up any one of the ladders nearby to grab books from the top or sort through the stacks of old newspapers and magazines. There were shelves dedicated to old movies in forms called DVDs, and there were video games, audiobooks, scrapbooks full of what Sylar called 'memes', and vinyl records. As far as Sae was aware, this was one of the last bastions of a forgotten past. The only other one he knew of was in Primitus, a tiny, insignificant portion of Glass run by people who hated the City. To step foot on that stretch of road would be seen as trespassing to the people there despite there being no barriers. How long ago this forgotten past was, Sae wasn't sure, and Sylar was vague about it. Sae wondered if even Sylar knew how long ago it was when these things were used by everybody. The library was lit by LED lights installed in the exposed wall between shelves, and there were tables and chairs set up in the middle of the room. A collection of board games were stacked up on a few of the tables.

Above the shelves at the front of the room, in the sliver of wall, was a plaque, which read:

All mortal greatness is but disease.

Sometimes Sae didn't read. Instead, he'd brush his hand against book spines, then retrace his steps and do it again over the same books, as if he feared they'd disappear if he didn't. Though he was allowed to come to the library any time he wanted, enough time above would make him feel disbelief all over again seeing everything the library had.

Sae's own personal scrapbook sat on one of the desks. He opened it up, thumbing through the pages until he came across a couple that had front page newspaper articles, all arranged chronologically. They were headlines that still filled him with awe and untamed curiosity. A deep yearning stirred in him, as if he wanted to witness the events described in the articles himself, and he sighed, knowing that the printed words were the only way he would ever be connected to this chronicled history.

Tensions rise as lines are drawn and negotiations begin
CIVIL WAR!
NYC in ruins after several bombs detonate
Standstill reached, but at what cost?
Skyrocketing inflation leaves millions desperate and without help
What is Glass and what will it mean for you?
The process of dividing Glass into separate sectors now in negotiations
The Web: Should we care about those left behind?
Why keeping the City divided into sectors is actually a good thing.

Sae continued flipping the pages in his scrapbook until he reached the end and closed it, reminded again of the things that had come before. His memory was refreshed, and he wished he could say the same about people above.

Something else on the table caught his eye. It was a copy of the old book, *Moby Dick.*

Must've forgotten to put it back.

He sat down, took it, and opened it. Subconsciously, he began reading it.

Call me Ishamael. Some years ago—never mind how long precisely—having little or no money in my purse, and nothing particular to interest me on shore, I thought I would sail about a little and see the watery part of the world...

Sae looked up from the book as his mind wandered. He had never gone sailing, but he wanted to. He had thought about asking Sylar to take him to the one by the Lighthouse Borough, but he knew Sylar would never step foot out of Glass for any reason, let alone allow him to leave.

Sae continued reading, not caring that it was the third time he'd read the book.

"THERE'S *no* way for you to get out of Glass, is that what you're saying?"

Inside a coffee shop, Violet stared at the tablet screen displaying her sister Vanessa. After finishing her morning shift at the nursing home, Violet was determined to find any excuse not to go home. It didn't matter that her boyfriend wasn't home yet, she didn't want to be in the apartment. She didn't want to hear the clicking sound of the keypad and see the front door slide open, and have to wonder if he'd just ignore her and watch TV or find a reason to yell at her.

"It's not that I can't, it's that I don't want to," Violet argued, flipping back her butterscotch hair.

"Well *I'm* not coming over there," Vanessa retorted. She had the same color hair as Violet's but shorter. Bright red lipstick glimmered over her mouth.

"Wait, why *not*? I thought you said you were considering it."

"*Considering* it. It's not the same thing as *doing* it. Our parents knew that when you go in, it's really hard to get out," Vanessa gestured to Violet. "Case and point."

Tears of anger raced into Violet's eyes, threatening to break apart her face.

It's just like her to do this to me. It's just like her...!

"You can stay in Spectra if that's what you want, but *I* think there's still something for me here."

"Really? Like what, Violet? Enlighten me."

Should I really tell her?

"I care about the people I work with. There's this one guy..."

"Violet, they're practically whining corpses."

Violet shook her head. Charles was on her mind, one of the only things tethering her to her job. "There's *one* guy I care about at least. He's...different."

"Different how?"

Violet sighed. "I don't know, just *different*. He's not a terrible person like so many other people here. He cares about me."

Vanessa smirked. "Careful. He might be lonely."

"Don't be gross, it's not like that."

Vanessa sat back and blew out an exasperated sigh. "I don't get you, Violet. I never did. Plus your taste in men suck."

Violet wanted to feel offended, but Vanessa was right in a way that was embarrassing to admit.

"On that, we agree. I just don't want to leave Glass."

Vanessa sat up straight again and her face turned dour. "If you leave Damien but stay in Glass, you know he'll come after you. You know too much about his work."

VIOLET

JUST MINUTES AFTER SPARKS LEFT, Damien appeared in the doorway that led into the lounge of the nursing home. Violet felt her insides jolt. Her heartbeat was so out of control she thought it would burst out her chest.

This was the first time Damien had ever stepped foot in the nursing home.

Oh no...oh no.

"Damien?" Violet whispered as she approached him.

"Don't get too excited, babe, I'm here on business," Damien replied, his eyes dancing around the room, as if looking for someone in particular.

"What...kind of business?" Violet asked, pushing against the rattle in her voice.

"That guy who just left...who did he come here to see?"

Oh no...

"Why?" Violet asked.

Damien stopped scanning the room and looked directly at Violet, blue flames in his pupils.

"Watch it," he fired. Violet staggered back a step. Damien recognized how bitter he came across and his face softened slightly and his voice lowered.

"It's important, Violet. It's for my boss."

"If I tell you, what will you do?" Violet's voice shivered.

"Nothing. At least not yet."

Damien had relaxed, but Violet knew that if she didn't cooperate, he'd flare up again, and she couldn't take any more for the day. She pointed at Charles, who had turned around to stare out one of the windows.

"Him. That's who Sparks came to see," she said, more bile building up with each word.

"What is he, his grandpa?" Damien remarked.

"His father."

Violet's answer triggered a crafty grin on Damien's face.

"Interesting," he mused. Without another word, he walked out.

Violet wanted to throw up. Wanted to go to Charles sobbing out an apology. Whatever Damien would do to Charles, Violet felt powerless to stop it.

VIOLET FELT TRAPPED in a relationship that would last whether she liked it or not.

She closed her tablet. No help was coming to her. She didn't dare reach out to her parents. She didn't want to face them after proving them right about Glass.

The coffee shop she was in was a fishbowl underground. A circular room with glass walls containing water and fish behind them, and the lights streaming down from above Violet were pale and somber. No one dared start a fight there. No one was stupid enough to shoot a gun there either. Violet felt it was one of the safest places in Glass.

Violet stared at the fish, reminded that, like her, the fish too were trapped. The only difference was that the fish were likely oblivious.

"Hey," a voice spoke up beside her.

A stranger with his hands stuffed in his pockets slid into the seat opposite Violet before she even had the chance to look at him. He wore a massive, white hoodie with the hood concealing half of his face. A pair of shades covered his eyes.

"Are you okay?" He asked.

Violet squinted. His voice sounded...*familiar*.

"Um, I...do I know you?" She asked.

A flimsy smirk from the young man. "I'm sure you've heard me before."

He turned his head so that he was facing the glass wall beside them and slipped the shades down. Then it dawned on Violet.

"Oh my god! You're...Wild, from Paragon!" She whispered.

"Keep your voice down, okay? I don't wanna get overrun," Wild replied with a smile, pushing the shades up.

"How can you be in *public* without getting overrun?" Violet asked.

"I can be invisible," Wild said, hand on his chest in mock offense.

Violet's coffee was brought to her but she didn't touch it. She couldn't believe it. There was Wild, one of the most popular people in Glass, sitting across from her and he was *talking* to her.

"Plus, I had to get out of the house for a little bit. Parents were driving me nuts," Wild continued.

What's he doing with his parents? Considering every-thing he has, how is he still living with them?

Then it struck Violet. Something she heard about a little over a year ago. There was nowhere you could turn where the news wouldn't be there.

"I'm sorry about Chase," she said. She wasn't even sure why she said it. She knew Wild as a celebrity, but not as a person. Did it stem from the good habits her parents had baked into her when she was a child? Maybe, but she still felt like she was in the wrong to bring it up.

Will he get up and walk away?!

Wild only shrugged with a joyless smile under his hood. ""Don't be. It's not like you're the one who...uh...unalived him. Do *you* have siblings?"

"Yeah, one sister."

"Older or younger?"

"Older."

"She's still alive, right?"

"Yes," Violet said, happy to say it.

"Good. It's...not fun to go through what I'm going through," Wild said.

Violet shuddered. "I can't imagine." It wasn't hard for Violet to have disturbing thoughts of her sister dying though. She wondered if that was a habit developed from spending too much time with Damien. "Please don't take this the wrong way, but why are you talking to me? Considering—you know—who you are, don't you have more important things to do?"

Violet figured that if someone like Wild was going to talk to her like a human being, she should talk to him back the same way. Joan—the wife of Damien's boss, Captain—and Charles were the only people she usually got to have a few normal conversations with and that fact was a crippling reminder of how lonely she really was.

Wild's eyes glazed over, and for several seconds, Violet regretted asking.

"Chase used to do the same thing. He used to sit and talk to strangers, get to know them and all. He had a good eye for finding good people. This happens to be one of the places where he did it most," he explained. He folded his arms and his voice turned lower.

"The bigger me and the other guys got, the more he did it. I think he was getting lonely because of how busy we were. When we started out, we were inseparable and we made everything together. We shared a home together because we wanted to keep each other close as often as possible. Once the views skyrocketed and the contracts were on the table, each of us started doing our *own* things too. I think he got lonely and wanted to connect with other people. I think—in a way—he missed hanging out with people without complications that come with fame."

Violet had good friends in Spectra. When she came to Glass, she got Damien. What Chase had craved, she craved.

An android came up to the table and put a twenty-ounce frappe in front of Wild. "There you are, sir."

"Thank you," Wild muttered with his head down. Once the server left, Wild raised the cup.

"Chase and I loved this stuff. Maybe a little *too* much. We'd have them while pulling all-nighters writing music."

Wild sucked up a big sip and smacked his lips and for the briefest moment, he looked content. Happy even, as if a dark veil was lifted from his face, before it fell back and his eyes were overcast again.

"But enough about me and Chase, let's talk about *you* for a sec. You seemed pretty stressed when I saw you," he said.

Violet flinched. "Okay, counter-question: why do you care? You're a celebrity, *I'm* not anyone special, I'm just... just..."

"Just a person. I know. How terrible," Wild chuckled. "Pretend we're the only friends we have for a minute. Maybe we can help each other out. It's obvious we could use a little help."

"I...I want to leave my boyfriend, but I don't know how with—without leaving Glass, and if I go anywhere else *inside* the City, he can find me."

Violet was out of breath by the time she finished, her last word almost muted.

"So he's...dangerous?" Wild asked.

"Kinda, yeah. He's with some bad people. He's with..."

Violet halted, mulling over her next words more carefully. She didn't think Wild was going to reveal she had told him any of this to anyone, but she still just met him. She knew the celebrity, not the person.

"He works for terrible people. He's horrible to me and he hurts others. Probably even does worse sometimes."

Wild chewed his bottom lip as an idea was knitted together. "Has anything happened where you needed to defend yourself?"

Violet blinked. Her mind drifted back to the moment when Damien came into the nursing home. Maybe it wasn't herself she needed to defend.

"I don't think so. Not yet."

"But you're saying it could happen?" Wild pressed.

A fist gripped Violet's heart, forcing it to beat louder. She lowered her voice.

"Are you saying I should...?"

Wild leaned in to talk to Violet in a hushed tone. He was completely serious now, the nostalgia and joy he had before gone.

"*I'm* saying you should do whatever you have to do to get that piece of shit out of your life before something worse happens. You've made it obvious he's that kind of guy. I never caught the son of a bitch that killed my brother, but unlike me, *you* can stop him before he does something. Maybe even hurts someone you care about..."

Charles.

"Don't leave behind loose ends if you think they'll catch up to you. Don't feel like you have to leave Glass because of him. I was born here. I met my friends here, made our music together, and experienced almost everything Glass can offer. I'd *never* leave," Wild said.

Violet never considered Paragon to be her hero, but listening to Wild reminded her of the phrase 'never meet your heroes'. What would someone who was an actual fan of Wild think if they met him and found out that he toyed with ideas of...murder?

Wild stood up with his coffee in hand. "I should go. I shouldn't be in one place for *too* long."

"Thank you. Really," Violet replied.

Wild flashed a sad smile, his bottom lip quivering. A hint of a tear slipped from under his shades. "Just think about what I told you."

After winking, he made a brisk beeline for the exit, quick on his feet. Something was spurring him somewhere, and Violet wondered how much of it was because of her. She finally took a sip of now-lukewarm coffee with Wild's words stamped deep on her brain.

...Do whatever you have to do to get that piece of shit out of your life.

Do whatever you have to...

Whatever...

———

WILD

Through the tunnel and to the escalator that went up, a dozen screaming voices spun around in Wild's head. All of them belonging to him, all of them chanting at him to seek vengeance.

Find the man who killed Chase.

Find him and kill him in the same alley.

After one time he went out in public since Chase's murder, he ended up opening his heart to someone, a stranger too.

There were risks to hunting down this animal. The other Jacks wouldn't approve of it because of the risks, but they didn't need to know.

It was time to finally make a decision for himself after so long.

23

DAGAN

DAGAN BLEW the dust off of a cassette tape he had found in the back room of his antique shop *The Time Capsule*, hopeful but not confident that it was going to work.

A lot of cassette tapes, CDs, DVDs, and VHS tapes in his store were already broken, cracked, or unplayable. Eventually he had to separate what was broken from what still worked. He tested portions of them every day to make sure they still played properly, and shed a tear if something didn't.

He swallowed a mouthful of Bathory, grimacing at the bitter taste of raspberry as it struck the back of his throat. He never liked Bathory, but he saw it as a means to an end, and that end was to preserve everything that was forgotten and share it with whoever came in until it wasn't possible to protect it from authorities anymore. Certain bureaucrats relished the idea of confiscating everything from him to burn away the past. It was the never-ending present of Glass that mattered most after all.

The only thing that seemed to protect all the things he had in his store was his history working within World

Linked, which had a department for collecting anything that was connected to the past somehow and incinerating it. Before Dagan left World Linked, he managed to take as much as he could with some help. Though he couldn't protect any of the people who came in and bought anything from him, they understood the importance of it. The politicians knew that if they sent authorities to confiscate everything in the store, people would have questions. And not only would people have questions, Primitus—which was a small stretch of road in the middle of Glass resembling a small town—would stand up for Dagan. There'd be conflict, and the conflict wouldn't end without violence, which would send shockwaves through Glass that the politicians had no desire to cause. Some called it an example of 'disturbing the peace'.

Dagan didn't want Primitus to stand up for him should his life and his work ever be in danger, but he was loved by everyone. His store was a signal of rebellion, which he feared ran too high of a risk of putting his family in danger, but his wife Marlene didn't want him to stop. As long as he kept the shop open, Primitus believed he was still strong. They felt safe knowing he and everything he had was still intact. It gave them hope. That and his encouragement as a preacher, another part of him that he had played with the temptation of giving up on many times.

His tired eyes under bushy eyebrows studied the tape he held in his hand, and with a deep breath, he slid it into the radio he had sitting on the counter near the back of the shop, praying the tape would work.

To his delight, the music played. Old jazz strayed through the store, and while the sound quality wasn't perfect, it was enough to make him want to cry tears of joy.

Despite the rich displays of literature and relics in the

shop, the store was right at home with the rest of the City. There were bars of soft green LED lights against the walls with neon posters flashing notes like 'Be Kind, Rewind'. A few arcade games lined up against the left and right sides of the store with names in big lettering that Dagan could read but couldn't understand.

Aside from the music playing, Dagan's personal hover drone CT-RX floated from shelf to shelf, pushing up against different things that it found misaligned. Perfection was in its programming. Marlene had it wired that way.

The doors of the store slid open and the chime alerting Dagan to visitors sounded. Thanks to how tall the shelves were and how they were formed to make a maze, it took a moment for Dagan to see whatever guests came in. His shoulders relaxed when he recognized Marlene coming around the shelves, a crucifix dangling from her neck. Her beautiful scarlet eyes blinked at her husband worried.

"When are you coming home?" She asked, setting her gloved hands on the counter.

"Did I forget something is happening?" Dagan asked, shutting off the music.

"Something is happening out *there*," Marlene replied, gesturing a hand to the doors.

"What do you mean?" Dagan asked, his eyes turning grim.

"There's some shady people scouting the area out. People we've never seen around here before," Marlene explained.

Dagan waved his hand. "They'll move on. Most people do."

"One of them went to the old Kostov home," Marlene said.

That made Dagan pause. The home Marlene was

talking about was the largest house in Primitus, which Lazarus Kostov used to come and stay in once in a while. He was the owner of Primitus until he died, and that didn't affect much, but a gnawing worry in the back of Dagan's mind did form when Lazarus stopped showing up. Was Lazarus's son ever going to turn up?

Maybe that time was finally coming.

"What do we do?" Marlene asked.

"For now...nothing. We keep our heads down, we do business as usual, and then when it's necessary to do something, we'll know. We can't give those people up top a reason to rain fire down on us," Dagan said.

24

CAPTAIN

IF GLASS WAS A GIANT, Primitus was an ant shadowed by that giant. Spanning only several city blocks, Primitus was what remained of a city that had been burned away a long time ago, and Glass was built around it, wrapping itself around these blocks as if to protect it. Calls had been made by people who had never seen the world before Glass to have it decimated and replaced with the same architecture as the rest of the City.

Very few people lived in Primitus. Those that did yearned for the simpler life the haven offered them without having to venture out into the Labyrinth and suffer in the Web in order to get it.

Captain's father bought the whole road, taking owner-ship of every home and business, but didn't lift a finger to change anything, as if he felt compassion and respect for it. It was the perfect place for Captain and his group to stay until relationships with the other crime families were proven stable. No gangs ever went to war with each other on Primitus' block because, like Primitus itself, they would stick out to authorities that weren't already bought and paid for by someone else within the underworld's network.

It was a glorified post where Captain could feel safer and more in control of his situation.

He stood outside with Joan, having sent Sparks, Ripley, Trevor, and Damien to scout out Primitus and make sure there were no spies or criminals hiding and waiting to pounce on him. Benji was visiting his mother at the hospital. It was a relief to finally have space with Joan without someone like Damien or Trevor breathing down his neck, reminding him of his and Joan's first days together.

What made Primitus special to Captain was that that was where those first days were spent.

Joan was perched on a silver glowing fountain rooted in Primitus' center. Water gushed from its top and bright neon colors of blue, purple, and pink bathed beneath the water at the bottom. Captain released a deep breath at the sound of the trickling water, his shoulders resting and the knot in his stomach unwinding.

The knot didn't unravel completely, however, because Benji wasn't back yet.

Joan smirked up at him. "Admit it, you care about him," she said.

"Maybe a little. So what?"

"You care about him a *lot*."

"Nope."

Joan leaped up with a giggle, their fingers intertwined, and Captain's heart rustled at the touch.

The only one who's able to break down these walls.

"I don't think most gang leaders would've let one of their own go visit their sick mom," Joan said.

Captain had no answer for that, so Joan continued.

"You gotta throw me a bone here. I never saw anyone

care about Websters the way I've seen *you* care. It's adorable," Joan teased.

Captain took a cigar from his breast pocket and bit the end of it. He reached for his lighter, watching people entering and exiting shops, some walking down the sidewalk eyeing him with suspicion. Everyone in Primitus knew who he was just like they knew his father, but the difference was that they knew what to expect from his father. They didn't know what Captain's presence meant. Down the street, he spotted Sparks crossing and his heart pumped revulsion. Damien trailed not far behind him, never taking his eyes off of him.

Tonight, I'm going to get my point across to Sparks.

"Okay, no secrets, right?" Captain asked.

Joan nodded. "No secrets. What's up?"

"Like Sparks, Benji is only here for the...short term."

Joan blinked. "Wait, what?"

Captain ignored Joan's surprise. He knew that was coming. He just had to keep pushing forward, hoping she'd understand.

"Obviously the Amon Tribe will want him for killing their men, which will make negotiations with them easy. I give them Benji, they give me what *I* want, and we can be friends."

"Oh," Joan let go of Captain's hand. "I gave you *way* too much credit."

"You're not actually upset, are you?" Captain asked.

Joan didn't answer. Captain followed her gaze, and it ended on Sparks, who was taking in Primitus.

"You should've told me from the beginning. 'No secrets' doesn't mean 'I'll tell you when I feel like it'."

Captain deflated, knowing full well that Joan wasn't wrong. "You're right, you're right. I'm sorry."

Joan heaved a sigh, never taking her gaze off of Sparks.

"Dude still gives me the creeps," she said.

"That won't be a problem for much longer," Captain assured.

"I hope not," Joan replied.

————

JOAN

Sparks had to go.

There were many things Joan still wanted, one year into living in Glass, but one thing she felt she'd lost ever since Sparks came into her and Captain's lives was predictability. That was something she longed for while growing up in the Web and something she finally gained when she got to Glass.

Heavy coal sank in Joan's stomach as she battled with the thought that, somehow, Sparks knew what he had taken. Neither of them had said a word to each other since he arrived in front of the penthouse, but the man's face had the power to say hundreds of words without opening his mouth.

The most disconcerting part of it all was that Captain didn't hear the words himself.

The roar of a car engine intercepted Joan's thoughts, and she saw a taxi pull up beside her and Captain. The windows were tinted red, blocking Joan's view of the inside. The passenger side door opened and out came Benji trembling with fear. The other doors opened and several men came out after him. One stuck out from the rest, gelled up green hair and a lapel pin resembling a hydra pinned to his scarlet jacket. In his hand, a gun.

"Amon?" Captain asked, flustered.

Amon? As in the freaking Amon Tribe!?

First Sparks, now Amon? I never want to see a taxi ever again.

Amon's eyes widened, surprised to see him, but he smiled.

"Well, well, well, if it isn't young Kostov!" He cried with his arms spread out, still gripping his gun. Benji stayed rigid, wringing his hands together and keeping his head bowed. Joan wanted more than anything to rush to him and help him, but this was gang business. Do something rash, and it meant death.

"What are you doing with him?" Captain asked.

There was no pleasantness in his voice, no mischief like there usually was. He was just as bothered as Joan to see Benji being held hostage.

Bothered, yes, but what weighed on Joan was the thought that this might be it for Benji.

25

CAPTAIN

I...SHOULD'VE *seen this coming*.

Captain had held out hope for an easy trade. Hand Benji over to Amon, and Amon would allow him to launder money in some of his casinos throughout the City. Benji was important to Amon, probably to a nonsensical degree, but if he meant *that* much to him...

The problem now was that Amon had already found Benji and was threatening his life in front of Captain. Regardless of what Captain wanted, he couldn't let it look like mistreating his associates was acceptable.

"What are you doing with him?" Captain asked. Amon's grin buckled. The crime lord's eyes darted to Benji as if expecting him to say something.

"Why look at him? You can look at *me*," Captain insisted, firm but still quiet enough to not draw attention. At this point, the rest of his gang rallied behind him. Damien, Trevor, Ripley, and Sparks lined up behind Captain, keeping their hands close to their guns. Damien stepped ahead of the others with his own gun positioned at Amon's head.

"What is this?" He growled.

Captain pushed Damien's gun down. "I've got this."

"He stabbed a bunch of Amon's own men like a pissed off devil!" Amon cried. "Did he tell you that?"

Captain nodded. Inside, he was panicking as though he was standing on a tightrope. Make the wrong move and he would go plummeting to his death below, but for now, he was on top.

"As a matter of fact, he did, because he's honest with me. He used a knife his brother gave him—who your men killed—by the way. Yeah, I know about that too."

Amon scowled at Benji but stopped once he saw Captain lean in closer.

"I don't care if he killed twelve of your men or thirty. What matters is he's *mine* now, and you were intimidating him in front of me. That won't bode well if we want to be friends."

What's Joan's thinking now, after what I just told her...?

The panic seared into Benji's face riled Captain up like a father when he sees his own son in danger. Suddenly, his plans didn't make sense anymore. In his mind, he raced to remember conversations his father had had with other crime lords and how he traversed those discussions. His back straightened, his shoulders widened, and he made a mental note to never break eye contact with Amon. There could be no room for error. This was it. The test before the bigger test. If he couldn't negotiate with Amon face-to-face, he couldn't negotiate with anybody.

I'm not giving Amon the satisfaction of having Benji, but there has to be something else I can give him.

"You told one of my associates that you don't negotiate with faceless men. That it's a man of honor who negotiates face-to-face. Well, my face is here *now*. This *pussy* is ready to negotiate," Captain claimed.

Ripley snorted and Trevor trailed out a whistle followed by a laugh. Damien laughed along with him.

Amon shuddered as his face twisted. Captain hoped that meant he was uncomfortable, but it turned out to just be buildup towards laughing.

"My, *my*! Amon underestimated you! Let's talk then..."

Right. Time to make this up as I go.

―――――

AMON

Amon's grandfather, once a fighter in the long forgotten civil war, was there when the great towers of Glass were nothing but looming husks, not yet the City that it one day became. The tools for his own criminal organization were already in his hands, financially backed by Sylar Han, who was responsible for the starts of many crime family organizations within the City and beyond. Amon's father was eventually raised to become a crime lord in the grandfather's place, and then Amon was groomed into taking on the family business.

Most crime families across Glass' history evolved and changed as leaders were switched or new ideas were formed. That wasn't the case with the Amon Tribe. The Tribe held on tight to tradition, keeping the precious rituals ingrained into itself by Amon's grandfather. Every member was tattooed top to bottom wherever there weren't artificial implants, and every new member took a blood oath of allegiance, oftentimes slitting their hand with a katana passed over to them to declare their loyalty. Punishment for breaking any of the Tribe's code came in the form of losing a finger. Desertion of the organization painted a massive, glowing target on one's back that never went away.

Loyalty, honor, and respect were the three most important traits within the Amon Tribe. Anything less was punished, some to the point of death.

Amon owned every casino in the City, each of them serving as safe spaces for people to buy fentanyl off the Tribe in private rooms, or for gangs to negotiate the trade of goods. For years, negotiations ran smoothly, but recently a few had gone awry, one even resulting in police busting a group that started to tussle when agreements failed. Each of the gang members and buyers involved were arrested, but the pills in their mouths ensured a quick and painless death for all of them before they were put behind bars. They couldn't be questioned and therefore there was no way the police could break them. The money trails that traced back to sources like World Linked and Samsara Financial—institutions wanting to keep their public records clean—remained protected.

At the end of the day, they were the ones who held all the cards in the game.

As Amon studied Captain, he wondered how much Captain knew about the game, how it was played, and how meaningless it was to work so hard to reach the top. He was a reckless, naive man. His father's greatest failure. Everyone in seats of power in the underworld knew that Captain had his father's council massacred in that club, destroying a significant piece of Glass' history seemingly without a second thought. Though Amon was never friends with any of the dead, the act forced him to wonder what else Captain was willing to do.

Amon must choose his words carefully in order to make this work.

What else could Amon ask for in place of Benji, which was what he *really* wanted? As he pondered it, it didn't take him long to understand that he was standing in it. Primitus. No regular person in Glass coveted Primitus, but to the criminal network, it was a land of opportunity and potential. There was no police presence in Primitus, and even the peasants with their weapons wouldn't dare stand up to the might of the Amon Tribe.

It was enough of a reason that if Amon told Captain that Primitus was what he wanted, he'd believe it.

"What are you willing to give Amon?" Amon asked.

Captain brightened, but only just a bit. "Why don't *you* tell me what you want? Benji is not an answer. Surely there *has* to be something else?"

Look at him. His face so false it's disgusting. This is a performance. The rest of them on the other hand...

Amon recognized Trevor and Ripley, but the jittery man most protective of Captain pestered him. Then there was the tall one, a face like stone, calculating and mysterious. There were signs of ulterior motives on him that Amon couldn't read but hungered to understand the language. He wondered if Captain had any idea about that, or if he was as blind and clueless as Amon suspected.

Finally, the girl...

Women were nothing more than a commodity to the Tribe. A pretty face to admire from afar or up close. Trophies to be won or cast aside when Amon's men grew tired of them. No high position in the Tribe was held by a woman because a stronger man had more worth. This was the way ever since Amon's grandfather crafted the Tribe.

"Why do you allow a woman in your organization? Is she some trophy?" Amon asked.

Captain's neck tightened, a pressure point hit. The woman was offended too.

"She is my wife," Captain drew out, dripping with poison.

"But she does the same as the others, yes?" Amon asked.

"You're damn right I do," the girl sneered.

"Ooh, feisty! Amon likes that!"

Out of the corner of his eye, Amon noticed Ripley jerk forward as if to rush up and tackle him, but he froze and stayed put, a last second decision made.

Ah, he likes her. I bet Captain doesn't know.

"Let's try that again. It'll be your last chance," Captain warned.

Amon sighed. He had to lie to wrap it up. He wanted Benji, even more than Primitus. His lust for revenge brewed stronger than any territory he could possibly want. Short-sighted? Perhaps, but it was always possible to achieve greater things in more ways than one.

He blew a kiss at the girl, who cringed but stayed silent. What could Captain do? If he killed him, another Amon would rise in his place, and Captain knew that. His father especially knew that. Even Sylar Han knew that. The Amon Tribe chose the hydra as their symbol for a reason.

It was also crystal clear to Amon that Captain needed him more than he needed to fulfill a petty grievance. Captain also needed to prove he had thick skin if building an empire in Glass' underground network was so important to him.

Amon glanced around at Primitus, as if noticing it for the first time. Some people lingered on the sidewalks, staring on with dread.

"Amon wants Primitus," Amon lied.

Not even a flinch of contention from Captain. In fact, he seemed relieved.

"If you're willing to give up ownership of a couple of your casinos to me so I can fortify my empire, I'll consider handing Primitus to you," Captain answered.

Amon frowned. "'Consider?'"

"'Consider'. I plan on talking to the other gangs to hear them out too. That's what a good boss does. Once I hear out *their* wishes, I'll weigh them all and get back to you."

This was an unexpected answer to Amon.

He is way out of his league if he can't even make promises. Still, he can play with the idea of giving up whole territory, but not the boy. Some honor there at least, Amon gives him that. He truly cares about Chi No Akuma.

Amon still had every intention of getting what he wanted. Benji will die and Captain along with him. Just not here, not with everyone else around them, but soon.

Why should Amon negotiate with those who are friends with traitors? Kill them both later and Primitus can be Amon's anyway.

"Then, for now, we have a deal," Amon said, holding out his hand.

Captain's face lit up and he snagged Amon's hand in a firm grip to shake it.

"Wonderful," he answered. After shaking Amon's hand, he held on to it, grip tight, and his face changed again. "You do not touch Benji. If you do, *any* deal is off."

Amon wanted to stick his knife in the man's throat, but he knew better. Instead—though it pained him—he kept his smile and nodded.

"You have Amon's word."

They let go of each other's hands.

"Oh, one more thing. Do you, by chance, have a way of contacting the Jacks and getting me an audience with them? I need to talk to them next," Captain explained.

"Amon can arrange that," Amon replied.

Daniel Kostov is a dead man. He just doesn't know it yet.

———

CAPTAIN

Captain meant every word.

Bending to Amon's wishes would have been a sign of weakness. Toying with the thought of Benji getting dragged away and shot by Amon burned Captain, as did the memory of Joan's face when he broke to her what he had planned for Benji. A memory that stayed at the forefront of his mind as he talked to the crime lord. Any residue of regret left in him for changing his mind about Benji didn't matter. Going back on his initial stance would be another sign of weakness.

Suddenly I don't envy my father's work as much as I used to.

Everyone was dumbfounded when Amon left. Captain felt Joan's fingers cross with his, like they did not long before. Relief radiated off of her in waves, crackling with energy that Captain felt every jolt of.

Oh, she cares about him too.

"Good job," she whispered with a wink.

"I knew you could do it," Damien complimented softly.

I made the right choice.

Then Trevor: "Good job, *jefe.*"

Then Ripley: "*Lo secundo.*"

Sparks said nothing, but he gave Captain a nod and a small grin.

"Thank you, Captain," Benji said, gratitude plastered on his face.

Only three words, and it was enough to lock Captain's voice away. Everyone was looking to him, most of them in awe of him.

This is it. Oh my god...this is it. Everything is going to change for the better now.

As he thought the words, he stole a glance at Sparks. He was acting, Captain could tell. His smile was a performance.

Captain faked his smile too, hiding the burning coals behind it.

Tonight, let's force something real *out of him.*

THE FRONT DOORS to *The Time Capsule* opened and the chime that alerted Dagan to visitors sang.

The first thing that caught Dagan's attention was how heavy the footsteps sounded. They echoed as they fell to the floor, as if the visitor had tied something to his feet to weigh them down.

Finally, the visitor came around a shelf, revealing itself to be a tall man with uncanny green eyes. There was an ugly scar on his forehead, as if it had been bashed against something.

He doesn't look like police or a politician. But he's not from around here either.

Then it hit Dagan. He recognized the man from the gangs that were outside earlier talking. Some agreement had been made and they parted ways without violence, but Captain's gang still tarried in Primitus.

Just what we need.

The man's attention was fixed on the shelves, his fingers brushing up against a pile of puzzle boxes, wiping the dust off as if he too wanted to see them clean. He finally stopped and took one to look at it.

Dagan raised an eyebrow when he recognized it. Put together, the puzzle formed a picture of a city long lost. New York City.

CT-RX, Marlene's drone, hovered over to the man. "Welcome, sir. May I help you find anything?"

The man smirked with a witty light. "I'm not looking for anything in particular."

"CT, it's okay. Keep going about your business," Dagan said.

"Are you sure?"

"CT."

CT-RX swerved away and continued roaming the shelves for any imperfections.

"Robots, right?" Dagan asked.

"Hmm," the man grunted, resuming his focus back on the puzzle.

Dagan cleared his throat and persisted. "You buy that, I'll throw another one in of your choice for free."

The man turned to face him, still carrying that witty look. He loosed a tiny shrug and shook the box around in his hand, listening to the rattle of the puzzle pieces. He seemed almost giddy as he came up to the desk.

"I loved that sound when I was a kid. My mom shook them before I opened them because she knew I liked it."

He set the puzzle down on the counter.

"I was never one for puzzles. Never had the patience for them," Dagan admitted.

"No offense, but you look like you have a lot of time on your hands. Maybe try again?"

Dagan didn't take offense. He was grateful that the man was good at conversation. "Maybe. Let me retire first."

"Who retires these days?"

Shaking his head, Dagan scanned the puzzle. "Go ahead and get another puzzle."

"Hmm," the man mused again, this time with a solemn grin, and retreated back to the shelves. He came back with another puzzle, took several large black coins out of his pocket, and slid them over to Dagan.

Dagan eyed the coins. They were common currency used by buyers in the black market. The only way in the world to pay without traces left behind.

"I'm sure you can find a way to convert these to something more...streamlined," the stranger said.

"You're lucky. Normally I wouldn't accept these, but business is slow nowadays," Dagan said, taking most of the coins and leaving one behind.

"You gave me more than necessary," he pointed out.

The stranger shook his head. "That's extra, for information."

Dagan raised his eyebrows and smirked. "Information? I don't even know who you are."

"Sparks."

"Sparks...?"

"Just Sparks."

Dagan rolled his eyes. It was pointless to keep prying. The man clearly had secrets.

"Okay....*Sparks*...what do you want to know?"

27

RIPLEY

FOR A CITY THAT LOOKS AMAZING, *it sure has a lot of trash.*

Ripley stayed in lockstep next to Trevor down a never-ending sidewalk downtown. Empty takeout boxes and strips of paper bounced and circled in the wind, nonexistent to the people walking through them and around them. Most were staring down at their phones as they moved, in sync with each other, drifting in the same direction like an army.

Ripley hardly ever touched his phone when he first got one, preferring to only use it to call Saint, the woman that took him and Trevor in after their parents died. The one Ripley had no problem calling 'mama'.

"Remind me why we're meeting them in person and not giving them a call instead?" Ripley asked Trevor in Spanish.

"That can be traced. A face-to-face meeting can't," Trevor answered in the same language, hands stuffed in his pockets with his head down.

Ripley picked at his diamond earring. "I don't feel great about these guys..."

"*Ponte a la cola.*"

"Then why are we talking to *them*?"

"They're the ones that *asustar* me the least."

"Obviously. They're *younger* than us."

"So?"

"I feel like there's something wrong with that somehow."

"Right here," Trevor said, stopping in front of a building. The building's entrance was wide, with a long row of spinning doors. The sign *Long Way Up* encased in gold sat a few feet from the front steps.

"A hotel?" Ripley asked.

"This is where they said they'd be. Conference room on the top floor," Trevor replied.

"*Mierda.*"

Trevor found the Purpletells' contact info when he and Ripley met with Amon a few days ago to negotiate for Captain. He and Ripley decided the right time to reach out was immediately after Captain's confrontation with Amon. His ship was slowly sinking and he didn't know it. Trevor and Ripley wanted to leap off that ship and swim away before it was too late for them too.

The two ascended the steps and entered the lobby. A security guard stopped them to scan them both for weapons, of which they had none. Had it been day one in Glass, Ripley would've gotten lost in everything that was the lobby. From its high, high ceiling with the massive glowing steel blue chandelier above the front desk, to the spotlights shining along the walls, it was amazing. The front desk was a massive rectangle in the center that Ripley and Trevor had to go around in order to get to the elevators.

Ripley found himself remembering fondly the

simplicity of the Web, even if most of that simplicity was 'family was the good guys and everyone else was the bad guy'. Trevor emphasized to him before they got to Glass that the City was their ticket to freedom. Their escape from the bondage of a starved, miserable life in the Web. Ripley was still waiting for that freedom he'd heard so much about. The only difference was that he had more food in his belly.

He didn't mind Primitus though. It reminded him of the Web in its simplicity but better.

Saint would love it.

What wasn't simple was Captain, making emotionally charged decisions and changing his mind in ways that might set a bomb off if he wasn't careful. Ripley was sure beyond all doubt that Captain brought Benji under his wing to throw him back at the Amon Tribe for an easy deal, but now that wasn't on the table anymore. Today, Captain proved that he cared about people more than even he liked to admit.

It didn't matter. The brothers were seeing the Purpletells to feed them information on Captain and earn their trust during a night on the town where they claimed to be shopping for food.

"Sure, he chose Benji's life, but one good choice doesn't equal a good man or a strong leader," Trevor had said to Ripley before they left to get to the hotel.

Thanks to Amon, Captain was able to call the leader of the Jacks, Ace. It just so happened that Ace and his friends were looking for the right excuse to destroy Jiang, their dance coach, whom Sylar found out was the last person with Captain's money. It was the perfect trade-off that promised more conversations later.

Ripley and Trevor stepped inside an elevator, but

before the doors could close, a man's hand shot out in between and stopped them. A bald man with gold earrings thrusted them aside and stepped through. Three other men followed him in.

"Which floor?" The bald man asked the brothers, his tone pleasant and his accent Russian.

"Top," Trevor answered.

"Ah, same." The man tapped the last button.

As the elevator rose, Trevor moved past him and casually pressed the button on the wall that halted the elevator mid ascend.

Ripley frowned. *What's he doing now?*

"Is there problem?" Bald asked.

Trevor retook his spot next to Ripley, keeping his gaze straight ahead.

"You're here to get the jump on the Purpletells," he said.

What? How does he know that?

Trevor was on to something though, because the elevator turned deathly silent. Ripley was sweating, and he knew everyone else was sweating too.

"What is that to you?" Bald asked, his voice sharp.

"My brother and I need to see them. Alive," Trevor said.

A fight was coming, and Ripley regretted not sneaking his gun in somehow. Several seconds ticked by in silence.

Then, the elevator erupted. Ripley spun and lunged at Bald, tackling him and shoving him up against the elevator wall. The force was enough to give Ripley time to pummel him in the stomach with a flurry of punches before going up to his face and striking him several times. Ripley grabbed his shoulders while he was still winded, turned him around, and pushed his body against one of the others. They both collided and collapsed in a tangled heap on the floor.

Two more to go. One was already fighting Trevor, wielding a long, glowing dagger that he had somehow gotten into the hotel. The other spun his own dagger at Ripley with a muted roar. The blade came first for Ripley's nose in a wide arc, which he bounced back from, feeling the disturbed air as it passed through.

Can't do that forever. Not enough space.

Ripley didn't have to brainstorm a solution. Trevor was wrestling with his opponent's dagger, clinging to the attacker's wrist using both hands. He forced both of them sideways so that the side of the blade sank into the back of the head of Ripley's opponent. Trevor used his attacker's surprise as an opening to bash his elbow into his face, repeatedly, until he let go of the dagger that was still in his associate. Trevor freed the dagger from the second man's head and hurtled it back at its owner, plunging it perfectly into the center of his chest.

"Grab the other one!" Trevor yelled at Ripley.

Ripley snatched up the knife from where Bleeding Head now lay and stumbled after Bald who had gotten back up, this time with two glowing daggers. In a graceful spin, he released one of his daggers like a boomerang and sailed it towards Ripley. He ducked, feeling the rush of air overhead, then leaped back up. Bald laughed, and Ripley knew immediately something was wrong. Red-hot pain exploded through his back.

Bald's knife was stuck in Ripley's back. Ripley had heard of daggers capable of spinning back the way it came like a boomerang or bouncing off walls and flying back to its owner. He was wishing now he had gotten one of those.

Tears of pain flooded Ripley's eyes. Sharp pain oozed down his back, spreading throughout his body.

Trevor caught up behind Bald, wrapped his arm around

his neck, and stabbed him in the chest. He had already dispatched the last goon, who lay bleeding out on the floor with multiple gashes in his throat. Bald slumped to the floor dead.

"Hold still. *Esto dolerá*," Trevor cautioned.

The knife was taken out of Ripley's back, inflaming the furnace Ripley felt. Tears were running down his face now and his teeth raked his bottom lip. He thought of Saint. He thought of Joan.

"Drink," Trevor ordered, forcing a vial full of Bathory to Ripley's lips. With a groan, Ripley let Trevor tip it in. A burning sensation caked the back of his throat and his eyes blurred again.

I hate this stuff.

"Can't say I blame you for getting hit. Glass has some special toys," Trevor said.

"Yeah, I was getting that," Ripley sputtered.

Trevor reached down for Ripley to take his hand, which he gladly took. His legs didn't tremble as he stood up. The Bathory was already doing its job.

"What were they?" Ripley asked, surveying the mess.

Trevor pressed the button to keep the elevator going. It shuddered before continuing. "The Talisman. I noticed the leader had a tattoo of their symbol on his wrist."

Ripley bent down and inspected the tattoo—two overlapping triangles—on Bald's wrist that was indeed there, mostly hidden by his sleeve. Captain had warned them about The Talisman before. They were a rival gang, small but deadly, that revealed themselves shortly after the death of the Jack, Chase. They sensed an opportunity to rise through the ranks while the underworld faced instability. Unlike Captain, who wanted to make friends with as many of the syndicates as possible, The Talisman were about using violence to send a message to the underworld that they wanted power. The leader of the Delanos, Alex, learned that after he lost his tongue to them not long ago.

Ripley felt relieved to have survived the Talisman without losing his.

———

The conference room was a dark cube, lit by white blocks positioned at every corner, and the hellish light blossoming from the fish tank in the left wall. There were windows in the back and a stunning view of the City. The clouds of the early night sky were sickly green, impaled by the bright lights of the metropolis.

At the center of the room was a long table. Waiting for Trevor and Ripley there were the Purpletells and their leader, Leon. Leon was a young man of below average height, with dense black hair that pointed up in all directions. Even in the dim light, Ripley noticed that Leon's grape red, sharp-shouldered suit was wrinkled, as if he had bunched it up first before slipping into it.

"Are they dead?" Leon asked, his voice cautious.

Trevor answered. "Who? Those guys in the elevator?"

"Big bald Russian guy, has a tattoo on his wrist," Leon said.

"You *knew* about that?"

"Uh, yeah! That was the whole reason why I had you come when you did!" Leon cried. He glanced around at his friends.

"It's okay, guys. They're dead," he assured them.

Everyone at the table sighed in relief, grateful smiles

spreading across their faces. Most of them went back to staring at their phones, tapping furiously away at the screens.

"You set us up," Trevor concluded aloud, sounding impressed.

And I almost died.

"Pretty clever, right? Those guys have been hunting us for *weeks*," Leon said.

"You knowingly put us in danger. Maybe the *Jacks* would treat us better," Trevor replied.

Panic pulled Leon forward and he clutched the edge of the table. "No, wait! Sorry. It's just that we're—like—kind of bad at this. But that's why we like *you. You're* in a position where you can give us information that'll help us! Listen... Captain doesn't really have an empire yet, right?"

"That's right," Trevor replied.

"Right, okay, and your concern is his consistency, right?"

"Consistency...*and* his ability to lead," Trevor corrected.

"Got it, so...keep coming back to us with info and we can use it to figure out the best ways to get around him and move our way up. We're still new to all this. We'd love to have you when your opportunity comes up to leave Captain. The Jacks have their contracts with World Linked. We," Leon paused and looked around at his friends, "don't have *anything*."

"Damn elites," remarked another Purpletell, this time a girl.

Ironic.

"Sounds like *your* problem," Ripley said. Trevor bumped him to shut him up.

Leon scowled at Ripley but left it at that. "We have

more guys than Captain, but based on what you've told me, that could change. Has he brought in anyone new?"

Here we go.

"Yes, actually. He has," Trevor said.

Just outside—unknown to everyone—was Ratchet, spying on them through a sniper scope from the roof of a nearby building.

28

ACE

ACE STOOD on a tower so high up his ears rang. Wind cut through his tiger-fur coat, every breath steaming. Below him, his hostage knelt.

The Jacks surrounded Ace—Blaze, Trey, Light, Gypsy, and Royal. The only one missing—besides Chase for obvious reasons—was Wild. Chase's death had driven him into hiding: no dance practice, no performances, no ops, just silence. Ace didn't blame him, but it felt like losing a limb. It felt that way for the rest of the Jacks too. Maybe not Royal. Ace never knew what was *really* going on in that psycho's head. Ace had asked Wild more than once if he wanted out completely—an option no other gang had, but Wild swore he was still a Jack and still Paragon.

Finding Chase's murderer went nowhere. The cops dropped the case without a lead after a while. Nobody that Ace knew had a grudge big enough to take a shot at Chase. Killing one of them was either a statement to the whole underworld...or just a lunatic wanting to feel something.

On his knees, wrists tied, was Jiang—the Jacks' dance coach. The music company, Hivemind, had saddled them with him, and Ace had never felt less in control. Jiang was older, cynical, always looking down on the Jacks for reasons he never explained. Hours of drills, repetitive moves, Bathory shots for adrenaline—nothing kept up with Jiang's screaming. When he threw a chair at Royal, that was the final straw. Paragon couldn't fight back, but the Jacks could.

"Was kind of hoping he'd be awake by now," Trey muttered.

"It's freezing," Gypsy grumbled.

"Your fault for not bundling up, freak," Royal said with a wicked grin.

Jiang stirred. His eyes fluttered open, confused at first, then showed fear. Ace felt a giggle rise in his throat watching the man squirm.

"Hey...*hey*, what's this about?!" Jiang rasped.

He yelped as pain shot through his torn lip. Royal twirled the ripped-out lip ring between his fingers.

"You *bastards*!" He cried, pressing his upper lip to the ragged flesh.

"How does it feel, Jiang?" Ace asked.

Jiang squinted. "Ace? Holy crap, Ace, is that you?"

"Possibly," Ace leaned on the cane he clutched with both hands.

"Look, listen! About earlier...I'm sorry, I'm really sorry!" Jiang's voice broke.

Ace pressed the cane's end into Jiang's chest. "Someone wants you dead for taking his money," he said. "He hired us to get it back. Only problem? We'll have to kill you after. Can't have you running around telling everyone that we're the Jacks."

Jiang's eyes went wide. "The Jacks are...*you guys*?!"

Ace and the others leaned back and laughed.

"As surprised as I hoped," Royal said.

Ace pushed harder with his cane. "You took seven hundred million from the Kostov family a few days ago. You're going to send it back before you die. Simple."

"I can't. I used it all," Jiang croaked.

Ace's stomach jolted. He bit his lip.

"On what?!" Blaze cried.

Jiang squeezed his eyes shut and spilled it all. "New TV! Workout equipment! Women, men, a bar for my lounge! Do I really have to list *everything*?"

"Yes," Royal said.

Ace sighed. "It doesn't matter. We'll sell it all and get the money back. As for you, you know now that the Jacks and Paragon are one and the same. I imagine you'd talk to the wrong people..."

"No! I won't tell anyone! Your secret is safe with me! It's—."

Jiang's breath cut off when Ace shoved him with his cane again and sent him over the edge.

The cold bit Ace's face and neck like needles. The air pressure roared in his ears. He stepped back from the edge, grimacing as Captain's name surfaced in his mind. Captain had things the Jacks would kill for, but Ace knew Glass: there was always a catch. Trust was a contract, and he'd signed his life away once already.

Jiang was gone off a roof. Captain could be next.

Give Captain his money, then tell him no. It's too soon to trust someone else, especially a nobody.

JOAN TUGGED her white tank top back on, sitting on the edge of the bed she shared with Captain in Primitus. She had never been on a mattress so soft. Even their bed back at the penthouse didn't compare.

"Love you," Captain said hurriedly as he left the room with his hands gripping the boot he tried to force on. The door slid shut behind him with a metallic hiss.

Joan thrust her own boots on with a snarl, cringing against the way they sealed her feet. The size of her feet was never a thought until she bought her first pair of boots in Glass. Even after a year, she still felt like an amateur, squeezing her feet into tight boots and fumbling with her jackets. One of the only things she missed about the Web was that she didn't wear anything on her feet most of the time, which gave her one less thing to worry about.

Today, she saw Captain change his mind and hold on to Benji, and the love she'd felt for him on day one was reignited. It was an exhilarating twenty minutes after the Amon Tribe left, until Captain rushed out of the bedroom and Joan was left reminded that nothing had *really* changed.

Joan hated herself for not bringing up the subject of kids before things got passionate. Like Captain, she was swept up in the spur of the moment.

She inhaled the cool, midsummer air once she stepped outside, and removed a cigarette from her breast pocket to light it. She drew it out and exhaled a thin stream of smoke. That was when she noticed Sparks leaving the *Time Capsule* shop, carrying two boxes.

Speaking of things that haven't changed...

Sparks looked a lot like so many of the men in the Web, with eyes like the ones she saw that stared at her before slinking away. The difference here was that Sparks wasn't slinking away. He was staying put.

Sparks stopped at the fountain and sat on the edge. He set the boxes down beside him and then leaned back to let out a deep sigh.

What if I can find *a reason for Captain to kill him?*

Joan felt her feet take her to the fountain, and the closer she drew, the more she felt like pieces of clothing left her, leaving her more vulnerable and exposed.

Right now would've been a great time for Ripley to be around.

Sparks didn't look up at her right away. His gaze stayed on the boxes.

Joan's gaze followed Sparks's and her curiosity piqued.

"What are those?" She asked, sitting down on the edge of the fountain with her legs crossed.

Sparks finally faced her and frowned. "Seriously?"

"'Seriously'," Joan shot back, bringing her cig back to her lips.

Sparks heaved a sigh and picked up the top box. "They're puzzles."

Joan cocked an eyebrow. *I'm gonna feel stupid, but...*

"They're what?"

Each of Sparks's next words sounded more exhausted than the last.

"They're pieces you put together to form a picture."

Clearly he wasn't interested in a conversation, but Joan didn't care. She was digging for information. Maybe there was something she could find out and bring to Captain, and this whole petty game can finally end.

"*Wow*, that sounds boring," Joan said.

A shadow flickered across Sparks's face. *Did I just offend him?*

"It isn't to *me*," he said. "My mother and I used to do them together all the time. I was...obsessed."

"Can I see it?" Joan asked, offering her hand.

Sparks handed the first box to her and she squinted at the picture on the front. It was the skyline of a great city. The towers weren't as tall as anything in Glass but they were still impressive. She pointed at it. "So, what's *this* then?"

"New York."

"That's the city's name?"

"Was. It hasn't been around for a while."

Sparks took back the box and tapped his finger on it. "Here, that's the Empire State Building." He slid his finger across the image and stopped on another building. "Right there is the Chrysler Building. Then there is the One World Trade Center."

It surprised Joan that she had never heard of any of that before.

Did dad know about this? Did he tell me about anything *more than just how to survive?*

Joan didn't know how old Sparks was. Joan also noticed that when he bled in Captain's office, the blood didn't glow. Glowing blood was a common side effect for people who took Bathory.

"Have you seen New York, like, in person?" Joan asked.

"No."

"If you've never seen it, how do you know it existed?"

If Joan's question stumped Sparks, he was doing an admirable job not showing it, but his jaw was set and his eyes were shy.

"Gotcha," she remarked before Sparks could finally answer. She filled the air with smoke again after removing her cig. "How do you know where the pieces go without an instruction manual or something?"

"You're supposed to figure out where it all goes on your own. Maybe I shouldn't have expected you to understand."

Sparks's biting remark didn't phase Joan, which she chalked up to years of being chased down by hungry, desperate people or being belittled and threatened. The Web gave everyone tough skin.

I *can take that. Daniel on the other hand...*

"You know that Da—Captain—would've kicked your ass if he heard you say that to me, right?"

Sparks shrugged. "To him, I might as well be a dead man already."

"Whoa!" Joan laughed, blowing more smoke. "You hit it *right* on the head! Might be the smartest thing I've ever heard you say."

Sparks ignored her, and instead stared into the fountain watching the bubbling water. He was calmer now, less uptight. The only sound was the water from the top of the fountain trickling down into the color salad glowing from the bottom.

"If you know how Captain sees you, why are you still here? Who *are* you?" Joan asked. She stabbed the end of her cig into the fountain to snuff out the light. Her heart was racing too fast now to focus on smoking, and her questions were taking her down an irreversible path.

"Why are *you* here?" Sparks responded gently, eyes still on the water.

Joan bit her tongue before answering.

"Captain found me when I came to Glass. He gave me a home, better than my last one," came the answer.

"So you weren't raised in Glass," Sparks said.

"Were *you*?"

"Yes."

"There you go. Next time, just answer the question instead of asking your own first."

"That's funny. You just did the same thing," Sparks pointed out.

I'm getting really tired of him being right.

"Fine. Ask away then," Joan snapped. Her hands were pressed against the fountain, her body ready to spring up in case the conversation got out of control.

"How'd you get here?" Sparks asked.

Joan guffawed. "That's a *long* story. I left my dumb dad. Captain found me, gave me a phone, new home, and my first taste of Bathory. I think that's all that matters."

Sparks frowned. "Then I guess everything I've already told you is all that matters too."

Oh no, not yet.

"Do you drink Bathory too? I saw that when you bleed, it doesn't..."

"Glow? No, I don't," Sparks confirmed. "Life is meant to have an ending. We can't all play god."

Joan never liked how Bathory felt going down her throat, but she still couldn't fathom the idea of quitting it. She knew when she first drank it that it did something to her, something special. She liked the eternal youth, being able to have the experiences Glass offered while she still felt and looked young. She liked that her life was in a standstill, frozen in time, an unending present. What awaited her in the future if she stopped? Decay, sickness, the threat of a weakening body and mind, the cloak of old age falling over her as she begged for more time. That was not a life she wanted to live.

"Maybe you're wasting your time talking to me then. Shouldn't you be out there—oh I don't know—banging chicks and buying a penthouse?" Joan asked.

"I'm right where I need to be," Sparks answered.

Please, I'm begging you, give me something.

"The hell is *that* supposed to mean?" Joan asked.

"What I mean is being part of Captain's crew is where I need to be."

Joan sighed and stood up. "Why? He treats you like crap!"

Now it was Sparks's turn to stand up, tucking his puzzle boxes under his arm. "You seem like a nice person, Joan. You're better than *you* think you are, but don't act like you know where you're meant to be either. You want honesty from me, but I don't think you're being honest with *yourself*. Let's start there, and *then* we can talk."

Joan's hand slammed against Sparks's chest when he attempted to walk away.

Why did I do that? What am I thinking?!

"I'd be *thrilled* to, after you just *tell me* why you're really here," Joan snarled.

Something about Joan's expression was working. Sparks relaxed and the ever present anger around his eyes recoiled.

"This is how I redeem myself and this City. It's run by people that'll do whatever it takes to hold the little guy back. Samsara Financial and the Jacks are just a few of the symptoms causing the larger problem."

"So, what, that makes you the solution?" Joan asked, taking her hand off Sparks.

A long pause. Then: "Maybe."

Damien's voice speared through the conversation. "Hey, Sparks! Captain wants you."

Joan didn't turn to face him. She stayed like a statue in place, keeping her eyes on Sparks. His face darkened in a way that chilled Joan. That fleeting gentleness was gone. The mystery man was back.

Sparks pushed the puzzles into Joan's hands. "Watch my puzzles," he said before leaving and following Damien.

Like an unwelcome stranger that refuses to leave, intrusive thoughts marched through Joan's mind. That part of her that embraced Glass, loved Glass, drank the Bathory, and was in lockstep with Captain coughed and wheezed, struggling to stay upright.

Joan let the puzzles fall from her hands and clatter on the ground, not wanting to do the one thing Sparks asked her to do. As if having just woken up from a deep sleep, she stumbled her way to *The Glass House*. The hypnotic lighting inside calmed her nerves and eased her muscles. Gentle music played from a jukebox in the corner and as she sat down at the bar, she felt peace being restored in her chest as if she was dipping herself into a jacuzzi.

She focused on Captain, remembering how caring he

acted when he first met her, right there in *The Glass House*. The way he treated her was unlike the way any other man had treated her.

"The usual, Joan?" The android bartender named BT asked. BT was a stripped-down version of most androids, with an exoskeleton-like body and two blinking white orbs for eyes. Someone at *The Glass House* once explained to Joan that should BT suddenly lose track of his programming and become a danger to Primitus, destroying him would be easier since he was nothing more than his basic components.

Joan's heartstrings were always tugged whenever she saw BT. He was kind, considerate, and surprisingly an excellent listener. He filled the void whenever Ripley couldn't, though not as well.

"Hell, yeah, BT," Joan replied. She removed a small flask of Bathory from her breast pocket, opposite the one where she kept her cigarettes, and stirred some of it into her drink. She then took the glass and dumped the contents down her throat. She shivered and grunted from the bubbling burn in her throat but managed a fiendish grin.

The fond memories she had of Captain from the day they met were as fleeting as the softness that was present on Sparks's face. Next to the rising pile of grievances Joan was fostering towards him, those memories became faint and tougher to capture. The Bathory she drank was shoving them down deeper into the recesses of her mind.

What if Daniel is throwing Sparks out right now?

Curiosity switched abruptly to apathy.

So what if he is? That's not my problem. It's Daniel's.

And yet, despite how cryptic Sparks was, a nagging thought chewed at her. Maybe he was just a confused man who liked putting puzzles together.

Maybe.

BEFORE

JOAN

IF YOU SQUINT JUST RIGHT, *they almost look like brothers.*

Joan watched Captain and Damien. Her husband of six months and his best friend had their arms locked together in a game of arm wrestling during a small, modest dinner party Captain threw for his gang in the penthouse.

Captain couldn't wait until he was famous in the under-world before throwing dinner parties, even if attendance was only seven.

There was Trevor, Ripley, and—despite at first insisting on not coming after Captain invited her—Carmilla watching the fight and cheering Damien on to spite Captain. Standing next to Joan, leaning against the kitchen counter and sipping her third glass of wine that night, was Damien's girlfriend Violet. Joan didn't see Violet often, but Damien tended to bring her along whenever Captain had parties like these. Violet always tended to go for whatever alcohol was out and keep her distance, faking a smile to look like she was a participant. It was no mystery to Joan that Violet was unhappy. She never asked why. She didn't need to.

Whenever Violet put her arm around Damien's shoulder, it was to keep him happy. Whenever she kissed him on the head, it was to keep him feeling content.

Joan gazed at Captain as he fought Damien's arm. *Content.*

"They almost look like brothers, don't they?" Joan asked Violet. She liked talking to Violet. She was no Ripley, but Joan had a nagging feeling that Violet needed someone else to talk to more than she did.

Violet scoffed, taking another sip from her wine. "Knowing them, they might as well be."

Joan poured her own glass and swirled it.

"So...are you still working at the nursing home?" Joan asked.

"Yep."

"Do you really like it there? I was thinking maybe I can get a position myself," Joan said.

Whoa, wait, what the hell *are you talking about?*

Violet finally looked at Joan, eyebrows raised. The ice in her eyes melted away, and the corner of her mouth turned up.

"Are you serious?" She asked.

Shit, what do I say now?

"Um, yeah. I don't really do much unless Captain has us go out and scout out territories. There's only been a few interesting ventures we've gone on so far, and it'd be nice to be more hands-on again," Joan said.

"What did you do before you met Captain?" Violet asked.

We don't need to talk about the Web.

"Honestly...not much. I wasn't great in school and I had a few odd jobs before Captain found me."

Lies, of course.

Joan thought of a way to turn the conversation back in her favor. "But," she turned to face Violet. "You didn't answer my question. Do you really like it at the nursing home?"

Violet blinked at her, then shrugged and sipped again. "I don't know. Most of the old people there just yell at me, except one guy."

"One guy?"

"Yeah. He *can't* yell because he can't talk, but we still communicate. He's grateful for the ways I help him, he's kind, and he's always happy to see me. I guess...if anything, something like that makes me feel like my job is worth it in the end. Plus, it allows me time away from..." Violet's voice trailed off, the unspoken heard. Joan looked at Captain and Damien again. Damien's fists were in the air, his face triumphant, while Captain crossed his arms and shook his head with a slight twitch. Damien had won the match.

"Hey," Violet spoke up, bumping Joan's shoulder, "If you want my advice, don't get a job at the nursing home just because it's 'something to do'. Do something that you believe will be worth it."

Carmilla sat across from Damien, offering her arm for the gangster to take.

"So? What's worth it to you?" Violet pressed.

Joan shook her head and her mind raced. She knew what she wanted. It was there. She had just never told anyone before. Not even Captain.

"I want to have kids," she answered, glancing at her husband.

"With *him*?" She asked, gesturing to Captain, who was oblivious.

Damien's arm cracked against the table as Carmilla—much to everyone's surprise—was the victor.

"What the hell? *How*?" Damien cried.

"That's what you get!" Captain yelled, pointing at his friend and laughing, a cigar in his other hand.

"A magician never reveals her secrets," Carmilla answered, rising up and taking a bow. She turned to Ripley. "How about you, darling? Care to try?"

Ripley raised his hands and shook his head with a subtle grin.

Trevor laughed, punching him in the shoulder as he tended to do. "The chick has you scared?"

Violet leaned to Joan and whispered. "If you ever reach a point where you can't see kids in the middle of...this, come find me. Maybe..." Violet shuddered as if a disturbing thought came to her.

"...We can help each other."

"WHERE'S MY MONEY, ACE?" Captain asked calmly.

"It's not that simple. Jiang blew a lot of your money on stupid stuff, so we're taking what he bought and selling it to get as much back as possible," Ace replied over the phone.

Captain's throat clenched. "Is he dead now?"

"You might hear about someone jumping off the Hive-mind building tomorrow," Ace replied.

Something warm stirred in Captain. "You're doing everything you can. I still want to talk more about arrangements if—."

"Yeah, about that."

Captain's throat clenched again. *Oh no.*

"Me and the boys talked, and we agreed that we want to take a break from breaking bread with others right now."

Captain leaned forward, hand gripping his phone tight. "We can talk about this. I'll help you with *any* concerns—."

"We tried working with someone else, and we just shoved him off a building. I like to think I'm also doing this for your sake, Captain. Do you want to find yourself falling off a building in the middle of the night?"

Captain bit down on his tongue, forcing back an insult he had ready. *Once he has his foot on the head of the underworld, no one will think to threaten him.*

"I understand," he managed, voice like gravel.

There was silence on the other end for a moment, prompting Captain to look and make sure he was still connected.

"I won't say 'never', but until we're able to get Wild to come out of his room, we're not agreeing to anything. In the meantime, we'll try to recollect as much of your money as possible and send it back to you. On that you have my word."

Captain winced as the sound of the gunshot that opened Chase's head all over the alley rang out in his head.

"Thank you," he said, but his mind was scrambled this time as his brain repeated the same abrupt moment over and over again.

He pressed 'Hang Up', not bothering to say a proper goodbye. In his vision, as if it was playing out on the windshield of the car he sat in, he witnessed the gun he used to kill Chase. He watched it go off, delivering a bullet through Chase's skull, the muzzle flash lighting up Chase's terrified face and the glowing blood splattering on the ground.

Behind him in the car was Sparks, with Benji holding him at gunpoint.

In the driver's seat was Damien, drumming his fingers on the steering wheel. "That's a 'no', then?"

Normally, Captain had a quip ready to send back to Damien. They'd been doing this together for years, but tonight was different. The four of them were in the parking lot of the nursing home where Sparks's father, Charles, lived. Through the long rounded window of the building, Captain saw Charles in a wheelchair watching TV.

Hovering nearby him was Damien's girlfriend, Violet, who was the only nurse in the room.

No man is unbreakable, not even a blank slate like Sparks.

Captain turned to Damien. "Go inside and wait for my signal."

Bang.

"You alright?" Damien asked, noticing the change in Captain's expression.

"Yeah, I'm fine. Just go," Captain urged.

Damien ducked out of the car and casually walked into the nursing home.

"Captain? What are you doing?" Sparks asked, leaning forward. Benji tightened his grip on Sparks's shoulder and shook his head.

"Making my point from earlier a little clearer," Captain replied, keeping his gaze ahead. He was fulfilling his own promise to make his threat clear to Sparks. It disturbed him that threatening the life of Sparks's father didn't seem to phase Sparks.

Maybe he hates him, like I hate mine. Still, I don't think he would want him killed, at least not by us.

Damien appeared in the nursing home window, his hand positioned on his waist. Violet noticed him, silently gasped, and dashed up to him, face painted in horror. Charles didn't even seem to notice. His eyes stayed fixed on the TV screen.

Damien put up a hand to stop Violet and slightly shook his head at her. He had his gun out now, standing close behind Charles.

Bang, Captain's mind sounded again.

Damien trained his gun at the back of Charles' head and eyed the car for a signal.

Violet was crying, pleading Damien to stop.

So she cares about Sparks's dad. What other ways can Sparks complicate my life before I'm done with him?

Bang.

Captain reached over while never taking his gaze away, flicking the car's headlights twice. Damien nodded when he saw the flickering and left the room without a word to Violet. The nurse looked back at Charles after watching him go, her cheeks wet.

A heavy lump was forming in Captain's throat. He couldn't shake the memory of what he did in the alley. He had had a successful afternoon, but the night was growing dark. What ran through his head taunting him wasn't normal.

Damien returned to the driver's seat of the car with an exhausted sigh.

"Will she be alright?" Captain asked him.

"She knows what my job requires."

"But will she *do* anything about that?" Captain pressed. He needed *some* kind of assurance tonight that things won't go south somehow.

Damien stayed staring at the window. "No. And even if she tries, I track her phone."

"Good. Let's go back home," Captain ordered. Damien started reversing the car out of their spot. The visions in Captain's mind finally began to quiet down, and he turned enough so that Sparks was in his view.

"Hopefully now you get me," he said.

In the shadow of the City's lights, there appeared the dimmest hint of a smile on Sparks. His eyes were greedy, as if he was ready to spring for Captain's throat and strangle him to death.

Captain looked away from Sparks and kept his attention

on the road ahead. He was armed, with two armed men there to defend him, but...

I might as well be naked and held at gunpoint.

"Why keep up this whole facade?" Sparks asked. "You're getting rid of me anyway."

"When did I say I would get rid of you?" Captain challenged.

"You don't have to tell me."

Damien shot a glance at Captain but it was hard to read in the dark. The air in the car was tight like a string pulled both ways.

"Better yet, just kill me *now*."

I've already made things hard by killing someone. I don't know who he is, so what if killing him makes things worse?

Everyone stayed silent the rest of the trip to Primitus.

———

Lazarus's knuckles were bloody. The man tied to the chair begged him to stop beating him and let his brother go. Several men standing nearby laughed at his cries, one of whom had another man on his knees caked in blood and sweat. A young boy was hiding behind shelves, crouched to see what was happening. Lazarus threatened to kill the prisoner's brother if he didn't tell him what he wanted to know. The prisoner stressed that he didn't know. Lazarus continued his assault on the man's face. The young boy spied, infatuated, almost gleeful. Then, in his crouch he slipped and smashed his knee against the shelf and the metal flinched.

"Daniel?" Came the unwanted response.

The young boy sucked in a gasp, scrambled to his feet, and limped fast to the hallway. The pain, however, was melting away at his weakened knee.

He couldn't unsee what he saw, and Lazarus spent the rest of his life trying to undo it.

CAPTAIN

JOAN WAS SWEEPING dirt from a toppled flowerpot on the balcony off their bedroom when Captain found her. Even though their stay in Primitus was temporary, Joan had insisted on bringing pots so she could keep trying to grow things. Captain had been glad to let her.

He lingered in the doorway, watching her work.

"Growing *anything* was next to impossible," Joan had told him about the Web. "Either the seeds were stolen before you could plant them, or some asshole trampled the plants flat."

Is this place much better? Captain thought. He'd yet to see anything thrive in Joan's pots.

"Want help?" He asked.

Joan paused but didn't look up. "Did you get rid of him?"

The question slapped Captain like cold water. Joan dumped the dirt into a bin, knelt, and kept sweeping. Captain moved onto the balcony, careful not to shadow her.

She's so much tougher than she looks. One of the reasons I love her.

Also, where are the brothers? How long do groceries take?

"If I dump him now...who knows what he'll do?" Captain said, voice low and breaking. "I threatened his father."

Joan glanced up. "His father?"

Captain nodded. "Even if he doesn't have bad intentions...I can't fix what I've done."

"Better yet, just kill me now."

And how do I know you don't have friends out there waiting?

Captain sat down and crossed his legs, palms smoothing over his knees as he tried to settle his breath. "I can salvage this. Maybe I can use him to get to the other crime lords in the City somehow. Show them I'm not a wannabe—show them I'm real."

Joan's mouth had already gone sour before he finished. "Sure, whatever," she said, rolling her eyes.

We can't go to bed like this. Today can't end like this.

Joan scooted closer to Captain until their knees touched. "I went to *The Glass House* after Damien took Sparks," she said, "and I kept telling myself he's *your* problem, not mine. But the more I told myself that, the more I realized—if you keep a leash on him, it becomes *my* problem too. Don't you think I had enough of that in the Web?"

Tears stung Captain's eyes and for a second he was back in *The Glass House* where he first met Joan. She was disheveled, raw, not yet the cleaned-up woman she was now, and Captain was still enchanted by her. He hadn't cared where she came from. He loved her: a nobody from nowhere.

His father had failed him. He wouldn't fail Joan.

Joan touched Captain's cheek and wiped a tear away.

"You're a good guy," she said. "I saw that today when you didn't let Amon take Benji."

Another tear fell from Captain's face. He remembered those eyes that admired him and loved him. He had given her access to eternity, and this was how she thanked him: by holding on.

For eternity.

Captain raised himself up and slowly planted a kiss on Joan's head. He felt her hair, as if feeling it for the first time. When he pulled back, Joan's face hardened. The softness that Captain loved so much drained away.

"Figure out what you're going to do with Sparks," she said. "Before he figures it out *for* you."

They stayed in each other's arms. Joan held on like she was afraid letting go would mean losing him for good.

When Captain tried to pull away, Joan didn't let him.

"DO you continue to experience ongoing nightmares about past traumatic experiences, and if so, how often? Not often...somewhat often...or *very* often?"

Wild was slumped in a big chair in an android's office that belonged to the Suicide Watch Division. These appointments were all the same. An android's face on a screen on the wall asked Wild the same list of questions. Wild had become so apathetic about coming in, he decided to mess with the AI and answer questions a bit differently. He had no problem dealing with the consequences later with a real human being.

"Very often, doctor. I still get nightmares about that time I walked onstage during a concert completely naked and pictures of me were posted on Culture."

"That sounds terrible, Wild. Let me document this data so that the record keepers can examine it," the android replied.

"Good. Tell them all about it."

"Are you still experiencing bouts of anxiety and a fear

of the unknown? If so, is it not often, somewhat often, or *very* often?"

Wild didn't answer, but the question rattled around in his brain. Anxiety? Sure. Who *didn't* experience that in Glass? Fear of the unknown? Absolutely.

But Wild knew that if he was honest about that, the Division would hold on to him. They'd keep experimenting on him as if he was a lab rat.

"You don't *actually* care," Wild muttered with his head in his lap. "All you do is go on and on and on with your stupid questions that you're *programmed* to ask. You're not *capable* of caring."

Wild looked up at the security camera set up in the corner of the room.

"And I know none of them are either!"

I can't be here! Chase's killer is still out there!

"I assure you, Wild, we care very much for your safety and want you to be happy again. We only have a few more questions to go before—."

Wild leaped up and started fumbling with his pants.

"Let's skip to the part where I tell you about the nightmare I had where you bend over and suck my—!"

The door to the room burst open and two men wearing white clothes with the Division's emblem pinned on their chests shuffled in and grabbed at Wild's arms before he could finish unzipping his pants.

"Let go of me! *Let go of me!*" Wild cried.

He felt something thin and sharp poke through the side of his neck, and his vision blurred before fading out completely. He hung limp as the two men dragged him out of the room.

THERE WAS no church in Primitus, so Dagan used the fountain at the center as his pulpit. About a dozen people, including families, usually came to listen to him; that morning as he preached about the story of Moses, barely half.

Yesterday, Lazarus Kostov's son and his crew had arrived, and no one knew why. All night in bed, Dagan held Marlene close, staring at the ceiling while listening to his six-year-old daughter Priscilla sleep in the next room, oblivious.

Now, back in the *Time Capsule*, Priscilla sat on the counter turning a Rubik's cube. Dagan stood beside her, watching Marlene bent over CT-RX, rewiring and cleaning. She had always loved fixing things.

For years, they'd sworn off children; the world was a dangerous place, and was becoming worse every day. Priscilla was an act of faith, and they were confident that Primitus was a good home for her.

Captain's shadow was making it a losing bet.

The door chime rang.

Dagan's heart climbed into his throat. His eyes shifted from Priscilla and Marlene, then to the man coming out between the shelves.

Red hair, leather jacket stitched with gold piping, boots that glowed faint blue with each step. Dagan knew he heard his name before.

Damien. One of Captain's men.

The gun under Dagan's jacket flashed through his mind and he forced it away.

The gangster peered at Priscilla, an unsettling grin forming on his lips.

"Can *I* try?" He asked, hand out.

Priscilla hesitated. Dagan bit back asking Damien why he was there. Push too hard, and Captain would hear of it. Marlene's eyes flicked up, cautious.

Priscilla passed the cube over and Damien's fingers danced on it.

"Great sermon this morning, preacher," he said without looking up.

"Really?" Dagan asked.

"Oh yeah, *especially* how the Egyptians were painted as oppressors. Those slaves were made to build monuments, yes, but how else would great cities rise?" Damien's voice was easy, covering up steel. "If the Egyptians even existed, they were gods. And when Moses led the slaves out, they only submitted to another master. *I* think the moral of the story is: there are only two ways to live. Serve a god, or you *become* one."

With a final click, Damien solved the cube. All sides matched. He handed it back to Priscilla.

"Daddy, look! He finished it!" She crowed.

Dagan picked her up and held her close. "Is that really what you took from the story?" He asked Damien.

Damien shrugged, wistful. "It's all subjective, isn't it?"

The gangster drifted down an aisle, perusing the puzzles, board games, and CDs. Dagan had to fight the urge to tell Marlene to take Priscilla and get out, but Damien wasn't the only threat.

The front door chimed again.

Damien whistled. "I've *gotta* take advantage of the 'everything must go' sale."

Sweat prickled Dagan's brow. "What makes you think that would happen?"

Damien turned, grin devilish. "Captain's putting offers out for this street. Hopefully you'll like the new owners."

"Leave them alone, Damien," said a voice that gave Damien relief. Sparks emerged from around the corner of a shelf.

Damien's face tightened, but he kept his composure. "Hey, Sparks. Just having a chat with the pastor."

"Captain's looking for you," Sparks said.

Damien glanced at Marlene. Dagan's fingers twitched, wanting to go for his hidden gun.

In a hurry, Damien bumped Sparks's shoulder as he stormed away. The door slid and hissed shut behind him.

Dagan let loose a sigh and hugged Priscilla close. "Thank you," he said to Sparks.

Sparks nodded. "Have you told her yet?" He asked, gesturing to Marlene.

"He told me," Marlene said, voice steady but tired.

"Good, because you're going to need to get started very soon," Sparks said.

Dagan was still shook. Panic stoked the furnace in his chest.

"There has to be something more I can do. As long as people like him are around—" Dagan jabbed a thumb towards where the door would be, "...my family will never be safe."

"I understand," Sparks said. "But you can't. You'll only put them in more danger."

Dagan put Priscilla down and stepped up to measure Sparks. "So there's *nothing*?"

Sparks's eyebrows went up. Impressed or offended? Dagan didn't know.

"Well," Sparks said, "there might be one thing."

VIOLET SPRINTED *to get to Charles, but Damien— standing behind the poor old man who was unaware of him —shoved his hand up to stop her.*

No! No, don't kill him!

Damien had told her that Charles's son, Sparks, was part of the same gang he was in, but was never meant to stay.

Violet's arms rattled as she clung to the kitchen sink, staring through red, raw eyes out the window at the neon signs and towers. Her stomach was twisted in a knot. She barely slept last night. The incident was a day old, and it replayed itself over and over again in her head.

If I see him again...!

A knock on the door startled her out of her spiral. Damien would've just let himself in. No one ever came knocking at their place.

Is it Wild? Did he find out where I live?

With shaking legs, Violet got to the door and tapped a few keys on the screen beside it to see who was standing on the other side. On the screen, a middle aged man with dark shoulder length hair and a salt and pepper beard, popped up.

"Can I help you?" Violet asked.

"A friend wanted you to have something. He said it can help you," the stranger replied.

Violet pressed a button to open the door, then pressed it again so that it stopped halfway. The man didn't move. His eyes were friendly, and he had a small, gentle smile. He handed her a small package. She was startled by how weighty it was.

"Good luck," the man said, and started walking away.

"Wait! Who's your friend?" Violet asked.

The man stopped and looked around the hallway, as if afraid someone was listening.

"You know his father," he said before scuttling away.

Violet gasped. *Sparks?*

The stranger was gone before she had the chance to ask more. She shut the door and leaned against it. Her heart was pounding out of control and pulsating in her ears as she fumbled with the package to tear it open. Once the top was torn off, something metal fell out and struck the floor.

A gun.

Slowly, carefully, Violet knelt and picked it up. She had watched Damien examine and clean his own gun enough times to know how to hold one. She pressed the button on its side and the magazine slid out.

Fully loaded.

Sparks sent this to me? But why…

It hit her.

Oh…

"*…Do whatever you have to do to get that piece of shit out of your life before something worse happens.*"

Wild's words rang loud and true in Violet's head.

36
CAPTAIN

I'M STARTING *to see why other people don't take him very seriously.*

Inside *The Raise*, Captain tried fishing for a reason to not establish a relationship with the Purpletells. So far, their leader, Leon—sitting across from him with several of his men—was jittery, insecure, and wanted to pursue the lifestyle of a gang while simultaneously hating on people who were rich.

Sitting to Captain's left was Damien, who had no objections to being there. Captain had tagged along with Damien and his father Isaac to *The Raise* several times. To his right sat Trevor.

"Oh!" Leon said over the obnoxious jazz noise, snapping Captain back to attention. "Did you hear about that idiot that jumped off a building last night?"

Jiang.

"Uh, yeah. What about it?" Captain asked.

"I just can't imagine anyone doing that here," Leon paraded his arms around to show off their surroundings.

"I don't get it either," Captain admitted, faking clueless-ness. He took a few puffs from his cigar.

A waitress with gloved hands came to the table presenting a tall bottle of red wine.

"Hell, *yeeeesss*," Leon drew out, taking the bottle and setting it on the table.

"Is this a toast to friendship?" Captain asked.

"Oh, no. Just a formality. I kinda have a thing or two to say about friendship with you."

Eh, still better than talking to Amon.

Captain raised a curious eyebrow. "Care to elaborate?"

Leon popped the cork of the bottle off without answer-ing, poured himself a glass, then tipped wine into Captain's glass before moving on to Damien and Trevor. Damien held up his glass but Trevor left his alone.

Once Leon got to his companion on the left, his grip on the bottle failed him and it crashed onto the table and dumped what was left on the tablecloth and his compan-ion's lap. Damien guffawed and his eyes bugged out, while Trevor remained silent and wary. Captain sensed a laugh in his throat but convinced himself to stuff it down. He wasn't in the mood to create friction with anyone, not after last night.

The man with the spilled wine on his lap possibly feared Leon because he barely reacted. He didn't say a word, didn't even look down. Leon pretended not to notice.

Everyone with glasses of wine clinked them together in solidarity and took a swig.

"Thing is," Leon started, wiping his mouth. "From what *I've* heard, you're not really a big deal. Dope, but not a big deal. *We* like to know that the people we vibe with have it all together, outside...*and* inside."

What exactly is he implying?

"I'm not sure what you've *heard*, but..."

"We've heard enough. Little birdie told me that you have someone you can't control."

How does he know that?

Captain took turns glancing at Damien and Trevor. No matter how paranoid he was, there was no way they had anything to do with that. Damien's first love was his loyalty to him. Leadership was never something he sought after, nor would he ever betray his best friend for it. He hadn't known Trevor as long, but he trusted him with his life more than his brother, who was harder to read.

"Did Sylar tell you that?" Captain asked.

"Oh no way," Leon laughed. "We're not awesome enough to have his attention, and we don't want it. He won't help us grow, but *you* can." He swirled his glass while never taking his eyes off Captain. "Here's the thing, I don't really want to be besties with you until I see you get your act together more. For now, all we ask is that you let us use Primitus to store some of our product. We're selling good, which means production has been going faster, which means stuffing all of it in my attic is less..." Leon stopped and faked pondering for a moment, setting his glass down.

"...Sustainable. I'll even let you try that product tonight. Maybe it'll convince you to have some in your territory."

Who told Leon about Sparks?

Captain wanted to keep pushing the question, but if he did, there was a chance—as much as he didn't want to believe it—the person he wanted to know about was sitting on either side of him. If he was, Captain was in no position to defend himself without getting shot within seconds of trying. What if that person was in league with Leon? If so, Captain had no chance of survival there whatsoever.

"I'm not asking to own the place. Just renting," Leon assured.

Captain grazed his bottom lip with his teeth and nodded. "Alright, screw it. Let's try what you're selling first."

"Awesome. Lose the cigar, you won't need it," Leon said.

In the corners of Captain's mind, however, he screamed a question.

How many of these guys are going to ask for a piece of that stupid street?

"ARE you sure it's okay for me to be up here?" Ripley asked as Joan led him onto the balcony of Captain's Primitus home. A modest garden setup inhabited the space, pots lined neatly along the railings—an echo of what Joan had tried to recreate in the penthouse.

Joan glanced over her shoulder, frowning. "What're you worried about?"

Ripley severed the thread before it could unravel. "*Nada, nada.* Why are we here then?"

"Well, I couldn't get anything to grow back at the penthouse. Tried for almost a year. I'm worried that the same will happen here," Joan groaned, lifting one of the pots and turning it over in her hand. Her fingers lingered on the clay like it was fragile, something that could slip away.

Ripley's first instinct was to step closer, to take the weight from her hands, but he held back.

"Are you asking for help?" He asked.

Joan gave a short, sharp laugh. "Don't be ridiculous. I've never asked for help in my life."

Ripley wrung his hands. "Funny. Me neither. No shame in starting today, right?"

Joan didn't answer. Her eyes had gone distant, emerald glass reflecting a place far behind them.

"Joan?" Ripley asked.

Joan blinked and shook herself. "Uh, yeah. Sorry. I know it's a long shot, but do you happen to know anything about gardening?"

"Mama taught me. Not my real mama, but someone who deserved the name."

Joan arched a brow. "Wait a minute, you *actually* gardened in the Web? Was it ever stolen?"

Ripley shook his head, wide-eyed. "Oh no. No one *dared* take from her. *Nadie.*"

"She sounds cool. What was her *real* name?" Joan asked.

"Saint," Ripley said, pride warming the word.

Joan's eyes lit up and her jaw dropped. "Saint? No frickin' way. You lived with her?"

"Yeah, I met her a few times. She was kind. Gave me some food once. Homegrown. Not the gray slop my dad and I ate. Crazy, right? If I'd ever gone to her place, maybe I would've met you."

"You probably did," Ripley said, his knees trembling as he leaned against the rail. "Most people in the Web see each other at least once."

Joan looked out at the skyline, the City looming like a great wall. "And now? You'd be lucky to really know anyone here."

Ripley swallowed. "Have you met anyone like Saint since you came here?" The words slipped out before he could stop them.

Joan blinked, her lips tightening. "No."

Ripley bit back his next thought. *Not even Captain?*

He didn't want her answer and didn't want to know. His smile faltered, and he realized he'd been smiling for her all along.

"If Saint was so great, why'd you leave?" Joan asked, setting down the pot and rubbing her hands together.

Ripley's hand found his diamond earring and played with it. "I didn't want to."

Joan's eyes widened. "Wait, really?"

"Blame my *hermano* that I'm here at all."

Joan cracked a bemused smile. "Seriously? I'd thank him."

"Thank him? Why?"

"Oh my god, dude. Why do you think?"

Ripley chuckled, though Joan's words dug at him. "That sounded like Captain."

He thought he saw Joan's face twitch in the evening light.

"Hmm," she murmured, tone flat. "Then why did Trevor take you away from Saint if she was good to you?"

Ripley hesitated. "It's Trevor's mission to find me a perfect life. Otherwise...he's got nothing."

"Reminds me of my dad."

"Why'd you leave him?" Ripley asked.

"Because I didn't want the life he was trying to give *me*."

Ripley looked at her. He saw the way her shoulders never relaxed, even with him on the balcony. He saw a woman who had clawed her way out of the Web—only to keep clawing, like she was stuck in quicksand. He knew that feeling, because he was still clawing too. Maybe all Websters really were cursed, dragging their past behind them no matter how far they ran from home. The nightmares, the need to glance over their shoulder all the time. They lived with them every day.

"Did you find the life you wanted?" Ripley asked before he could stop himself again.

Why the hell are you asking her that? That's none of your business!

Joan's eyes scanned the balcony, lingering on the pots as if one of them might give her an answer. She sighed.

"Yeah," she said finally, without looking at Ripley.

Ripley waved his hand. "Sorry. Maybe I shouldn't have asked."

Joan laughed lightly. "It's fine. I get it. To be honest, my life would be even better if I could figure out how to grow some damn plants." Her eyes brightened again, and Ripley felt warmth creep back into his chest.

"How much do you know about growing these things?" Joan asked.

Ripley's smile returned, steady and real this time. "Show me what you've got, and we'll go from there."

THE YELLOW LIGHTS of *The Raise* looked like goo to Captain.

Captain was splayed out on his side of the booth. Damien was sitting on the floor beside him with his head in his hands. Trevor was up and pacing, having not inhaled Leon's product, which turned out to be something in the vapes Leon had handed out to everyone. He never explained what the drug was in the vapes, but it was enough to knock Captain halfway out. A warm sizzling thrummed in his chest and he was floating.

"Damien? Damien!" Captain cried.

"I'm here," came Damien's voice, lost and tired.

A tidal wave of memories crashed over Captain, keeping him pinned to the booth. Sparks. Benji. Joan. Charles in the wheelchair, Chase's face staring back at him with dead eyes.

"I screwed up, man," Captain croaked.

"You don't *ever* screw up," Damien slurred.

"I screwed *up*, Damien! I took it too far with Sparks last night."

"You needed to show him...you're not screwing around."

"*Figure out what you're going to do with Sparks...before he figures it out for you.*"

"I should've just...let him rot in prison..." Captain moaned.

Damien didn't answer.

"*...Before he figures it out* for *you.*"

"What if Joan is in danger now?"

Sparks was in Primitus right now.

Sparks is in Primitus with Joan!

Captain tried using his elbows to lift himself up but he was paralyzed. The ceiling was drooping and dripping and the lights were gelling together in one bright blob.

"I have...an idea," Damien managed.

Captain craned his neck but it was no use trying to see Damien. "You do?"

"The Purpletells want you to get Sparks under control, right? Just kill him."

"I don't know if that'll help," Captain said, but already the idea was tantalizing. It was a tussle, however, to connect the dots of Damien's logic in Captain's fogged brain.

Damien elaborated. "The only thing Leon knows is that Sparks is a thorn in your side. What if you...what if you get as many of the gangs as possible together in one place...in Primitus...so you can have your final negotiations with them...and *kill* Sparks right then and there? Show them you *do* have control."

"...You're a *genius*, Damien," Captain hiccuped.

Damien guffawed. "I know."

"It'll take a little more time to get the other gangs together."

"I have...*no* doubt you'll get it done," Damien said.

"Better yet, just kill me now."

Sparks's words sliced a razor through Captain's confidence in the idea.

A ringtone blasted in Captain's ears and he winced and groaned until finally it stopped. He heard Damien speaking in a hushed tone.

"Daniel, I gotta go," Damien's voice echoed.

"Go? Go where? Don't leave me," Captain said.

"It's Violet, I guess someone is trying to get inside our apartment. Sorry, man."

"Damien?" Captain called out, his voice never reaching beyond a whisper.

"Watch him," Captain heard Damien say to Trevor.

"Damien?"

Damien didn't answer. He was gone.

IF SAE HAD the power to freeze time with a wave of his hand, Glass would be unfazed, unchanged. A point in time trapped in stasis.

So many people around me should either be dead...or dying. I should be dead. Then time can move on.

He got a laugh out of Sylar mentioning this to him once. Sae asked him if life was boring him to tears since death wasn't in his future.

"*Boring* me? There is no *boredom* in eternity," Sylar had said, the lies clear in his eyes.

Sylar lied often, but he was more honest with Sae than anyone else, making his honesty and his lies easier to distinguish between. Sylar was more honest *without* words than he was *with* them, and—though it took years—Sae was able to piece together that he was like a brother to Sylar, one who was filling the gap for someone else who was now long gone. A *real* brother, Sae suspected.

Sylar was no pest to have around. Quite the opposite actually. He was great at conversation, and the days he told Sae nothing but the truth were the best days.

Sae owed Sylar so much, for so many reasons he didn't remember.

Sylar saved him, for reasons he didn't remember.

There was no time marching forward, but the longer Sae drifted, the more time in the past dissipated, until the faces of his family and whatever friends he may've had were consumed by the purple light shows in the sky. The only thing left that connected him to family was his scrapbook, gifted to him by his long-gone grandfather.

Sae sauntered down the sidewalk in downtown Glass to the same elevator that'd take him to a skybridge near Primitus. He wished he had the ability to freeze time with a wave of his hand, to silence everything around him. He wanted to be alone with his thoughts. Alone so he could try and see forgotten faces.

The earpiece he had nestled in his ear crackled. For a few seconds, he thought Sylar was reaching out to him. He stepped onto the elevator and the doors slid shut with an obnoxious *whoosh*. He keyed in the combination on the wall and the elevator shook before it pulled itself up. He grabbed hold of the safety handle dangling above him. On the wall beside him, was a screen displaying the news, covering the death of Jiang Band, Paragon's now-former dance coach. It was being ruled as a suicide, and the news coverage was taking the opportunity to dig deep into every aspect of his life to find answers as to why he'd commit the unspeakable.

Ace, the leader of Paragon, appeared on the screen in an interview. "We are...deeply saddened to hear this news. Jiang was our teacher...and a friend, and the best trainer we've ever had. I'm sorry." Lips quivering, Ace turned to leave with the other Jacks filing right behind him. Sae knew right away that everything from Ace was an act. He had seen enough fakeness from Sylar to recognize it.

"You're treading on some thin ice," a scratchy voice over the earpiece blared.

Sae peered around the elevator as if someone was going to leap through the wall at him. His heart hammered against his chest. He had been near Primitus scoping the street out last night, and Sylar wanted him to do it again.

"Who is this?" Sae asked, reaching to push the earpiece in deeper to hear better over the stutter of the elevator and the sound of the news.

"Is this...Captain?"

A garbled laugh vibrated out the earpiece. "You may not be a good spy, Sae, but Captain can't even see what's right in front of him."

The elevator rattled again as Sae gasped, recognizing the voice in his ear now. The elevator screeched to a jarring stop with a high-pitched squeal and the doors slid open, revealing the skybridge. Rain beat against the glass arch that protected it. A drone passed over the arch with nightlights on, cloaking Sae in white light for several seconds before it moved on.

"*Arbor*? I thought you were dead, what...how did you survive?" Sae asked, stepping off the elevator. He walked to the glass, peering down at Primitus stretched out below him. His eyes searched and searched for his friend, as if he would find him looking up at him.

He wanted to know everything that had happened with Arbor since...

"This needs to be quick, I can't chat," the scratchy voice said.

Sae sniffed and wiped at his eye. "I feel like you owe me one."

"*More* than one. But not yet, and I don't know when."

"Soon?"

"Even sooner if you answer a few questions, and that's only if you're..." The voice trailed off, and Sae wondered if it was just getting drowned out by the beating rain outside.

"Arbor?" Sae called, raising his voice to be heard.

"Call me Sparks."

O...kay.

"Do you love Sylar?" The voice asked.

"I—." Sae stopped. *Think about this.*

'Love' might be a strong word. Do I 'like' him? Yes. Do I love things about him? Yeah, but...

"Why?"

"I wanted to know so that I can figure out if you'd be willing to help me...behind his back," the voice said.

"Why don't you tell me what that help looks like first?"

"Like I said, just answer some questions."

"Will my answers kill Sylar?" Sae asked.

"No," the voice cracked, marred by static at first. "I just want to know why you're spying on Primitus and what Sylar knows about Captain's actions so far."

"Will you kill *me* if I answer those?" Sae asked.

"No," the voice said again, this time soft and empathetic.

Sae thought about his scrapbook again, and the tight tension in his chest slowly came undone. He hoped—though even he knew that hope might be futile—that a better reunion was in their future.

"Sylar wants me to spy on Primitus to keep an eye on Captain. He thinks he's a loose cannon who might 'disturb the peace'. He already knows about Captain's talks with Amon, and he figured Jiang was killed by the Jacks because Captain told them he has his money. His death *really* made Sylar mad. Jiang was a reliable client for years...among other things."

Sae liked Sylar, but he hated most of his friends, Jiang included. All of them were sloppy, unintelligent, oblivious freaks that didn't earn a single dollar they had, instead becoming rich through trust funds Sylar set up for them.

"Lovely. Anything else?" The voice pressed.

"Not really," Sae lied. He learned it from Sylar. "I'm just supposed to keep doing this until Captain leaves Primitus. Speaking of which, why do you care about what happens to Captain?" Sae asked.

"I'm part of his gang," Sparks's voice confessed.

Seriously? He could've joined any gang in the City.

"Why his?" Sae asked.

"I can't answer that right now. I don't have enough time," Sparks said, anguished. "Do you really not know anything else? Please, Sae."

Sae sighed and rubbed his aching temple. Any relief he might've had that Arbor was still alive was overwritten by his elusiveness and his obvious but unclear plans. The best course of action for now was to give him what he wanted.

"Ratchet saw two of Captain's guys meet with the Purpletells last night. He's pretty sure that Captain didn't know about that."

"Captain thought they were getting food," Sparks said.

"Obviously he's being backstabbed then," Sae replied.

How anyone would want to join the Purpletells is freaking beyond me.

"Keep doing your watches, but just tell Sylar nothing is happening," Sparks's voice said.

Sae raised an eyebrow and flattened his hand against the glass of the arch. "Clearly something is *going* to happen."

"Goodbye, Sae," Sparks said, sad and quiet. "If it's any consolation, I'm glad I got to talk to you again."

"You too," Sae said. He wanted to wake up from whatever dream this was. This dream that brought an old friend back just to slap him in the face and tell him there's no joyful reunion here. No going back to normal. Normal left when Arbor was presumed dead.

"Hello?" Sae tried through the earpiece, but there was only a dead silence on the other end. Sparks was gone.

Sae cautiously peered down at Primitus's street, the shining fountain in its center illuminated through sprays of rain.

Even if I tell Sylar he's here, he still has his five Calypsos. He'd have a plan for that too.

...He always was good at that game.

40

DAMIEN

DAMIEN LURCHED out of the self-driving taxi. His vision and mind were still not back to normal after inhaling a drugged vape. The idea that someone was trying to break into his home was the only thing keeping him moving on his feet, flailing and groaning as he went. He tried calling Violet again several times on the way home, but she didn't answer.

Damien never feared for Violet's safety until today. She was someone to come back home to, a woman that qualified as 'tolerable' compared to others he'd been with before.

What Captain had with Joan was something Damien still longed for and never felt he was accomplishing with Violet. Joan seemed to not only tolerate Captain's work, she supported it. That wasn't Violet. Once the right woman finally comes along, Violet was going to find herself outside in no time.

Damien almost changed his mind on the way, close to having the taxi turn around and go back to *The Raise*. There wasn't anything of value in his apartment he cared to keep, and Violet was a placeholder.

Damien got ahold of his gun after some wrestling and

entered the apartment building. He ascended up the elevator that took him to the right floor. He peered around the corner at his door to check and see if someone was lurking there. The door was shut.

Damien's eyes narrowed. *Okay, what's really going on here?*

Violet doesn't have it in her to lie to me.

When he used his key card to open the door, he saw Violet standing in the middle of the living room, sweaty and her breathing out of control. Her eyes were traumatized and she gulped when she saw him.

Maybe someone was *here.*

"Are you okay?" Damien asked, his voice still slightly marred by the drugs.

Violet nodded hard despite what Damien saw. He cautiously stepped into the apartment and the door slid shut behind him. He gazed at Violet as if *she* was an intruder.

"What happened?" He asked.

Violet drew a gun from her waist and leveled it at his head, her shoulders rising and falling like angry ocean tides. An insatiable thirst for justice clouded her face.

Huh, maybe she can change.

———

VIOLET

Damien didn't appear as appalled as Violet expected him to. He seemed off, as if he had run into a wall and was recovering from the impact. He was leaning against the wall beside the door, fighting to hold himself up. His pupils were dilated.

Is he...is he high?

"What are you doing, babe?" Damien slurred.

The gun shook. Her hands vibrated. She jerked the trigger and a bullet rang out. Her ears exploded from the deafening noise.

Miss. It was a *miss*.

The bullet hole near Damien's face smoldered in the wall.

"You're even stupider than I thought," Damien said. He pulled his own gun up. Violet slammed the trigger again, the skin of her finger this time slicing between it and the trigger guard. The bullet carved its way through Damien's cheek, and the man dropped to the floor with his hand clutching his ruined face. His gun was lying away from him now.

Violet's stomach convulsed as she realized it was going to take more than one bullet to finish him off. She adjusted her aim, squeezed one eye shut, and the final bullet shattered through Damien's forehead.

Violet was free. But only from him.

PART THREE

41
AFTER

THE WEB WAS a catastrophe of misshapen buildings cobbled together, and winding paths through the city that made for a convoluted maze. Most roofs were flat, making it easy for people to set up tents or sleep under the stars, which they preferred over sleeping inside their filthy homes.

On top of one of these roofs was an old man in his sixties, poking a small fire with a stick. The fire's light lit up his long, graying beard and revealed sunken eyes and gaunt cheeks. Around him, he held a blanket, and his young son on the other side of the fire held one too. The boy stared at his father through the long mop that was his hair. It was late at night, the stars were shining bright, and it was quiet, besides the wind that beat against the crackling flames. If the wind picked up any more, it would be enough to snuff the fire out.

Past the man, the child could see Glass, standing tall in the distance. He could see the flashing neon lights and the towers that stretched far up into the sky. He thought he could hear an ever so faint throbbing of music. It played in the back of his head, almost like a tiny vibration. That vibration had been there for so long, he couldn't remember a time when it wasn't.

It felt like an invitation that wasn't meant for him but rubbed itself in his face.

"Do you think I can go there some day?" The child asked.

The father looked up and peered at the City over his shoulder, as if it was threatening to come closer and envelop the two of them. He stared back at his son and shook his head.

"I'd put those thoughts to rest, son. It's not worth it," he grumbled.

"But why, papa?"

"That...*place*...isn't good. *Nothing* good comes from there."

"But you lived there before, didn't you? Why can't *I*?"

"I lived there once, yes. But at the time it was... different."

"Different how?"

"I don't know how to describe it. It was different. Simpler. But it wasn't the City that was different in a better way. It's what came before it."

"Before it?"

"A community called Primitus, before...before Glass was built around it. It swallowed Primitus up. Primitus used to have more people living in it, but some of them moved out and into the City because they wanted to participate in it."

"But you weren't one of them, were you papa?"

"No. I didn't want to live in the middle of this place I didn't understand. I wanted the quiet. I wanted to see stars again. Like tonight."

The old man pointed up at the stars in the sky and the

son looked up too. They were beautiful. He liked looking for patterns in them, and if he couldn't find any, he'd imagine them.

"What was Primitus like, papa?"

"Primitus was a beautiful little town. Everybody knew everybody, and they all looked out for each other. They helped each other."

"Did you help people too?"

"Of course I did. I don't mean to brag, but I was pretty good at it." The father willed a small, mischievous smile. A tiny hint of light before it disappeared. The child giggled.

"Once a week, everyone in Primitus would go out together and pick up trash in the street, we'd have movie nights under the stars, we listened to football on an old thing called a radio, and we'd give God praise while gathered around the fountain."

A tear fell down the father's face as his nostalgia took hold of him. The child tilted his head and thought about what his father said. Everything he said was nothing he had ever seen before. Movie nights? Football? A fountain?

All of these things sounded simultaneously strange and wonderful.

"What if I went to Primitus some day? Maybe I can find those things."

The father shook his head. "You won't find those anymore."

"Well, maybe I can still go to Primitus."

The father shook his head again, harder this time. "Primitus doesn't exist anymore. Glass destroyed it."

The child shivered at his father's words and the small gust of wind that patted him.

Is there anything *out there for me?*
Somewhere...?

42

VIOLET

VIOLET COULDN'T LOOK AWAY from Damien's sightless eyes.

His body leaned against the wall. Blood pooled underneath him.

Dead. Oh my god. He's dead.

In Damien's pocket, his phone rang. This was the third attempt by someone to reach him.

It has to be his boss. Oh no.

"*Violet?*" Vanessa asked over Violet's phone.

"Huh?" Violet gasped.

"*You need to run that by me again. What. Did you do?*"

"I..."

"*Violet!*"

"I killed Damien!"

"*You what?!*"

"I...I was scared! He threatened to kill Charles and someone gave me a gun and I used it to...oh my gosh!"

"*Violet, you need to leave Glass.*"

Violet shook her head, flinging her hair left and right and getting it all over her face as she paced.

"No! No. I told you I'm not leaving!"

"*If you're caught for the 'm' word, no one will ever see you again.*"

Tears gushed. Boulders weighed down her stomach.

"*And what about Damien's boss?*"

As if on cue, Damien's phone rang again.

"*What is that?*"

It hurt to breathe, her face was soaked, and Damien's cloudy eyes stared back at her.

"How do I leave?" Violet whispered.

Just then, someone started banging on the door.

43

CAPTAIN

CAPTAIN SHOVED his way through Damien's door before
it finished sliding open, the influence of the drugs gone. His
nose was greeted by the stench of blood and sweat.

When no one answered the door, he had used the spare
key card Damien gave him a while back. He never thought
he'd have to use it.

Behind him was Trevor. Damien wasn't answering
Captain's calls and the last time Captain saw him, he said
there was someone trying to break into the apartment.

What is that smell?

"Captain," came Trevor's voice, quiet, hollow, bearing
witness to something Captain didn't yet see.

Captain jerked his head around, opened his mouth,
then froze.

Damien was there, against the wall, unmoving and
silent.

No...I just saw him, he's...no...

Those same eyes he saw in the alley a year ago stared
back at him.

Captain's knees buckled. His insides melted, dragging

him down into Damien's blood. His hand caressed Damien's icy cheek.

He was dead.

No tears came. The pain in his gut was like fire, burning away his stomach, leaving him numb. His mouth shivered trying to form the right words.

I'm so sorry.

But he had no control over his voice. His voice was broken.

Trevor, who had left the room to scout out the rest of the apartment, returned.

"Looks like Violet escaped out a window in the bedroom. There's a staircase outside. Wasn't she the one who called him here?" Trevor asked.

Captain reached into Damien's pocket and pulled out his phone, then used his friend's thumb to unlock it.

He mentioned once that he tracks her.

He opened Damien's phone tracker app. There was Violet. A red dot on a map, heading in a straight line through Glass. It was shooting in the direction of...

The border. She's trying to escape!

"We need to go," Captain announced, leaping up and tearing his way to the door.

"We're going after her?" Trevor questioned.

"She either killed him or she knows who did."

TREVOR

TREVOR REMEMBERED CHASING a man down in the Web for a loaf of bread once. Ripley was back home on the floor, starving. Trevor didn't care that the man might need this bread too. What mattered was keeping his brother alive.

He finally caught up to the man and tackled him down. The bread went rolling through the dirt. Though the man tried to fight Trevor, Trevor was faster and stronger. He shoved the victim's arms aside and brought his fists down on his face. Over and over again, he struck the bread man, splitting skin and fracturing bone in his nose. Once he was weakened, Trevor got up, snatched the bread, and ran back home. Ripley got to eat that night.

Trevor understood Captain's drive. He was angry, grieving, and down one friend. The difference though was that when Trevor chased people down in the Web, there was something at the end that could help Ripley. The merit of *this* chase, on the other hand, was simply revenge.

Everybody was right about Captain. He's not cut out for this.

Back at *The Raise*, while Captain was drugged up, Trevor got close to Leon.

"Why'd you tell him about a 'little birdie' feeding you info? You could've blown this whole thing," he snarled.

Leon grinned, not phased by Trevor. "But I didn't, and now he'll be more on edge than ever, making him vulnerable. Trust me, dude, I know what I'm doing."

Trevor sniffed as he weaved his way around traffic in the pouring rain while Captain barked directions at him.

What he did was help create a monster.

VIOLET'S TAXI stopped at a block where a flight of stairs leading underground would take her to the subway station. A blinking sign above the steps displayed the train's destinations, one of them being the eastern border of Glass that led to Central.

Violet scampered out of the car and bolted for the stairs, stumbling once while going down, almost launching herself towards the floor below.

"Train to eastern border, set for departure in five minutes," said the female announcer over the speaker.

Violet jerked her head around to watch for anyone that looked like they could belong to Damien's inner circle as she hustled across the station towards the sleek, silver train sitting still on the tracks as people boarded it. She fell in line with everyone else, still checking for Captain and his group.

Not here. Maybe they haven't figured it out yet.

A hint of hope rose up in Violet's throat when she stepped on the train. She snatched one of the straps above and held on. Tears snaked down her face and she balled a fist against her heart, which was raging so hard it felt like it was going to tear its way out of her chest.

I'm almost out...almost out.

The train shuddered, the lights flickered, and the doors slid shut before the train started moving.

Violet's hand went for the gun at her waist and she checked her sides. Nothing out of the ordinary. No one was even looking at her.

The ride lasted for what felt like hours. She sat and stared out the window at the City outside, which was swaddled in an angry twister of rain.

She yanked her eyes away and focused on the light show on the ceiling instead. It was hypnotic, immersive. She found herself drifting, sleep borne out of fatigue cloaked her eyes.

In the back of Violet's mind, the deep thrum of the City sounded.

Where are you going? Come back.

Violet gasped, her eyes shot open and she flung forward, her fingers trembling against her forehead.

I've got to get out of here now!

————

CAPTAIN

Captain clamped his hands against the sides of his head and screamed over the noise in his mind. At least, that was what he *wanted* to do as Trevor drove through vicious rain that tried to veer them off course.

That snarky grin, his snippy remarks, and the faith he had in Captain—that faith that didn't come from anyone or anywhere else. That was Damien. His father didn't believe in him like that. His mother clearly didn't since she left. When Captain was left alone in the world with his father's scheming friends, Damien was still there.

Captain wanted to call Damien's phone, wait for an answer, see if maybe what he saw back at that apartment was just a decoy. It wasn't beyond the realm of possibility.

The problem was that Captain was already holding Damien's phone, watching the red dot as it flew towards the border on a subway train.

Then Captain's phone went off and he dove for it, hoping it was Damien. Instead, it was Benji.

Captain's first instinct was to ignore the call. Seconds later, Benji's name popped up again and his phone vibrated.

Captain sucked in a hot breath and hit 'Answer'. Benji was babbling before he put his phone to his ear.

"*Captain, the hospital called. My mother is dying, there's nothing more they can—.*"

"This isn't a good time, Benji," Captain interrupted.

I'm not stopping this chase.

"You'll have to see your mom without me, I can't make it," Captain said, and hung up.

———

VIOLET

Violet was already at the door when the train started to slow. Waiting at the end of a wide tunnel were the eastern border gates, guarded by a desk cop and an officer.

Just show them your ID...get out of here...

Deciding not to risk alerting the guards by running towards them, Violet walked. The police noticed her, squinting as if they weren't sure she was real.

"I need to get to Central," Violet wheezed.

The officer at the desk started filling out a sheet on a tablet.

"Reason?" He asked.

"Uh, I'm seeing family," Violet said.

"ID, please," the cop requested.

Violet pulled up her ID on her phone and showed it to the cop. Next, he took a scan gun, scanned the QR code on the ID, and her information popped up on his computer screen.

"Do you have a history of infectious diseases including..."

"I don't," Violet answered quickly.

The cop glanced up at her with arrows in his eyes. "Was that an interruption?"

Violet straightened her shoulders and shook her head, feeling like her face was peeling off, threatening to expose all her secrets.

"Sorry. Ask away," she said.

The cop only stared at her, growing more belligerent. He bit his bottom lip and his nostrils flared.

"You're hiding something. I can see it all over you, you're shaking," he said.

The guard stepped closer, one hand hovering over his own gun. He was readying himself just in case.

Violet's heart lamented in her ears and her hands shook so hard she had to put her phone back in her pocket.

"What was the reason you gave for going to Central again?" The cop asked.

"I said I'm seeing family," Violet said, teeth chattering.

"You did say that," the cop mused. He turned to the guard.

"Let's take her in for further questioning. This one's lit up so green, the Labyrinth can see her from here."

No...no!

The guard at the gate already had cuffs in hand. He strode up to Violet, his figure taller and wider than she was.

"No...no, you can't! I didn't do anything!" Violet cried.

"That we know of," the desk cop motioned to the guard, "check her."

The guard patted Violet down, each touch causing her heart to flare. Then he found the gun.

"She's armed," the guard announced, sliding the gun out of the holster.

Violet's eyes flickered between the desk cop and the guard.

Either I run or I let them take me...or Captain kills me.

Violet elbowed the guard in the stomach, which did little thanks to the body armor. She attempted to run, but the guard was quick, snatching her shoulder and holding her in place under an iron grip.

"Innocent people don't try to run," the guard sneered.

Violet struggled to no avail. An icy cold dread poured over her and her chin began to tremble. She was forced to the ground, and she felt the metal of the cuffs pierce her wrists.

Is this really it...?

————

CAPTAIN

Captain turned the corner at the subway where Violet would've gotten off the train. A small crowd had formed to watch something that was happening at the border gates.

The red dot had been frozen in the same place on Damien's phone for a little while now, which meant Violet was being held back. What he saw caused him to pull back around the corner and put his back to the wall.

Two officers had Violet on the ground and were handcuffing her.

The crowd murmured in disapproval of Violet and shook their heads as a guard led her down the subway.

"Move!" The officer yelled. People parted to give him room. Violet's head was down, not even noticing that Captain was there.

Trevor put a hand on Captain's shoulder and squeezed it. "There's nothing you can do now. Not without getting yourself in trouble," he said.

She'll go to prison but still live.

Damien is gone. He's really gone...

KOA HATED playing chess with Sparks.

Sparks always won, but he drew the games out to last long stretches in order to torture Koa. He wanted Koa to recognize he was losing before the final move struck. Koa second-guessed his moves every time, and often beat himself up for making the wrong ones.

The majority of Koa's life was spent as a butler, doing what other people expected from him and not much else. The one he used to serve taught him a lot, but none of those lessons involved learning how to plot against his enemies. Nevertheless, chess was addicting to him because he wanted to know how to play, and some day how to finally beat Sparks.

The two of them were playing in a virtual world set in a dark room that oozed cool blue light. Koa had on a virtual reality earpiece at his desk in the back of his implant repair shop, a small business he started after his last master died. Sparks was using an earpiece to play too, his avatar appearing as real as he did in person. Koa hadn't seen Sparks in person since he joined Captain.

Koa finally broke the silence. "So."

"So," Sparks repeated.

"From what it sounds like, it seems to me that Captain is a better person than you thought," Koa said. Sparks had told him about Captain's deal with Amon, how he was able to save that kid.

Sparks's shoulders twitched, signaling a shrug.

"His goals are still the same. What's *really* on your mind, Koa?"

Koa sighed and rubbed his temple. "I guess I just want to make sure that in your obsession for revenge, you don't hurt people that don't deserve it."

"People who don't deserve it aren't getting hurt though," Sparks insisted.

"Not *yet*."

"Is this about Violet?" Sparks asked.

"Violet could get hurt—or *worse*—because *you* made sure she got that gun."

"It was too risky to kill Damien myself. It was either him or my father."

"But giving Violet the means to kill him puts her in danger. That was never part of the plan," Koa barked.

"A lot of things were never part of the plan. These things happen, Koa, it's the nature of it."

"What about Sae, now that he knows?"

"He won't be a problem. He was the least risky way to learn what Sylar knows already about Captain's movements."

"There has to be another way."

"Not at this point. Unless it's to walk right up to the doors of Samsara Financial and..."

"No, not that," Koa said. "Glass has taken so much from

you...it took the same things from *me*. Don't let it take the rest, or I would have *nothing* left."

"Maybe you won't lose the rest if you leave now and pretend you never knew me," Sparks suggested. "I won't stop you if you walk away."

Sparks glanced down at something Koa couldn't see. Something was alerting his attention. "I have to go," he said, reaching for his ear.

There was a click and Sparks's body darkened, a window popping up over it that said 'Logged Out'. Koa glanced down at the chessboard. After studying it for another minute, he spotted Sparks's path to victory. One of his knights had the opening to move two squares vertically and one square horizontally, knocking out Koa's king.

Sparks won the game again, and—without saying much —this argument.

Vengeance was clingy, especially when family was involved.

BENJI'S MOTHER, Lauren, was dying in a bright white room. No life support. No staff nearby. Benji was kneeling beside her bed holding her hand while Captain hovered next to him, aloof.

Joan watched through a window in the hallway. Lauren's lips were moving but she couldn't hear anything. Leaning against the wall next to her, with his hands stuffed in the pockets of his worn jeans, was Ripley. His amber eyes were haunted and tired. Trevor and Sparks were on the other side of him.

"You good?" Joan asked Ripley.

Ripley blew out a sigh. "*Quizás.*"

Joan shook her head. "Sorry, I don't know that one."

"Maybe...probably."

Joan nodded and the two stayed silent as they watched Captain and Benji. From where she was standing, Joan could see Lauren fading away.

"They just roll these people into a room to die alone," Ripley said. He muttered something in Spanish, which Joan didn't understand fully except, somewhere, the word 'dignity' was involved.

Joan folded her arms. "Apparently no one who dies here gets buried either. They just reduce the body to ashes. The family isn't even allowed to keep them. Bastards."

"Papa spent more than half of his savings for my real mama's coffin. We buried her in our backyard, held candles, and..."

Ripley stopped and kept staring ahead, rubbing his diamond earring. Behind the window, Lauren breathed her last breath. To Joan's surprise, Benji's face didn't change. Captain did, however, wrap his arm around the young man's shoulder as Benji bowed his head. Captain was saying something to him. Whatever he said, it seemed comforting to Benji.

Am I seeing a potential dad?

"Where's Damien?" Ripley asked Trevor. Sparks stirred to attention.

Trevor's dark eyes blinked at Ripley and Joan with dismay.

"He's dead."

Joan's heart did a backflip. She forgot about Captain and her family fantasies.

"Oh my god. Are you for real?" Joan gasped.

"Yeah," Trevor answered, his voice full of gravel. "Violet killed him."

No...Violet...

"Do you know why?" Sparks asked.

"I don't," Trevor replied.

A question rose in Joan's throat before she caught it. She was afraid to ask.

Then again, if I don't ask, it'll never go away.

"So, what happened to Violet?" Joan asked.

"Captain tried going after her, but she was arrested while trying to leave Glass," Trevor said.

Tried going after her.

Joan stared back at Captain, something like bile building up in her chest. The idea of Captain catching up to Violet...what he would've done...

Her husband was staring back, with fatigued, angry eyes. After everything she'd heard and seen, she couldn't even smile to alleviate the tension. She had nothing.

Between them, there was nothing.

JOAN

JOAN FOLLOWED her father around in the Lighthouse Borough, carrying a basket full of fruit and bags of nuts. Her hair—not yet dyed—was black and trailed down her back, over her shoulders, and hovered over her eyes.

Ninety-nine percent of what was shipped to the Lighthouse Borough, a port by the Web, went to Glass while the remaining one percent was left for people in the Web to buy—if they even had the money to pay for it. Though the market in the Borough had a lot to offer, a lot of people didn't have the energy or motivation to leave their homes and come see, fearing high prices and disappointment.

That wasn't a problem for Joan's father, Urban. He visited the market every week almost immediately after the ships arrived. Oftentimes, he managed to save up the money to buy nicer things that he would then trade later with port guards for even more money and a first look at supplies that had just come in. Urban—a tall man with black eyes that made anyone stop when they saw them--wore a collared shirt displaying a snake coiled around a cross with a long black double-breasted overcoat over it. These were clothes he was proud to have snatched before anyone else at the market.

Urban was trying to fix an old car he kept in one of the warehouses at the Borough, promising that one day it'd be ready for them to use to get away from the Web, the Labyrinth, and everything else having to do with the City. Joan's mother's disappearance didn't kill Urban's motivation to fix the car; it only made it grow. It wasn't just about leaving the Web anymore. It was about finding her mother too.

"Right, what do we got here?" Urban stopped at one of the setups in the market and buried his hand in the mango cart, rifling through them until he pulled one out that wasn't bruised all over.

"Beautiful specimen, isn't it, love?" He asked, showing the mango off to Joan.

Great, he's doing the accent again.

Urban used to dip into an Aussie accent around Joan's mother when she was still around. He was good at it, and it made her laugh. Now, he was trying to use it around Joan and it annoyed her instead.

"Yeah, dad, it's great," Joan replied dryly.

Urban turned to the marketkeeper. "Just one coin, right?"

"Two today," the marketkeeper answered.

Urban dug into his pocket, pulled out two black coins, and handed them to the marketkeeper.

"Bloody hell, it was just one three weeks ago," Urban complained.

The marketkeeper eyed Urban with disdain. "You're pretty entitled for someone who lives *here*."

Aw, crap.

Urban raised an eyebrow and took a heavy step forward. "Come again, mate?"

"And you look pretty good for someone who lives in *this* hellhole," the market keeper continued. "What does everyone else think of you walking around wearing that coat like you own this maze?"

Urban glanced at Joan who slightly shook her head at him, then looked back at the keeper.

"Well, if you *must* know, mate, I don't give a *shit* what other people think. Everyone else can choose to live their lives however they want. Most are just not smart."

"Let's just go, dad," Joan urged.

"You should listen to your daughter. If the port guard sees this, they could—."

The keeper was cut off by Urban shooting his hand out and grabbing his throat.

"You mention my daughter again, you see what happens," he seethed.

"Dad!" Joan cried.

A few men watching over the market noticed the commotion and approached the cart. Urban saw them coming and casually let go of the keeper.

One of them was quick to question him. "What's going on here, Urban?"

"Nothin', mate. Just a little misunderstanding. Really, I can just—."

"You can just watch that big mouth of yours, or it'll get you in trouble," the guard warned.

Urban's jawline tightened and his eyes bulged. His neck strained and he sucked in a sharp breath. Joan grabbed his hand and started tugging him away.

"Let's go, dad," she hissed.

To her relief, Urban didn't argue and allowed Joan to take him away from the market. Once they got inside their hut, Urban let loose a string of curse words, some in different languages Joan didn't understand. His fists cracked the dining table.

"I had that under control, love!" He roared, his black eyes aflame.

"Oh yeah, *totally*! And drop that *stupid* accent!" Joan screamed.

Urban sank in the chair by the table and clapped his hands on the wood. "I'll never take you with me to the market again," he moaned, losing the accent.

"Oh no, how horrible, whatever will I do?" Joan said, setting the basket down on the other side of the table. She released a bitter sigh, exhaling the frustration and tension she felt at the market. A boldness to tell her father the truth reignited.

"I don't want to be here anymore," she said.

Urban groaned, sliding his face through his hands. "We've already talked about this."

"Don't care! I want to go to Glass!"

"Your old man can get you what you need *right here*. You don't need Glass."

"Your version of getting me 'what I need' puts us in danger!" Joan cried.

Urban sat back, mouth agape. "And you think Glass *won't* be dangerous?" His fake accent found its way back in. "There's monsters *everywhere*, love. At least in the Web, they're easier to spot."

———

Joan walked up to the border gates, clutching the documentation papers in her hand trying not to bunch them up too hard in her grip. The guards standing by watched her with wary eyes.

Will the papers be enough? Will they fool them?

She raised her hand for one of the guards to look at the papers, her breath catching in her throat. The guard's mouth moved but she didn't hear anything. She couldn't react in time when the guard raised his gun. A bullet sounded and pierced her skin...

"Joan!"

Joan blinked out of her daydream nightmare and looked down at Mack, a young man with a mop of brown hair and comically large glasses. He frowned at her and muttered something.

"Sorry, yeah?" Joan asked.

"Did ya hear *anything* I just said?"

"No, yeah, I...need to memorize the info on the ID papers so that I'm not reading it in front of them."

"Memorize, memorize, memorize..." Mack's voice trailed off until he was muttering again.

He sat at the computer in his bedroom, which was sealed shut by a password, a thumbprint, and a face scan. He was one of the luckier ones in the Web, having pulled together some things that allowed him to live a more comfortable life than others, but even then it wasn't much. The computer was a gift from a woman named Saint, who insisted his abilities would be best paired with it. It turned out she was right.

Out of an old printer beside the computer, the ID papers shuffled out. Mack snatched them up and held them out to Joan.

"Here."

As soon as Joan took them, Mack slapped his hands together, wringing them nervously. "You're really going to Glass, eh?"

"Gee, what gave you *that* impression?" Joan teased.

"I just...uh, hear a lot of bad stuff about that place. Not safe."

"I think I'll be fine," Joan said, not wanting another argument. They were getting exhausting. Now that she had what she needed, she started her way towards the door.

"Does your dad know?" Mack asked after her.

Joan spun around. "No! And you're not going to tell him. If he comes and asks you—and he *will*—you tell him you *don't know* where I am."

Mack hesitated, still wringing his hands and avoiding eye contact.

"But that means lying."

"Mack!"

"No knowing where you are, got it! I tell him nothing!"

"Good!" Joan sighed and relaxed a bit.

"Thanks, Mack. I appreciate this. Seriously. You've always been a good friend."

Mack smiled but still didn't look directly at her. She knew that he liked her, in a way that he could never bring himself to admit. After suffering a head injury from rolling off the roof of his home, Mack got to keep his technological genius, but his mind was scrambled in a way that made him hard to connect with. Sometimes he forgot where he lived, and someone had to lead him back home.

"Good friend," Mack repeated, then started muttering again.

Joan opened the door and left, closing it behind her. She was afraid that if she stayed any longer, she would start regretting her choice.

———

Joan never saw her father again. She never saw Saint again, or Mack, or any of the boys that used to catcall her, or the girls that used to pull her hair until she was yanked off her feet and her face cratered into the mud. The Web was a world she wanted no part in anymore.

Leaving the Web was the easy part. No one kept track of people leaving the Web and entering the Labyrinth. Trying to get into Central was another matter, which was why the papers were supposed to allow Joan entry into both Central *and* Glass.

On the subway train that took her through Central, Joan peered out the window, seeing Glass draw closer and closer, the tops of the towers becoming impossible to see. For a moment, the way it was rushing up to her looked like someone who finally found a lost loved one, eager to embrace her in a hug.

In the back of Joan's head, she heard something she had heard since birth, except stronger now. A rhythmic thumping like a beating heart that seemed to emanate from the City. Beyond that, a faint whisper.

Welcome, welcome! We've been waiting for you...

She wanted to laugh in relief as she drew closer to Glass. She was welcome?

That's *a first*.

She was *welcome* there. Glass was where she was meant to be.

Stepping off the train with about a dozen other people, her stomach growled. She was more than familiar with hunger pain, but this pain was the worst she'd felt. It was as if her body knew that where she was going, there was more food than she'd need.

"Ugh." She clutched her stomach as she approached the border gates where guards were waiting. "Shut up."

"What?" One of the guards asked.

Joan shook her head. "Nothing. I have these."

She showed the guard her papers and waited with bated breath.

The guard looked over the papers, nodded, and handed them back. "Everything checks in."

A crooked grin dashed across Joan's face. She was free.

What she saw on the other side of the gates left her frozen in place for what seemed like forever. The sights took her eyes captive. The bright lights and disco colors consumed her vision.

Joan was in the middle of it all and had no idea where to go or what to do first.

CAPTAIN WATCHED DAMIEN'S FATHER, Isaac, pour himself a glass of whiskey, silent after he broke the news about his son. The man was a spitting image of Damien. He wore a long, glimmering gold night robe that pinched Captain's weary eyes. They were both standing in Isaac's backyard on one of the upper levels of the City, able to gaze down over the fence and see the rippling, twinkling lights of the downtown area below. Isaac's swimming pool danced in the pale lights streaming from the bottom.

Isaac's face never changed. Not when he saw Captain coming around to see him in the backyard, not when Captain broke the news about Damien, and not after pouring himself a glass and taking a sip.

Does he feel...anything?

It burned Captain to stay standing, rigid by the pool with his arms at his sides. He wanted to sit down and flush away the pounding in his head with a swig of Bathory.

The problem was that he had already tried that.

"Violet is dead too, right?" Isaac asked, tone like gravel.

Sludge slowed Captain's blood. He tasted something bitter when he looked Isaac right in the eye and lied.

"Yes."

Isaac blinked at him with tombstone eyes. He took both the bottle and his glass and sauntered into his house. The door slid shut behind him and clicked.

Captain hadn't shed one tear since finding Damien's body. Now countless of them were threatening to break from his eyes.

What I saw could've been faked. It's not impossible...it's not...im...

He glanced down at the pool. Something about the moving water and the warm lights glowing beneath it was hypnotic and comforting to him. The pool beckoned to him, as if it was his way of escape out of the nightmare.

Maybe if I let myself fall in, I'll wake up.

Captain pinched the skin on his side and winced at the pain. It was real and sharp, and it almost broke the wall he'd built to hold the anguish in his eyes back.

I need to know for sure.

He had never gone back for the body. Surprisingly, Isaac didn't even ask for it.

Only one person knows what really happened. She ran for a reason.

Captain left Isaac's backyard, stumbling like a drunkard on a late night. The others were expecting him back in Primitus soon. They would have to wait a little longer.

VIOLET

In her prison cell, Violet sat huddled on her bed. Her arms wrapped tight around her knees, pulling them to her chest. Her eyes stayed fixed on the floor, sweat soaking through her prison clothes. She had lost track of time. She didn't even know if it was day. The prison was always dark—an endless night. The laser wall over the cell's entrance didn't block sound. Every laugh, curse, jeer, and cry echoed through the halls and chilled Violet's shoulders.

Violet shut her eyes, then opened them, realizing there was almost no difference in what she could see. The mess hall wasn't much better, its dim lights casting shadows that made the greasy slop they called food look dark and color-less. Violet still remembered the taste of it—metallic and greasy with a hint of chicken—sticking to her teeth forever.

Even Spectra was better than this. There had been real food, real drink, real pleasures. It was almost comical to Violet, how she'd gone from living in a modest city, to living in the greatest city known, to now living in hell.

A knock jolted her out of her thoughts. She looked up, squinting through the darkness. A shadow stood on the other side of the energy shield. It was tall but not imposing. Violet's breath caught. This wasn't a guard.

"Hello?" She whispered, her voice a fragile tremor.

The shadow didn't answer. It stayed there, unmoving, as if thinking. Then it raised its hand, pressed the button beside the cell, and the shield wall flickered out. The shadow stepped inside and got close enough for Violet to make out who it was.

Captain.

Violet shot to her feet, her heart catapulting up her chest, and tears of panic burned her eyes.

She glanced at the door. The shield wall hadn't come back up yet. Normally, it reset automatically unless someone disabled it. A small, dangerous flicker of hope snapped through her. Maybe this wasn't what it looked like.

"What are you doing here?" Violet whispered.

This time, she got an answer. Captain's voice came out hoarse. "What did you do?"

Violet swallowed hard, pain flaring in her throat. Playing dumb was pointless.

"You found him, right?" She asked.

A shuddering breath escaped Captain. "So that was really him?"

Violet frowned. *He doubted?*

She was damned no matter what, but if she had to be, she'd rather tell the truth.

"It was him," she said.

Captain sniffed and his head shook.

"And you did it?"

Violet's voice failed her, so she nodded.

"Why?" Captain's voice broke. No malice, no rage. Just pain.

"I—uh—," Violet's eyes fell to the ground. "I did it because..."

"*Because?*" Captain barked, tears in his voice.

Violet's body quaked harder, threatening to topple her. "He almost killed...C-C-*Charles*."

Captain's tone sharpened with confusion. "That old man?"

Violet nodded again, violently.

"He threatened the old man because he was following my orders," Captain said. "Why not kill *me*?"

He took a step closer. "Why didn't you kill *me*?" His last word broke, thin and fragile.

Violet hadn't even thought of that. Killing Captain was unthinkable. Damien was within arm's reach every day. He was the one who kept her caged.

Her eyes flicked to the way out, then back to Captain. If

she stayed, she'd die. If she ran, she'd die. She already tried leaving Glass once...

The shaking in Violet's body slowed. Her jaw unclenched. She met Captain's eyes.

"I have no regrets," Violet whispered through her teeth.

Captain inhaled deeply. Malice finally surfaced, crawling into his face.

"I see," he said, but he didn't move.

Violet stayed silent. There was nothing left to say.

"I'll be honest with you," Captain said after a moment. "I understand why you hated him."

Violet didn't move. If Captain was baiting her, she wasn't taking it.

"As long as he was there, you had no control over anything. Things just happened, and you had to...roll with it. You were done," Captain said.

Violet's pulse kicked. The instinct to run came roaring back, and Captain's smile told her he saw it.

"I'm done letting things happen to *me*."

His hand moved. Violet gasped. A gunshot tore through the air, and her world went black.

WILD PACED BACK *and forth with his tablet, racking his brain for a song he wanted to write with his brother Chase. It'd be their first song. Their fifteenth attempt at one anyway.*

Chase was sitting atop a car near him smoking a vape, looking out at the City, up high on one of the upper levels of a parking garage where they could be alone without noise or traffic and still get outdoor air that helped Wild think.

"I think I figured out one of our problems with the song," Wild said.

Out of mock surprise, Chase raised his eyebrows. "This should be good."

"So it turns out, it's hard to find good words that rhyme with 'pearls'. When you rely on that word to carry the song, things get dicy."

"What words have you found?"

"Curls, girls...urinals..."

"Let me stop you right there. I think the mistakes started when you looked at my necklace and thought 'oh hey, that's a song'," Chase pointed out.

"Write what you know I guess."

"That's a stupid saying. If all of us only write what we know, every story in the world would bore us to tears."

"They always say that your best writing comes from what you know."

"Yeah, that's after you write everything else. What you know will always involve itself in the story somehow, but that's not why you start."

"Okay, Chase the Philosopher. Give me stories that you've never experienced."

Smoke unfurled through Chase's grin. "There's two guys, best friends with mind powers. One has telekinesis, the other has empathy. The one with empathy can feel what everyone else is feeling and if he's not careful with his own feelings, he can make people go insane."

"Where does the relatability come in? Besides maybe you drive people insane?"

"Even the smallest thing can trigger terrible, terrible consequences for everyone else."

"Huh, I didn't realize you ruined so many people's lives."

"We're the Jacks. Ruining people's lives is our specialty."

"You got any more of those stories?" Wild asked, tapping a few notes into his tablet.

Chase leapt off the car and walked with his vape still in hand. "Two vampires, a brother and a sister who have to protect their oldest ancestor from sinister forces after he rises from the dead."

"You're losing me," Wild said.

Chase stopped and faced his brother. "Am I? What do we and vampires both have in common?"

Wild had never read any books involving vampires and he could count on one hand how many movies he had seen.

Still, there were a few facts about vampires that were universally known.

Finally, the answer found him.

"We never die."

Chase stomped his foot. "You got it! We know what it's like to never die, unless some idiot is killed or...kills himself."

"Don't say that too loudly," Wild scolded. "And where did these stories come from? Are you actually writing them?"

"Started both, haven't finished either yet. Remember what I said about starting with what we don't *know. One thing that* nobody *knows, that almost* no one *experiences...is death. My advice is, write a song about the* meaning *of the necklace, not how pretty it looks."*

Chase raised the black-and-white pearl necklace around his neck, running his thumb over the pearls.

"White means life, black means death. It's a reminder to me that no matter what humans achieve to stave off death, no one is safe from it forever."

Wild rolled his eyes. "You keep using the 'D' word."

"I'm just living in reality."

————

WILD

Wild stood alone in his room at the Suicide Watch Division with his head bowed, his filthy purple and turquoise hair hanging loose towards the floor. His mouth moved silently at first as it fought to make the sounds he'd been wanting to make all day.

Pearls...that's what we called it...Pearls...

The first words of the first song Wild and Chase wrote together croaked out, barely audible. He inhaled from his cigarette, which was graciously given to him by one of the security guards. He shook his head as he exhaled, inwardly begging his voice to work.

Chase's killer is still out there.

His voice started to return. The words he whispered came out clearer. The more he sang, the more passionate he sounded. There was a clicking sound as his door whooshed open. They were going to take him away and force him to take a pill again. It was meant to calm him down. Numb his thoughts.

He always believed singing was the cure to numbness.

A familiar *click clacking* sound beat across the floor and Wild looked up, surprised to see Ace coming in, tapping his cane. Two guards stood behind him at the doorway.

Ace looked Wild up and down, his smile smug as always. "You look good," he said.

Wild snorted, a gleeful smile tearing through his misery. He sprinted for Ace, threw his arms around him in a desperate hug, and buried his face in his friend's shoulder.

"There, there," Ace purred, rubbing Wild's back. "Let's get you out of here."

"I have to find him, Ace...please...I have to..." Wild cried.

"I know."

A GROUP of people stood in a circle around the fountain at the center of Primitus gripping each other's hands. All of them were singing.

Ripley watched them from a distance, one hand on his earring and his back against *The Glass House*. He and the rest of the gang—what was left of them—returned to Primitus without Captain after he insisted on visiting Damien's father alone.

A few of the people in the circle glanced at Ripley, silent anger simmering under their eyes. One of them was Dagan, the man everyone in Primitus looked up to. Ripley looked away, but still felt their eyes on him. He sealed his eyes shut, and a tear broke free and slithered down his cheek.

The voices of the people around the fountain rose higher.

Ripley got out his phone, his hand quaking, his thumb barely able to speed dial. He put the phone to his ear, and listened.

"Please wait while we transfer your call. This line will take additional time."

Saint answered after several rings.

"Ripley?" Her voice cracked.

"Hi, Mama," Ripley answered.

"Are you okay?"

The singing grew louder, forcing Ripley to stand and turn the corner between buildings in order to hear Saint better. The singing was like an inescapable force that was going to get him, no matter how far he fled.

He leaned against the wall on the side of *The Glass House*, using his other hand to pick nervously at his earring.

"I miss you," he squeaked into the phone.

"I miss you more. How's Joan?"

"She's fine, Mama."

"You don't sound so sure."

"She needed help with her garden and I was able to help her...thanks to you."

Ripley could hear the smile in Saint's voice. *"I knew what I taught you would one day come in handy."*

Tears watered Ripley's eyes and he sucked in a shattered breath. "I don't know if I can do this anymore."

"Do what?"

Ripley's body slid down the wall until he was on his butt, hugging his knees.

Even then, the singing somehow rose more.

"Ripley?"

Ripley brought the phone back to his ear. "Sorry."

"You know you can come see me whenever you want. It gets lonely out here sometimes," Saint said.

Ripley swiped at his eye. "The more I think about it, the more appealing it sounds."

"I did say once you weren't missing anything over there."

"You were right, Mama. It's just more of the same."

"*Just keep thinking about coming to see me, kiddo. I love you.*"

Ripley snorted. "I love you too."

A metallic voice switched out Saint's. "*We're sorry, your call has been disconnected due to high levels of interference. Please try your call again. Thank you.*"

"Saint?" A voice spoke up.

Ripley saw Trevor standing a few feet away from him, a bottle of beer in hand. "And?"

"Why waste time on her? She's behind us now."

Trevor moved closer to Ripley and crouched to be level with him.

"I brought you here to live better than the old lady does, and you're still calling her."

"That *señora mayor* took care of me, and she didn't have to *steal* bread to do it," Ripley argued.

"You would've done the *exact* same thing if you were in *my* position." Trevor raised a questioning eyebrow. "Right?"

Ripley sighed and hung his head between his legs.

Trevor groaned and took a swig from his bottle. "Loving the gratitude, by the way."

Ripley faced him. "I love you, *hermano*. But this place isn't for us. We don't belong with Captain *nor* Leon. They're like the scumbags in the Web, just with nice clothes."

"You're never going to find a perfect leader, and a leader is what we need to survive here without getting sent back," Trevor said.

Ripley frowned. "Why do we need someone to lead us? I thought we came here to live *beyond* surviving."

Trevor stood up, keeping his gaze down on his brother. The music at the fountain finally stopped, ushering in a heavy silence. Sighing, Trevor toasted the air with his bottle.

"So did I."

The engine of a car vibrated, shaking the night air. Trevor peered around the corner to investigate.

"Captain's back."

WHEN THE DOOR to *The Time Capsule* opened and the alert sounded, Dagan's hand automatically reached for the gun on his waist, taking no chances. Captain was not in a good mood when he came back to Primitus last night.

In fact, he didn't even look himself. What that meant, Dagan wasn't sure and he didn't want to be caught unprepared. He didn't even like leaving Marlene and Priscilla at home anymore.

The footsteps were heavy, striking the floor in a moody rhythm. Sparks came stepping around the corner of a shelf.

Dagan raised an eyebrow at him. "Oh. It's you."

Sparks nodded, brushing his gloved fingers along the puzzles sitting on a shelf. "The man that bothered you yesterday...he'll never bother you or your family again."

Dagan frowned. "So that woman...?"

Sparks gave him a look. It told Dagan everything he needed to know.

Dagan shook his head. "I'm not a fan of being responsible for murder."

"But you weren't," Sparks said.

"I gave her the trigger."

"Something tells me she still would've found a way. Don't talk about it. We don't want someone coming in and hearing the wrong thing."

Dagan put his head in his hands. *That poor woman.*

"Why do you care about my family so much? I thought you were a criminal like Captain," he said.

Sparks's fingers stopped on one particular puzzle and he slid it off the shelf.

"I'm not like Captain," he said, putting the box on the counter for Dagan to scan. He fished in his pocket for coins and put three on the counter. "It's time to start the plan."

Dagan's heart skipped a beat and he rested his hands on the edge of the table to steady himself. "So soon?"

"Or your family will be in danger."

CAPTAIN

THE PLAZA WAS a wide square in the center of Glass, rich in color and spectacle. Several fountains were in the middle, spraying rainbows in the air. Dozens of businesses surrounding the Plaza had giant screens advertising VR headsets and augmented reality inserts. There were food trucks parked along the sides, the smell of cheap food permeated the square. Androids walked around, handing out pamphlets for different clubs and underground brothels to anyone who was willing to accept them.

In the distance, near Glass's prison, a rainstorm brewed.

Captain and Benji stood together waiting. Benji was wearing a VR headset that was shaped to accommodate his cybernetic eye. Captain wanted to help Benji move past his mother's death, while also hoping to find peace after losing Damien. Anything to take his and Benji's minds off the 'D' word.

When he got back to Primitus the night before, he told the others his plans to negotiate with the Delanos and the Garks, then ask all the gangs he had successful negotiations with to meet him in Primitus in two days. He was able to contact someone from the Delanos and agreed to meet up in the Plaza.

Captain also made it clear to Trevor and Ripley that they not tell Benji about Damien's death for now. Benji's loyalty and enthusiasm was unquestionable, but he was far from one of the toughest among them. Even so, Captain couldn't lose him, after everything he did to protect him.

"So, I'm sure you're wondering where Damien has been," Captain said.

Benji adjusted one of his earplugs under the headset to hear Captain better. "What?"

Benji wore earplugs whenever he walked around outside. He said it was because the noise was too overstimulating to him. Captain didn't understand it, but it wasn't an inconvenience to him so he accepted it, for now.

"I said I'm sure you're wondering where Damien has been," Captain repeated.

"Now that I think about it, I didn't see him this morning," Benji realized aloud.

"Uh, yeah, he's...away because of a, uh, family emergency. I'm sure you really miss him."

Benji shrugged and put his plug back into place. "Not really."

The words stabbed through Captain's heart like a shiv, but he kept from showing it. He knew Benji was different. Different in what way he had no idea, but he knew it wasn't all Benji's fault.

Captain's phone rang and he checked the Caller ID.

Samsara Financial.

Blinking himself out of his mind fog, he answered the call. His greeting dripped out in a drugged whisper. "Hello?"

"Captain Kostov, what a beautiful voice."

Sylar.

Captain's sleep-deprived eyes widened. Paranoia overtook him and he swung around. Was Sylar watching him? Were any of his goons watching him?

"What do you want?" Captain asked, searching the crowd bustling around him.

"*A little more...discreetness would be nice,*" Sylar said.

Captain glanced at Benji, who was oblivious to the conversation.

"How am I *not* being discreet?" Captain asked.

"*Chasing young women across the City...bribing prison guards so you can kill inmates...*"

A couple men, dressed in suits, glowered at Captain from one of the fountains. A few other people walking through the Plaza halted, turned, and stared at him. Eerie blue lights winked in the right side of their heads. Their eyes were glaciers.

"How do you know I chased a woman across the City?" Captain asked, reaching for his gun while circling around so that he was in front of Benji.

"*I have eyes and ears and mouths and lovers everywhere, Captain.*"

The same person that told Leon about Sparks maybe? What if...

"Do one of your lovers happen to be a guy named Sparks?" Captain asked.

Above. A slender woman with black lipstick and shadowy eyeliner was standing atop a balcony gazing down at him while leaning on the railing. There was a gun in her hand.

"*Who?*" Sylar asked.

"Forget it," Captain growled. "Why are your people staring at me?"

"They're there as a precaution. In case we're not on the same page."

Hold on a second...

The Plaza was empty except for Sylar's plants, guns shining in their hands. The music playing in shops had stopped, and the androids shut down. Captain yanked the headset off of Benji.

"Hey man, I need your head here."

"What's going on?" Benji asked. He reached for one of his earplugs and peeled it back.

"How did the Plaza get cleared out?" Captain asked Sylar.

"This City understands when to pull back so that a disturbance of the peace can be handled without a mess."

"Is that what you think I am?"

"You're getting close. Be careful what you do, or you'll turn the rest of the gangs against you. How do you think the Nine Circles massacre makes them feel?"

"Whoa, whoa, what's going on *here*?"

Coming out between two of Sylar's men was Amon, red wool jacket swaying as he approached Captain and Benji.

"Captain? What is he doing here?" Benji asked, stepping back.

"Don't worry, I've got this," Captain said.

"Is that *him*?" Amon asked, pointing at Captain's phone.

"Um..." Captain stuttered.

"Hello, Sylar," Amon crowed.

"Amon," Sylar replied flatly after several silent seconds.

Amon shifted his gaze to Benji. "And hello, *Chi No Akuma*. It's been too long."

"It's only been two days," Benji pointed out.

Out from Amon slithered a humorless chuckle and he

refocused on Captain. "The Delanos have entrusted Amon to give you a message. They want *nothing* from you, unless you can rally the support of a few others. What you did at *Nine Circles* apparently spooked them. Reminded them of your ferocious *kuma* of a father way back when. They never did like him."

"What did I tell you, Captain?" Sylar said.

Captain brought the phone back to his ear. "Hold on a minute." He pressed 'Mute' on his phone.

"They'll like *me*," Captain said to Amon.

A flash of light glinted in Amon's eye and his mischievous grin crept back. Something wasn't working this time. Captain's voice was more on the defensive, less defiant like their last meeting. His head swirled with flashes of faces. Damien's. Chase's. Violet's. Captain wished his head could be scrubbed through, freeing him of these memories, these decisions, this gnawing pain deep in his stomach that warned him something was very wrong.

I'm fine...Joan is fine...Benji is fine...it's going to be okay.

Captain released a sigh, and though it wasn't enough to expel the clawing in him, it gave him enough relief to feel like he was standing tall and proud again.

"Give me two days and I'll get *every* major gang in the City together in Primitus to discuss how things will be from now on. After that, our network will never be the same again. We'll be stronger than *ever* before and we can put the past behind us."

Amon twisted his lips into a hungry grin. "What if you won't be able to convince the others?"

Captain stepped forward. "I will."

Nodding in approval, Amon shook Captain's hand like he did two days before. "Very well. Amon will see what you can do."

"You will," Captain assured, letting go of Amon's hand. Amon turned and disappeared behind the onlookers. Captain unmuted himself on his phone. "Sorry, what were we talking about?"

"I like a good revenge story, Captain, but you need to stay focused if you're going to gain any ground. I've been in this business longer than your father. More people have been disappointed than have found success."

"That's not the Glass *I* know."

"Then you don't know Glass."

"Watch me," Captain replied, his jaw set and his throat tight. The grief that ate away at him was nothing now but a shadow of a memory.

"Always," was Sylar's reply as his people broke off in different directions. Regular people started parading back into the Plaza. The music in stores roared back on, and the androids powered back on and continued doing what they were programmed to do. Captain's phone beeped as Sylar hung up.

"Captain, are we going to be okay?" Benji asked.

Captain slid his phone in his pocket. Damien was gone, but like his father, he would move past it. He was too close to achieving what he wanted for so long: the creation and evolution of his own criminal empire that would become the face of Glass's underground network. The fact that Sylar was confronting him like this meant he was scared.

Captain grinned at Benji. "We're going to be just peachy."

TAKING A DEEP BREATH, gun in hand, Wild pushed open a door, revealing a spacious bedroom with a massive king-sized bed. Pink and white pillows were piled high on it and the covers were a silky magenta. A young woman flung herself out of the bed, clutching a blanket tightly around her, her eyes filled with horror and shame. A man in his underwear fell off the other side of the bed, scrambling for his shoes.

"Wild, don't!" The woman cried.

The man begged. "Listen, man! I'll go! You'll never see me again!"

In Wild's ears, an obnoxious robotic male voice narrated. *"Uh oh! Looks like someone was being a BAD BOY to your lover! You might just have to put him in his place!"*

Wild flipped the safety off on his gun and aimed it squarely at the man's head. The man shielded his head with his hands.

"No, please! I'm sorry, I'm sorry, I'm sorry!"

Just then, a chiming sound threw Wild's focus off, and a

window popped up on the right of his vision with a message.

sparks_521 sent you a private chat request.

The man in his underwear did all he was programmed to do at that point, whimpering and writhing on the floor, while Wild stared at the message.

Who is this?

He stared for a while before approving the request. The scenery around him changed, transitioning him away from the simulator. Now he was staring into a black void.

He called out, "Hello?"

"Thank you for approving my request," came the raspy reply. The voice was everywhere, bouncing off of invisible walls and vibrating Wild's ears.

"Who are you?" Wild asked.

"Just call me Sparks. I need your help."

"*My* help? For what?"

"I need you to convince your friends to accept Captain's offer. They'll know what you mean. He'll want to meet in Primitus."

"And why should I do that?"

"Because you'll learn what happened to your brother."

Wild's heart skipped a beat. "Do you know what happened? If you do, *tell me.*"

"You can't find out unless you go to Primitus. If I tell you *now*, you'll have a smaller chance of getting what I know you want...revenge."

Wild shook his head in disbelief but he couldn't argue with Sparks. Sparks obviously had ulterior motives, but Wild didn't care. If he was willing to give him answers he wanted or at least show him the way to find them, whatever else Sparks was planning didn't matter.

Sparks continued. "Tell your friends they'll get those

answers about Chase too. When you get there, don't push for them. They'll come."

A tear fell from Wild's eye. "You promise they will?"

"I promise they will."

Wild nodded and he raised his head.

"I'll kill you if you're wrong."

"I'm not wrong."

The black void dissipated like smoke, and Wild found himself back in the simulator, the man in underwear still cowering on the floor.

Wild cleared his throat, aimed his gun at the man on the floor, and pulled the trigger. He reached up and logged out of the simulator, plopping himself back in a beanbag at Ace's penthouse.

Time to talk to Ace.

JOAN

JOAN TRIED whiskey for the first time at *The Glass House* on the night she entered Glass.

Joan wanted to find a quiet place where she could figure out what to do next. On a glowing map in the Plaza, she spotted Primitus, a small stretch of road not too far from where she was. She was amazed by its simplicity when she got there. A shining fountain glistened in its center, casting an ethereal glow over the road.

The Glass House was small and quiet, just like Joan was hoping for. At the counter, she met an exoskeleton of an android named BT. Mack had tried creating his own androids, but most of them never survived past a minute, with the only exception being an ugly turtle-shaped monstrosity, its only way to communicate being a gargled, metallic screech. It was shut down and dismembered immediately.

A TV screen on the wall above BT displayed the news, with a big story breaking.

"Chase Weathers, beloved member of the pop band Paragon, was found in an alley with a bullet in his head tonight. Police are investigating how this might have happened and who was responsible..."

'Found with a bullet in his head'? Never heard death called that before.

Joan lifted her whiskey glass in a private 'cheers' to herself and took a swig. Her hand was on her throat in half a second. Her lungs caught fire and her eyes bulged as she hacked and coughed.

"Having a problem there?" BT droned.

So, the robot is capable of sarcasm I see.

"Shut up," Joan groaned, but a smile broke through her misery. Maybe it was the relief settling in that the Web was behind her.

"You could've asked for something milder," BT reminded.

"I've settled for mild all my life." Joan took another sip. It went down easier this time.

There was a noise as someone sat on a stool close by her. The bright white in the corner of Joan's eye prompted her to look. Sitting a few stools away from her was a white-haired young man wearing a white, high-collared jacket. He was soaked head to toe from the rain outside.

He didn't seem to notice or care. The excitement on his face was infectious, and the relief in his ruby eyes radiated out like a sun.

"Oh, that *sucks*," White Hair said, slowing down the last word as he stared up at the breaking story. He waved for BT. "BT, a round for the bar, on me," he declared.

The other people in *The Glass House* stared at him, some confused, others appearing irritated. To Joan's knowledge, when people did this, it *thrilled* the rest of the bar.

Not this one. Most of the patrons seemed to hate that he was there.

Joan pitied him.

When BT rounded up the drinks for everyone and carried them around the bar, some people didn't take them when offered.

"I'm not taking anything from that guy," one of them remarked.

"Sorry, BT. Not from *him*," another said.

"Tough crowd," White Hair said, loud enough for Joan to hear. His grin stayed undisturbed, but his tone was sharp as a knife's edge. He took his own whiskey and raised it.

"In Glass is life, and in life is our transcendence to greatness."

Okay, weird.

White Hair snapped his head back and downed the whiskey. BT got to Joan last, placing another glass in front of her.

Is it stupid to say something? Maybe...?

Joan cleared her throat and picked up the new glass. "Hey, um, thanks."

White Hair noticed, then raised his glass at her with his crooked grin.

"Finally, some gratitude," he slurred.

He moved on watching the TV without giving Joan attention, but she was intrigued. No one liked him, he knew it, and he didn't care.

I like that.

"That's it?" Joan asked.

White Hair didn't look back when he answered. "Hm?"

"You buy a lady a drink and then leave her alone?" Joan said.

White Hair's eyes were still glued to the TV. For a few seconds, his rambunctious smile was watered down. Under the weight of the water all over him, he was like a ghost that was—itself—haunted.

"Did you know him?" Joan asked, gesturing to Chase on the screen, trying again to jumpstart a conversation.

Geez, I guess I am lonely.

White Hair shook his head, and his grin came piecing back together.

"No. I just don't recall Glass reporting something like *this* since Angel," he said.

Do I pretend to know about that or do I ask?

"How did he die again?" She asked, hoping it was subtle enough.

That finally got another look from White Hair. "Where are you from? Really?"

Joan gulped, racking her brain for an answer, hoping to remember names she saw on the map in the Plaza.

White Hair pushed himself off the stool and sat next to Joan. "Now that I think about it, I've never seen you here," he said, wagging his finger. "*No one* outside of Primitus comes to this place except my father and me."

"What did I say?" Joan asked, choosing coy over defensive.

White Hair clutched his chest in mock surprise. "The dreaded 'D' word, Ms...?"

Joan bit her tongue before her name came out. *Careful.*

In the end, she used the name that was on her forged papers. "Hillary."

"The dreaded 'D' word, Ms. Hillary! *No one* says that word in Glass." White Hair paused for several seconds as if something new hit him. "Well, at least not *most* people."

I'm confused now.

"What, you mean 'die'?"

"'Die', 'dead', take your pick, it's all the same to everyone here. So where are you from?"

Think of something, dumbass!

White Hair leaped to conclusions before Joan could snatch up a lie.

"The Web then," he said under his breath.

"How did you figure?" Joan asked.

"Those hands have seen better days," White Hair said, pointing at them. They were indeed scarred in a jigsaw of white, ugly stripes. Years of pummeling, getting pummeled, and tearing through broken glass and dirt.

"No one gets their hands messed up real bad like *that* here. I mean, *wow*, those are some nasty scars! One sip of Bathory right after usually does the trick to get rid of cuts," White Hair said, waving his hand to demonstrate. His grin still didn't fail him, and Joan was unable to look away.

"Maybe I just didn't have Bathory on me at the time," Joan suggested.

There's gotta be an out somewhere.

White Hair reached inside the breast pocket of his coat. "And finally, *no one* goes around without this," he said slowly as he pulled out a small bottle full of red liquid, each word falling on Joan's head like rocks. He set the bottle down on the counter between them.

There is no out.

"'Hillary' isn't your real name, is it?"

Joan's face betrayed White Hair, and his grin widened. "You can tell me. I really don't give two shits where you came from. If you made it to Glass, you deserve to be here. So...?"

Joan twitched, but remembered that she was the one who spoke up first.

"It's Joan," she said.

White Hair nodded with a glint in his eye. "I'm Daniel, thanks for asking. Daniel Kostov." He pointed at the bottle. "Guess I have to tell you about that."

WHY DID VIOLET KILL DAMIEN?

That question gnawed at Joan all night. The pale face Captain had come to bed with was stitched into her brain. Sympathetic tears watered her eyes every time that face resurfaced.

Comforting people was never something I was good at.

Hands buried in her coat pockets, Joan climbed the wide steps to Glass's only jail, splashing through shallow puddles. With Captain in town with Benji, now was as good a time as any to find answers without rousing suspicion.

How many criminals does this city have to need a building this big?

Two officers stood at the doors, rifles slung across their chests. One raised a gloved hand to stop her.

"Hold up," he ordered through his visor. He circled her and patted her down. Joan lifted her arms, rain running off her sleeves.

"No phone. No weapons," the guard said, stepping back. "You here to report something, or visiting someone?"

"Visiting," Joan replied, shivering.

"Who?"

"Violet Gardner."

The guards exchanged a glance. The rain hissed against the concrete as they stood there in silence.

"What?" Joan asked.

The first guard finally spoke. "Violet Gardner is no longer with us."

Joan's insides turned brittle. "What are you talking about?"

"She did it herself," the guard said flatly. "You wasted your time coming here."

He wasn't a machine—just a man with a prosthetic arm —but the way he delivered the news made him sound like one.

"Are you sure *she* did it?" Joan pressed.

The guard stepped closer, raising his rifle just slightly. "Are you questioning us, ma'am?"

"Maybe I can look. Maybe someone overloo—."

"No one overlooked *anything*," the guard snapped. "Now *leave* or we'll take you in."

The second guard lifted his weapon, ready for escalation—until another voice sliced through the rain.

"Stop."

All three turned toward the entrance. The front doors had slid open, revealing a tall, black-haired man with almond eyes studying Joan. A transparent umbrella rested in one hand; in the other, he squeezed a stress ball.

Holy crap...that's—

Beside him stood a younger man in a black raincoat, his almond eyes mirroring the first. He was also holding an umbrella.

"You don't need to lie for our friend Captain," the tall

man told the guards, stepping into the rain. He stopped a few feet from Joan, the storm drumming on his umbrella but never touching him.

"Do you know who I am?" He asked.

Joan's pulse quickened. "You're Sylar Han."

Now that she was face-to-face with the man, it felt different. He was taller than Captain—as tall as Sparks. Joan and Captain's philosophy together had always been 'no secrets', but Sylar looked as if he wore secrets beneath his skin.

"Not too shabby, right?" Sylar said, a smirk flickering across his mouth.

"Come on, Sylar, I want to go back home," the young man complained from the doorway. The guards stood right beside him—two drones without commands.

Sylar sighed, exasperated. "In a minute, Sae." Then, to Joan:"Brothers, right?"

"Never had one," Joan said.

"You got lucky," Sylar murmured. "So, you came to see Violet?"

"Yeah," Joan replied carefully. *What does* he *want?*

"Well, I'm sorry, Mrs Kostov. Sadly, Violet really *is* gone." Sylar's eyes sharpened. "She didn't off herself. Your husband killed her."

Joan's heart lurched, as if someone had reached inside and shaken it. Her skin went cold. Her mouth opened, but no sound emerged.

Even through the rain, Sylar could see her unraveling. "I'm sure you wish I'm lying."

Joan swiped the back of her hand across her wet face, though the tears didn't matter in the downpour.

"I want to," she whispered.

Sylar twirled his umbrella. "Truth hurts. That's why everyone here lives without it!" His tone softened. "But hey —at least they get to live forever, right?"

Intrusive thoughts forced their way into Joan's head: Violet trembling as Captain approached her cell. Joan wanted to turn and storm away from Sylar, but her feet wouldn't obey.

Sylar tilted his umbrella, letting it cover her head. "I've been digging, Mrs. Kostov," he said quietly. "You have no birth certificate here. No school records. No license. Nothing that ties you to Glass."

Joan's throat tightened.

"You're from the Web, aren't you?" Sylar asked.

Joan's eyes widened.

Sylar went on. "You, and two others from Captain's crew. I know."

"What are you—going to do?" Joan asked, her voice trembling.

Sylar smirked. "Nothing. I'm just going to wait and see what happens. But I do hope you understand—you don't belong here. None of you do. But, you're smart. I'm sure you and the others will do what's best." He paused. "For your sake."

When Joan didn't respond, Sylar drew the umbrella back and nodded to Sae. "Let's go."

The two of them descended down the steps toward a car waiting at the curb. Joan stayed where she was, frozen at the entrance. The guards didn't move. No one spoke.

No one was there to tell her it wasn't real.

This was the nightmare she'd tried to wake up from— the one that followed her all the way to Glass. As she stepped down the stairs, the rain pelted her face. Beneath it, something hot began to rise in her chest. Even through the storm, she could feel it—warm and restless. A feral thing stirring from hibernation.

JOAN

IN JOAN'S HANDS, she held Captain's flask of Bathory up to the City lights. The lights were luminous, and hypnotic, submerging Joan. She felt as though she was underwater.

Energy spread through her whole body, anticipation swelling and swelling. Around her finger was a ring. She had just gotten it moments ago. Captain finally made his move to seal each other together for life.

For eternity.

He was rich. Kind. He helped Joan become a part of Glass. That was enough for Joan to believe she was better off with him than anywhere else.

"My father was the head of a crime family," Captain told her a while ago, when they agreed there'd be no secrets between them. *"Drugs and weapons were part of his trade, but the biggest thing was his SpeakWare implants that allow mute people to talk. Now that he's gone, I own the blueprints for that tech."*

Joan knew what her father would've thought about Captain. Joan also knew she didn't care.

She unscrewed the cap off the flask.

Plink.

A drop of rain on Joan's nose. The start of a storm. The City had a lot of those it seemed.

Captain didn't notice. He was staring at his new fiancee, wide-eyed, anticipating. Joan gave him one last smile, then tipped the contents of the flask down her throat. She stared up at the fermenting clouds in the evening sky as she drank.

Her throat blazed, an attempt at words failed in a wheeze, and all the lights around her grew sharper, threatening to impale her. Her hand squeezed a fistful of her newly-dyed hair.

Captain's hands were on her shoulders, shaking her.

His lips moved but the sound of his voice never reached Joan.

"Mm...uh...?" Joan moaned.

Captain's voice and the sound of the rain returned in a rush. "Come on," Captain laughed, sprouting up his umbrella. "Let's get out of the rain!"

It *was* raining. Hard. Joan was already drenched by the time the safety of Captain's umbrella found her head. The two ran across the street, splattering ponds.

What was all that?

By the time they got to the other side, Captain was still laughing and Joan was still processing.

Once they got under a roof, *both* were laughing. Joan threw herself around Captain, cackling against his chest. There was sweet, sweet relief. The sweet taste of freedom like honey on her tongue.

Captain reciprocated, his arms wrapped tightly around her and his head rested on hers.

"I love you," he said, for the first time.

"AND THIS *SPARKS* underscore *five-two-one* didn't show his face?" Ace asked Wild.

Wild shook his head. "No, I only heard his voice."

"Hmmm."

Ace turned with his cane to face the holographic water-fall where the wall should've been in his office. The carpet glowed the same shade of red as Bathory.

"He obviously has ulterior motives," Ace said.

"I have a feeling they won't impact us," Wild replied.

"How do you know that?"

"Because he *needs* us to learn what happened to Chase. What's the point in killing us after?"

Ace frowned. "Captain wanted us to join him just the other day. What if he's using one of his men to get to us so that we'll see him anyway?"

This was why Ace was the leader. He questioned every-thing before making decisions.

"Even if you decide not to go," Wild said. "*I'm* going."

Wild jabbed his finger in his own chest. "*I'm* going to

find out what happened to Chase, because *I* still care about him."

Ace closed in on Wild, carrying his cane with him.

"Clearly, you don't understand me, old friend. I speak for not just myself but also the others when I say that we still care a *lot* for Chase and what happened to him." He placed a hand on Wild's shoulder. "We just wish that you didn't disappear."

Wild had been away for so long that he almost forgot how old Ace sounded despite looking early twenties. Ace was late by a couple years taking Bathory for the first time, but when he did, he did it with the rest of Paragon, celebrating the moment together as their next step towards eternal life. Chase was the last one who sipped from his flask that night.

Ace shut his eyes, his hand still on Wild's shoulder. "In the beginning, there was Glass. All things come from Glass, and apart from it, not one thing can live. In Glass is life, and in life is our transcendence to greatness."

Wild sniggered. "Is this from that cult you're a part of?"

"The Children of Glass isn't a cult, Wild. It's the next generation that Glass is raising up to be its gods, and you're going to be one too."

I'm many things. So was Chase. I could never be a god.

Ace returned his attention to the waterfall which, despite being holographic, still generated an authentic roaring sound.

"I'll get in touch with Captain and tell him we'll meet him after all. We'll *say* it's because we want Primitus."

Wild smiled. For a moment, he remembered his conversation with that girl in the coffee shop. He wondered if she got *her* closure too.

And if she can, so can I.

"LIFE IS MEANT *to have an ending. We can't all play god.*"

Some *of us can.*

Joan was arguing with the memory of Sparks. Standing alone on a walkway overlooking a street downtown, she exhaled cigarette smoke. The rain hadn't let up. Her clothes clung to her like a second skin.

"*You seem like a nice person, Joan. You're better than even you think you are, but don't act like you know where you're meant to be either. You want honesty from me, but I don't think you're being honest with yourself.*"

I am honest with myself.

I love Daniel.

Coming to Glass had always been her dream. Having children where she knew they'd be safe was a runner-up.

There's no future in the Web. The Web is not normal.

Joan's chin shot up as a chiming sound exploded from a large billboard overhead. She blinked. On the billboard was the face of a woman. Butterscotch hair, hazel eyes.

She's beautiful, was Joan's stray thought.

Then her breath caught. *Violet?*

A hyper voice blurted from the board's speaker, echoing through the humid air. "Always remember to treasure your life and take Bathory. Don't be like this woman who chose to unalive herself." Underneath Violet's picture, a familiar phrase scrolled across the screen.

'In Glass is life, and in life is our transcendence to greatness.'

"Why do people do that?" Someone nearby asked, a man walking with his girlfriend.

"Dumb bitch," remarked another.

Below the walkway, a crowd of people booed at the face on the billboard.

One foot floundered back, shoving Joan away from the railing of the walkway. Her eyes stayed locked on the billboard until the face materialized away, replaced by one of the Jacks, Royal, holding up a fragrance bottle.

I loved *Daniel.*

"She didn't kill herself," Joan cried to the people nearest to her. "She was murdered!"

Everyone near her froze and stared at her with bright eyes, wide and scared like they were being threatened by an animal. A young woman, with a massive white purse slung over her shoulder, glared at her. "Watch it," she warned before walking away. Everyone else scattered to distance themselves from Joan.

Sylar's voice lingered, oily and precise: *You don't belong here. None of you do.*

Fresh tears spilled from Joan's eyes. She reached inside the breast pocket of her pink trench coat and pulled out her Bathory flask. She hadn't taken it all day. Bathory was a powerful drug, but it required daily use. It was well past the time she needed a sip.

"*Samsara Financial and the Jacks are just a few of the symptoms causing the larger problem.*"

Yeah...

Joan whipped her flask down on the railing with a cry, shattering the glass and watching the liquid splatter and drip.

Should I run?

Violet tried, and she failed. Sylar knew who she was, and he knew she didn't belong here. Joan had no reason to believe that he lied to her about Violet's murder, but she didn't trust him enough that he was simply just going to let her go like he implied.

Was this how Violet felt when she wanted to run?

It devastated Joan to know that that question will never be answered.

Live forever. Have children. Be happy. All bullshit...

More tears. *If I'm going to die some day, where will I be by then?*

"*So, what, that makes you the solution?*" Joan had asked Sparks.

"*Maybe.*"

Let's see if Sparks is.

Joan stormed off the walkway, hands crammed into her pockets, head down. All around her: a puzzle she didn't fit into.

"CAN you do me a favor before the meeting tomorrow?" Captain asked Ace on the phone.

He was sitting in the passenger seat of his car—driven by Trevor—with Benji in the back. The lights and people of Glass flew past them as the car cruised down the street towards a surprise meeting with the Garks.

"Depends on what it is," Ace replied.

"I need to get a message to the Delanos, but they won't hear me out. Maybe you can use your *obvious* influence to assure them they have nothing to be afraid of with me. Tell them they should meet me in Primitus. If they know you'll be there, maybe it'll calm their nerves."

"We've always been in good standing with them...I can try."

"I think you'll succeed," Captain said. "I have something their leader, Alex, might want. I can provide him one of my father's SpeakWare chips. I heard about the incident between him and the Talismans. I think he'd love feeling like he has a tongue again."

"*I think so too,*" Ace replied.

"Wonderful. And what about getting my money back?" Captain asked.

"*We got as much as we could after we sold Jiang's stuff, not just the stuff he used the money to buy. Expect some transfers in a few minutes.*"

Captain relaxed his head against his seat, sighing in relief. "Love to hear it, Ace. I'll see *you* tomorrow."

"*Don't waste our time,*" Ace warned.

"I won't," Captain said. Though his voice was flat, he was euphoric.

He hung up, then tried calling Joan for the third time.

No one knew where she was. Captain was hoping Ripley of all people would know, since—besides Captain— Joan got along with him the most.

I'm starting to understand why Damien tracked Violet's phone.

"Why didn't we take Sparks with us?" Trevor asked.

"If the Purpletells think he makes me weak, others might too. Besides, after tomorrow, he won't matter. He'll be..." Captain paused, then continued. "...Dead...by the end of the meeting."

Trevor glanced at him, more impressed than surprised. Benji sat forward.

"Captain..."

Captain faced him and cut him off. "You had him at gunpoint in the back of my car the other night. I threatened his father. Do you really think we can be *friends*?"

Benji's eyes—including his prosthetic one—were flying everywhere as usual, but he stiffly shook his head. "No."

"No," Captain repeated. "He's the weak link in our group, and as long as he's still with us, my empire will never happen."

Benji is not Damien. But he can be.

Captain faced the road ahead again and sighed.

"Tomorrow, I correct a mistake."

ONCE A FOOTBALL STADIUM, *Rage Quit* had become a fortress—Glass's beating black market heart. Holo-signs flickered and screamed from every surface, peddling the things that *Rage Quit* sold: weapons, drugs, data, and people. Food was served everywhere. Drinks were around every corner. The betting pits were always thriving. Even representatives from World Linked stalked the crowd, hunting for partners.

All this while the authorities looked the other way, so long as their share of the profit kept flowing in.

Royal leaned against the torn railing of the mezzanine, bundled in his red, white, and blue fur coat. He drew from his vape and exhaled a pink vapor that hung like a halo above him. In *Rage Quit*, no one cared that he was a member of Paragon. They cared that he was a member of the Jacks, and they kept their distance. Royal wished they didn't. Loneliness was real, and—inside Royal—it was a crisis.

Then he saw Alex Delano and grinned. Alex was slouched on a couch below, mechanical hands buzzing faintly as he put them on his knees. Dense shades hid his eyes, and his hair stood up in a crude mohawk. His jacket shimmered with blue light—no shirt underneath. As Royal got closer, he noticed something new. There was a scar running straight through Alex's neck, and the square green chip pulsing where a voice box used to be. Next to him sat a hooded figure, face shadowed. A magenta V-neck glowed beneath its checkered jacket.

Royal raised a brow. "Oh my god, Alex?"

Alex's voice was broken and metallic. There was nothing human about it. "Good. To see you too. Old friend."

Royal almost laughed. He knew the tech—a bootleg version of SpeakWare, the AI speech implant Lazarus Kostov had perfected before his death. Nobody else had ever succeeded to replicate it cleanly.

Royal dropped on the couch across from him, eyes gleaming. "Who ruined your beautiful neck? I'm not mad. I just want to hurt them, that's all."

Alex grimaced and the hooded woman placed a hand on his shoulder.

"After you. Lost Chase," Alex rasped, "our alliance went. On hiatus. Then the leader of. The Talisman. Found me. He cut. My tongue out. He wanted. To send a message."

Royal blinked and sat back with his arms spread over the top of the couch. "Well, damn, message received. Did he cut your arms off too?" He gestured to the prosthetics. "You know, to capitalize each sentence?"

Alex's head tilted, almost unnaturally. The servos in his neck whirred. "Better to be. More machine. Than a man without his voice."

Royal smirked. "What a shame. You were so—*beautiful.*

I think I get it now. You don't want to meet Captain in person like this."

Alex nodded stiffly. "I also heard. About the murders at. *Nine Circles*. How do you know he won't. Kill us too?"

The woman pushed back her hood. "Excellent question, darlin'."

Royal's expression soured. "Elsa," he sighed.

"Guess who," she teased, flashing a grin under the red lights. Her dark, buzzed scalp gleamed.

Royal inhaled his vape again. "Oh, Alex. You could do *so* much better than this tramp."

"At least I don't resort to name-calling," Elsa argued.

Royal rolled his eyes. "I almost wish you did. It'd be nice to hear you say my name every once in a while."

Elsa raised an eyebrow. "Which one?"

"Elsa, it's okay. You don't have to. Waste your breath," Alex said, putting his metal hand on her leg. He turned back to Royal. "She's been with me since. The incident. Her own gang. Is growing."

"Don't tell me you went with—."

Elsa cut Royal off. "The Poker's Many Faces. Catchy, yeah? The Children of Glass need some younger—prettier —faces down here representing them."

Royal groaned and signaled to the android bartender nearby. "Whiskey. On the rocks."

"Remind me again why you're forming your own gang?" Royal asked Elsa.

"To shove out the old trash," Elsa said. "If we don't step up, the only people who'll have their wealth are the people who've been here forever, and their families—like Captain."

"The Children of Glass are nothing more than activists, not crime lords. Why couldn't you just stick with what you're best at...being an annoying bitch, like the rest of the Children?" Royal said.

"It's clear to me now that waving around signs and chanting won't get anything done. The underworld has such a foothold in the City that it will take some of us joining it for any change to happen."

"Sure, fine. You keep at it then, I guess," Royal said, retrieving whiskey from the bartender who had returned. "Business has been slow for the Jacks. The underworld is more tense than ever. Lazarus's death...Chase's death...The Talisman coming into the picture...it's all becoming a bit of a tight squeeze and we need to find a way to wriggle ourselves out."

Royal leaned forward with his hands clasped together, a creepy grin glazed on his face. "Captain is desperate for the underworld to respect him. He'll hear you out. Especially with that—uh—little square shaped problem in your throat. He might even give you a proper SpeakWare chip—if you ask nicely. No offense, but every time you talk, it makes me want to—."

I get. It," Alex bemoaned. "Maybe it's. For the best. My own family. Is losing faith in me. We were. Robbed last month. Under my watch."

"Then ask Captain for the chip while he's still breathing. Or before his empire outgrows you."

Elsa ruffled Alex's mohawk. "I'll go if you go. The Pokers deserve a slice too."

Royal rolled his eyes again but didn't argue. Elsa and Alex were linked at the hip and there was nothing he could do to detach them—that he knew of yet.

"Fine," Alex said at last, "But I'd. Better not. Regret it."

Royal grinned and crossed his legs. "You will, once you get a good look at Captain. Just keep your eye on the prize."

INSIDE THE GARKS' mansion, Captain was reminded that —in Glass—there was no such thing as having too much. The high-ceilinged hallway lit by crisscrossing red lights in the ceiling, the glowing bright blue fishtanks in the walls. The spacious living room with sleek black couches, a reflecting table in the middle, and an electric fireplace spouting unnaturally scarlet flames.

Captain's face stared back at him in the floor. He saw himself staring back everywhere. It was as if the home looked up to him.

He allowed a sliver of a grin.

The Garks' mansion was on a hill isolated from the streets of the City.

Imagine that, Captain mused. *Being able to look down at the City from here like you're God.*

As Captain followed the three armed security guards escorting him, Trevor, and Benji up a flight of stairs. Benji was the most engrossed in their surroundings. He was wringing his hands together and his head turned left and right, absorbing everything and grimacing. Was he over-whelmed or fascinated? Captain couldn't tell which.

This could be his *future too.*

Stopping at a door in the upstairs hallway, one of the guards tapped a few keys in a console installed by it and the door whooshed open. Inside the room, long tables were set in a rectangle, and the blinking colors of prosthetic limbs glittered on the people that sat at them. There were plates piled high with food, and plenty of wine to go around. Behind the rectangle of partiers was a glass wall, and beyond that, the sprawling cityscape underneath a dark-ening sky. A couple men stood nearby, ready to serve when-ever they were needed.

Smirking nervously at Captain behind a chinstrap beard was Eli Gark. His hair was slicked back in a stiff shower behind him, gelled up beyond need. He took a bite of mashed potatoes before washing it down with a drink, but his gaze stayed locked on Captain as if he was a bear out of its cage.

"Mr. Kostov," Eli bellowed, wiping his mouth with his sleeve.

So cute that he tries to sound like he has bigger balls than he does.

Captain dug for some witty remark to say to liven things up, but came up with nothing this time.

As Captain strode to the center of the room, Eli gestured to his party, and a chorus of guns appeared, the barrels directed at Captain's head. Benji and Trevor both drew their own guns, and one of the security guards at the door planted the barrel of his into the side of Trevor's head.

"Mr. Kostov, tell your men to stand down," Eli ordered.

Captain lowered his hand at Benji with a slight shake of

his head. Benji hesitated but ultimately caved. The guard who had Trevor at gunpoint followed suit, then Trevor.

"That's it. Do what he tells you."

A double heartbeat within a second. Captain faced the direction of the new voice, and there was Amon, sitting at one of the tables with a wineglass in his hand. Unlike other guests, he didn't have a gun out.

Is he following me?

"Did you know I would be here?" Captain asked the gangster.

"We *all* suspected you'd come," Eli answered for him.

"Oh, really?" Captain touched his chest. "Where's *my* seat then?"

"It seems Amon was right," Eli said, more to himself than to Captain.

"Right about what?" Captain shot a glance at the Tribe leader. "What were you right about? Have you been talking to Eli about me?"

"Maybe," Amon replied with a smirk.

"What's wrong, buddy? I thought we had a deal."

"You never said Amon couldn't talk about you."

Maybe Benji should add a thirteenth kill to his board.

Captain turned back to Eli. "How else was I supposed to see you? I've heard you never leave here," Captain said.

Eli snapped his fingers and a hover drone flew to his side with a wine bottle secured to its underbelly and poured a new glass for him.

"I like this place. Sylar Han can't get to me here," Eli replied.

Everyone seemed to bristle at the name. Even some of the guests lowered their guns, concerned as though Sylar was on his way right now.

Hold it. What's this?

"You're afraid of Sylar?" Captain asked.

"You're a fool if you aren't," Eli sneered. "After that Jack was killed, Sylar has been keeping a much closer eye on everybody to see who will try to snatch up the power cards that had been left on the ground. *We* came to the decision to stick closely to what we already do and stay out of trouble."

This. This *was why I was right to off Chase.*

Captain folded his arms. "And as your business continues to die because you won't offer something new, Sylar will swoop in and drain the life out of the rest of it. Maybe even drain the life out of *you*," he replied, every word as dry as shaved ice.

"What if I can help you keep Sylar out of your hair *and* put new life in your enterprise? You won't have to be afraid of showing your face down there anymore."

"How do I know I shouldn't be afraid of *you*? Lazarus's men were and they're *dead* now because of *you*," Eli countered.

Captain stepped closer, arms still folded. "Well, fun fact, I don't like traitors." He scanned the people around him and shook his head.

"I recognize most of you. I used to see you all the time at parties like this when my father threw them. I know you've seen me before, but for some *godforsaken* reason, you guys decided to pretend I wasn't still here after my father left the show."

Bees buzzed inside Captain's head when he continued. "How can you be so surprised to see me? Did you really think I'd just bow out? Live a normal, nameless life? Did you really think I mattered *that* little?"

"Choose your next words carefully, Mr. Kostov," Eli said, as if trying to soothe a wild animal.

"I am...'Mr. Gark'," Captain said. "None of you deserve

anything from me, but it's my *passion* to work together towards a new phase. One where Sylar loses his control over us. To do that, I need to share something my father wouldn't: the blueprints for the SpeakWare tech."

Eli's eyes widened but he stayed still, as well as the rest of the room

How about a little bit of respect now?

"I'm the only one who has them. Since they're custom made, I can't just give a bunch away, *but*," Captain paused and held up a waiting finger. "I *can* give you a copy of the blueprints."

Eli leaned back, grinding a toothpick between his teeth. "Why would you do that?"

Captain circled himself around so that he was taking everyone else in, relishing their anticipation and surprise. He had himself a captive audience.

What a dream come true.

"Sylar thinks he can keep tipping the power scales however he wants, but if I share something even *he* doesn't have, and you're able to grow your business again by selling it, he'd be an idiot to mess with you. Yeah, he'll still benefit from this new success within the underworld, but at least you and I will have something he can only *wish* he had," Captain explained.

Eli flicked his toothpick away and took another sip of wine. Clearing his throat, his first words came out fragmented. "People can try selling valuables to me, but I like knowing the kind of person I'm buying from. I've always liked making deals in a more...unorthodox way."

An early memory came to Captain. He was thirty, standing by his father who was talking to Eli during one of his parties. Fragments of a conversation knitted themselves together.

Eli liked to pit dealers against a few of his own people to test their strength and study their decisions as they fight.

"You want to watch me fight," Captain said.

"I want to watch *him* fight," Eli replied, pointing past Captain.

Captain's stomach sank lower and lower as he followed the finger's path, which ended with Benji. Benji leaned to Trevor.

"He's pointing at you, Trevor," he said.

"I'm pointing at *you*, you moron," Eli snarled while others—including Amon—laughed. Trevor looked as unhappy as Captain felt.

"Why *him*?" Captain asked.

"Why does that bother you? Amon calls him...uh...what was it again, Amon?" Eli asked.

"*Chi no akuma*," Amon answered through a gleeful grin.

"Yes, that. If he can kill twelve of Amon's men on his own, he can take on less than half of my own men. Unless you're afraid he'll fail?" Eli said.

Captain believed that Benji had in fact killed some of Amon's people, but he didn't witness it. How much of it had been blown out of proportion?

Benji sidled up with Captain, but there was no fear on him. He was focused, with determination that Captain had never seen on him.

"Are you sure you can do this?" Captain asked.

"Yes," Benji said.

"Very well. It's been a while since I've been entertained like this," Eli said, and he clinked his glass with a fork.

The men in jackets standing by made their way around the tables, a few of them cracking knuckles.

"Mr. Kostov, clear the space," Eli warned, waving his hand.

With a frustrated grunt, Captain backed up until he was with Trevor.

"What if they kill him?" Trevor whispered.

That's what I'm afraid of.

Even quieter, Captain answered, "Then the blueprints will go to someone else, and I'll see to it that the Garks die out."

There were four Jacket Men in total, circling around Benji, estimating their distance and assessing openings. Not a single person in the party moved. Amon was pulling himself over the table infected with glee.

Still no fear on Benji.

Should that worry me?

"Go," Eli said.

Uh oh.

The center of the room detonated in a frazzled, disorienting blur of movement and cries. Captain expected Benji to get hit quick, knocked out, maybe even stabbed. What happened instead was that none of the men were able to get a single hit in. Benji expertly dodged, swerved, and pivoted from every attack, his eyes wide and focused as he did so. When *he* was the one dealing the blows, they landed, splintering noses, cracking teeth, and busting shoulders. One man belted out a scream when the bones in his arm shattered after it snapped in Benji's death hold.

It was enough to make Captain shiver.

In a desperate attempt to catch Benji, the last man's fist carved through the air to slam into Benji's chin but Benji shifted away. Still, the man was able to graze Benji's earlobe.

Benji's jaw dropped, as if offended. Offended turned

into seething. He spun around and locked eyes with the earlobe grazer, snatched up a plate from the table, and smashed it over the man's head. He fell in a heap.

No one—except Amon—clapped. Captain and Trevor glanced at each other, stunned beyond words.

"You're going to need a *challenge* for *Chi No Akuma* to be bested," Amon said.

Eli nodded with a thin grin. "I think I know one. Ling?"

He snapped his fingers, and a woman from the table stood up, dressed in a knee-length black coat with a fur collar and cuffs belted at the waist. One of her eyes was a glowing blue prosthetic. She pulled on a set of gloves that ticked and sparked, and waltzed around the table to get to Benji.

That was when Benji got scared.

"Wait, no. I don't hit women," he said.

You've got *to be kidding me.*

There was laughter and booing. Amon was roaring, as if it was the funniest thing he had ever heard. Eli was focused on Captain, disapproving. Suddenly, Benji was a victim despite his victory, and the butt of every joke in the room. It was a bad, *bad* reflection on him.

And a bad reflection on me.

The crime lord's nails dug into the skin of his palms. He didn't regret most things he'd done in the past few days. He didn't regret killing the council even though others dangled that over him. He didn't regret killing Violet. He didn't even regret bringing in Sparks because of what his execution tomorrow could mean.

But one thing he was beginning to regret was...

No, stop.

Ling's gloves sparked again as she threw a punch, ramming her fist into Benji's stomach and holding it there as bursts of electricity jolted through him, and he had no option but to stand there and take it.

I'm beginning to regret...

"Benji, just hit her!" Captain cried, rage blinding his self-control to keep quiet. Ling continued swinging and jabbing and thrusting her taser-gloved fists into different parts of Benji, rendering him useless as the electricity consumed him.

All you had to do was the SAME thing you did to the OTHERS!

"This isn't going to work. You're going to have to step in!" Trevor urged.

"That would show weakness," Captain argued.

"*This* is weakness," Trevor pointed at the one-sided fight. "You step in, you get to show Eli that you're not just capable of holding your own in a fight, you're also willing to stand up for your fellow man."

He gripped Captain's shoulder. "Eli wants the blueprints no matter what. It doesn't matter who's giving them away. But if you want him or people like Amon to respect you...you need to show them why."

I thought I was already doing that, was what Captain wanted to say, but he stopped because he knew better. Being a charismatic talker—having the right words to say— was good on its own, but it wasn't enough. These people needed to see him get ugly. They needed to see blood.

"Okay," Captain said, and he dashed up to Ling and Benji.

BY THE TIME Captain reached Ling, the fury in his shove was enough to send her off her feet with an alarmed cry. He was breathing hard, his lungs catching fire as his anger boiled.

"Go stand by Trevor," he sneered at Benji. A wounded and flabbergasted Benji slunk around Captain and hurried away, while Captain stood back and allowed Ling to gather herself back up. Like shooting, Captain learned most of what he knew about hand-to-hand combat from Damien. One of his key lessons: never let the opponent make the first move.

"If you let your opponent make the first move, they get the illusion of control. That's dangerous. Make the first move and put everything into it. It'll set the tone for the rest of the fight."

Captain lunged after Ling, ready to clobber her face. When he swung to strike, however, Ling managed to duck out of the way and bash his shoulder. Sudden pain gushed through his body.

Thanks, Damien. Great advice.

He should've thought about taser gloves.

With the other arm, Ling's fist sailed for Captain's face, but this time he was able to jerk his head back, feeling the rush of air and the heat of the sparks as the glove passed just inches away from his throat. With a determined cry, Captain responded by striking Ling's own throat.

"Find a way to disarm your enemy. Go as light or as aggressive as you need to."

Well, this enemy's weapons are gloves, that's not gonna be easy.

Captain just barely finished the thought before electricity ravaged his body again, this time with a gloved fist in his gut, stumbling him backwards close to Eli's table. Ling had recovered quicker than he expected. He had no time to punch back before she delivered an uppercut to his chin. His vision blackened for a second and had it not been for the table behind him, he would've fallen. In a mad dash, he felt around on the table for something he could use as a projectile.

Finding a wineglass, he hurtled it at Ling. She evaded it, and Benji and Trevor leaped away as it shattered against the wall near them.

If I could hit her with something, she'll be too hurt to use the gloves and then I jump in!

Captain snatched up another glass but Ling caught up and smashed her gloved fist against his nose. His vision went out again for a second. Agony shredded his head.

"Mr. Kostov," Eli called out. *"Where* is your father's strength? Because I'm not seeing it."

What everyone was seeing now—to Captain—was what they all thought of him behind closed doors. It *had* to be.

Captain leaned his elbows against the table, then flung himself up with his feet out to knock Ling back, giving him the space he needed to advance. This time, she moved to sweep his leg.

Oh, big *mistake.*

Captain sidestepped the sweep, and when Ling rose back up, his knuckles thrashed her hard in the nose. Shock and pain racked her face. Her hands throbbed and twitched as she forced herself from reaching up to clutch her nose.

"Once you disarm your enemy, don't be afraid of going crazy, maybe a little over-the-top. You're throwing all the pain your opponent dealt you back in their face and they'll deserve it..."

Flinging his arms around her, Captain tackled Ling to the floor.

"So throw hard."

The blows to Ling's face were hard and heavy like flash bangs. The only thing he held back on was keeping from striking her prosthetic eye. Skin tore. Bone shuddered. Ling's mouth was agape with voiceless pleas through blood-stained lips.

Her face melted away and Violet's took its place, peering up at him, filled with terror. Captain only stopped for a second, then grinned and kept going. He only stopped for good once his knuckles started throbbing.

Violet's face evaporated, and it was Ling's again. The crowd around him—at first graveyard silent—erupted into cheers and claps and hoots and hollers. All around Captain he saw smiles.

Smiles!

The respect he had been looking for.

Even Amon was clapping like everyone else.

Why did I let Benji *fight?*

Captain stood up and turned back to Eli, who—to his

glee—was also clapping. "Tomorrow morning then?" Captain asked through harsh breaths.

"Tomorrow morning," Eli agreed. "But even better. Have the rest of your friends come here and we'll celebrate this agreement. We love the excuse to throw a party whenever we can."

Captain's phone buzzed and so did his heart. He held up a halting finger to check it. *Joan?*

Where r u?

She was fine. Captain's breath, still weary from the fight, petered out in a broken but relieved sigh.

"Mr. Kostov?" Eli prodded.

Captain stared again at Eli, then glanced around at the partiers and their bated breath. Ling was on her knees guzzling Bathory to dull the pain, quietly moaning like a wounded puppy.

So...this is what being a god feels like.

"I accept," Captain answered.

The thrill of being wanted. The thrill of not just being seen, but seen for what he believed he was, *knew* he was. It was like inhaling fresh outdoor air in the middle of a rainforest. The burden of the past few days and the mildew of Captain's grief over Damien's death retreated in a frenzy, as if Captain was contagious with a virus.

Everyone cheered and raised their glasses. Tension was rolling off of them as they returned to the weightlessness of their time before. This time, Captain was the center of their attention. Captain remembered the statue of Sylar in Samsara Financial's courtyard and how the arms of that statue were outstretched. With a grin, Captain outstretched his own arms, embracing the cheering.

Glass...in the palm of my hand...

"Good job, Captain!"

That voice. It seized Captain by the legs and yanked him off his feet, dragging him away with his fingertips embedded in the floor.

All you had to do was the SAME thing...!

Benji, elated and jittery as if he hadn't just been electrocuted over and over again—as if he hadn't just embarrassed himself, and in turn, Captain—was *congratulating* him.

One thing I'm beginning to regret is...

Just past Benji's head, Amon watched them both, eyes gleaming, teeth shining. It was as if he knew what was brewing inside Captain.

"You humiliated me," Captain said to Benji, quietly enough so as to not be overheard.

Benji frowned, head fidgety, eyes bouncing, and cheek twitching. It was a pathetic display of shock.

What was I thinking believing he could be a part of something like this? He thinks he can thrive in my empire?

Amidst the noise of Eli's guests, Captain's words trailed their way to Benji, seemingly without being intercepted by anyone else.

"I should've given you to Amon."

RIPLEY HAD NEVER SEEN Joan in a real dress before, which was why he gaped when he did. She was sitting on the side of the fountain in Primitus with a cigarette between her fingers. Next to her was a latte still full.

Weird. I thought she said she hated coffee.

A ballroom length waterfall of gold silk flowed down Joan's body. The top of the dress fell off one shoulder and accentuated the blue diamond necklace around her neck. Finishing the outfit was a pair of black velvet opera gloves. What also struck Ripley was that Joan's hair was now a short bob above her shoulders.

Ripley got a message from Trevor that he, Joan, and Sparks were expected to arrive for a party being thrown at the Garks' mansion. He was relieved to finally have something to do, but he was never one for parties.

Nevertheless, like Joan, he also made sure to dress for the occasion, wearing a gold and black lapel three piece tuxedo.

As Ripley drew nearer to Joan, he noticed something

else. The skin around Joan's eyes was red, as if she had been crying. Ripley decided for now that it was best not to ask.

"Hey," he said, hating himself immediately.

Joan glanced at him, and her face turned sadder. "Hey," she replied, her tone forced.

"I didn't know you had something like that waiting around for a night like tonight," Ripley pointed out.

Joan stared straight ahead again, inhaling from her cigarette and blowing out a stream. "It wasn't *my* choice."

Um...

"Well, you look very nice anyway," Ripley said.

Was that a smile there?

"Thanks. You don't look too shabby yourself," Joan replied.

"This wasn't exactly my choice either," Ripley admitted, smoothing down the tux.

Turn the page. Ask something else.

"I thought you hated coffee," Ripley said, gesturing to the latte.

"I felt like trying again," Joan replied after a puff of smoke.

"I haven't seen you all day. Where've you been?" Ripley asked.

Joan shook her head. "Needed some time away from all this."

Ripley looked around for a moment, hoping Sparks would finally show up so they could all go. He had been told about the party a while ago now.

"And what exactly is 'all this'?" Ripley asked, gesturing with a hand.

Joan shook her head again and stood up, allowing the gold silk to fall around her legs. "I'm sorry, Ripley. I really am. But I can't do this right now. I would never forgive myself if..." Joan's voice cracked. "If..."

Ripley wanted nothing more than to grab Joan and rattle the truth out of her. Something had spooked her, and it devastated Ripley that he couldn't find out why.

Before he could say anything else, Sparks's raspy voice spoke up. "I'm ready."

Both Ripley and Joan turned to face Sparks and gasped at what they saw.

"*I SHOULD'VE GIVEN you to Amon.*"

Benji's earplugs muffled the noise around him at the party. The voices, the laughter, the shouting, and the cheering were all lumped together in a low, indiscernible hum. Benji missed how quiet Central was.

"*I should've given you to Amon.*"

Benji flinched as though he had been slapped, a feeling he was very familiar with. The pain from that, however, never lingered like Captain's words did, which repeated in his head over and over again, rewound and replayed. Benji was scavenging for any clue that Captain was using sarcasm —something he wasn't good at picking up on. He learned that many times with Amon.

"*I should've given you to Amon.*"

Was it sarcasm or was he serious? Because he couldn't be serious...right?

Why would he say something like that? He saved me from Amon the other day.

"*You do not touch Benji. If you do, any deal is off.*"

That's what Captain said to Amon and he meant it.

"I should've given you to Amon."

Benji squinted up at the shelf behind the bar he was sitting at, situated against the wall in a room where Eli's party was blaring.

"I should've given you to Amon."

Stop.

"Hey buddy, are you okay?" The bartender asked, blinking at him with cybernetic eyes.

"I should've given you to Amon."

What did he mean? What did I do? Was I...

I was supposed to beat that woman, wasn't I?

"I should've..."

Benji nearly leaped out of his seat when a hand slapped his shoulder hard, popping him out of his spiral.

Sitting next to him, the owner of the hand, was Amon.

"He'll be *just fine*. Get us both a whiskey, on Amon," Amon said to the bartender, his voice muffled thanks to the earplugs. The bartender nodded and started preparing drinks.

Benji diverted his gaze from Amon to stare at the bar shelf. Better than looking at him.

He adjusted the setting on his earplugs to hear Amon better. "What do you want?" He asked.

"To catch up! To find out what the life of the *Chi no Akuma* has been like these days," Amon answered.

An anxious seed was buried inside Benji's stomach, growing vines.

"I'm not the *Chi no Akuma* anymore," Benji said.

"Really?! Could've fooled Amon a minute ago the way you were taking all those guys down! You still have it in you! That spark!"

Benji faced Amon but his eyes danced around. "I don't

want to hear from you what I have! One of your men killed Jade!"

Amon accepted his whiskey glass and circled it, allowing the ice to swirl. His voice turned dour. "Oh, child. You know that's not true."

Jade's bloodied face. Bodies everywhere, some even missing limbs. Benji was waiting for his brother to wake up.

That wasn't the day he killed Amon Tribe members.

Amon found Benji on the floor next to Jade, stunned but not shaken. He surveyed the carnage, a scene unlike anything he had seen before. He closed in on Benji, who made no sound, made no face. It was as blank as a new whiteboard. Clean like a ghost.

"Akuma," was the only word Amon said.

"You and your brother were loyal to the Tribe. When Jade died, we knew we had to trick you somehow into believing he was still alive, otherwise you'd become worthless. Too dumb to serve. Amon couldn't just let you go, *Akuma*. Amon couldn't let go of such *power*."

Benji's breathing quickened and the anxious seed sprouted more and more vines, cramming the space in his chest.

"But I still got to talk to him! He went everywhere with me!" Benji exclaimed.

"Of course he did!" Amon sniggered. "It's amazing what can happen when we plug a brain into a computer and create an AI with a person's memories."

One of Amon's men screamed at Benji, furious that he failed to assassinate a deserter of the Tribe, who was able to sell valuable information to an interested buyer. Benji winced from the man's screeches, but he continued to stare blankly at him, understanding he was angry but felt nothing.

"Are you stupid? Am I not getting through!?" Cried the

man. He reached up and yanked the headset off Benji that contained the Jade AI, threw it on the ground, and crushed it under his boot.

"How about now?! Am I getting through to you now?!"

Triggered by seeing the headset destroyed, Benji unleashed a wretched cry and Jade's knife came out. The man who destroyed the AI was the first to go, then some of the other men were next. Throats were slit within seconds. One man managed to catch Benji's eye with a knife of his own, but Benji kept going and killed him while only seeing through one eye.

Benji peered down when Amon put something on the counter in front of him. Jade's knife, still coated in dry blood.

"You dropped this by the way. *Chi no Akuma* is still strong, but not nearly as strong without it."

Benji was shivering, the plant inside him fully grown.

"I can't take this," he stuttered.

"Oh," Amon took Benji's hand and opened it to slide the knife handle between his fingers. "Amon thinks you can."

Amon wants me back. Captain doesn't want me anymore.

I don't want to be with either of them.

"Did you cut the brand out too?" Amon asked.

Benji shook his head. He had never shown it to anyone. Captain always frightened him, even when he first came to the penthouse. Benji understood that former loyalty to one gang meant no trust from another.

"Hmm. Then there's still hope for you yet." Amon downed the rest of his drink, wiped his mouth with his sleeve in a satisfied grunt, and stood up. "Amon will be around."

Benji stayed sitting at the counter, knife in hand, quavering from head to toe. The weight of Captain's words to him earlier—as well as Amon's just now—clashed in a riotous symphony.

THE PARTY WAS as big as the ones Captain remembered attending with his father. People were everywhere, chatting, laughing, and sipping wine. Amethyst drapes hung between tall windows lined up on creamy white walls. Breaking up the wall in the middle—matching the white—was a massive balcony where one could gaze down upon the lower levels of the City atop the platform that the mansion rested on.

A long table with all kinds of food was set on one side of the room with a white tablecloth thrown over it. In the center of the room was an enormous mirror on the floor where people could dance. Small, blue flames licked the ridges of it but didn't burn.

On the other side of the room was the bar where Benji was sitting, with a display shelf behind a black counter and a blue light fixed above it. Dotted in the ceiling were clusters of arctic blue crystals lighting up the room.

I could host something like this soon, Captain thought. *Multiple times a week too.*

He glanced at the doors to the room, impatient for the rest of his group to show up, especially Joan.

He stood with Eli, Amon, and several other men, a drink in hand that he hadn't yet tried. Loitering near him was Trevor. Eli was talking to Captain, but he wasn't picking up on most of the words.

Right before the party, Captain was finally able to get ahold of Joan. They argued over the phone, with Captain begging Joan to wear a dress he had picked out for her a while ago. She wasn't really into dresses, but he wanted her to step outside her comfort zone for just *one night*. Tonight had to be perfect in *every* way.

Tonight is going to be perfect, Captain assured himself.

Eli stopped talking when he—along with everyone else near him—noticed that the room had grown quiet. All eyes were on a newcomer, standing in the doorway.

Captain didn't recognize the man at first. His black hair, gleaming in the light, was tied back into a shoulder-length ponytail. His face was clean-shaven and handsome. What made every eye in the room turn on him, however, was his outfit. It was exotic looking, a tunic in design, that fell to his knees, with a high collar and slits in the side that went up to his waist. The fabric was a rich, deep red silk that stood out against his tight black pants and short, black boots. A holographic golden-red dragon was embroidered on the fabric; its tail wrapped around the waist, the body crossing the torso diagonally, and the head going behind the collar to rest on the left shoulder. Suddenly, to everyone's surprise, the dragon lifted its head and roared.

The man smirked and strode into the room, and Captain noticed his shiny green eyes.

It was Sparks.

"And here I thought I've met everyone in Glass," Eli said as Sparks caught up with him and the others. The dragon head bobbed up and down as his shoulders rose and fell. His green eyes scanned Eli and Amon like they were slabs of steak he was eager to devour. A shrewd grin dripped from him, icing Captain's spine. Captain shivered, shedding his pride from a moment ago, when he was basking in the attention and respect he was getting.

Right now, *all* that attention was on Sparks.

Captain's toes were curled in, aching from the cramped space in his shoes. What will Sparks say? What was his motive?

Why didn't I do something sooner?

"Hmm, maybe you should leave home more often. You might be surprised," Sparks said.

Amused, Eli snorted and waved one of the servants over for a drink. "Maybe. Now, who exactly are you?"

Sparks took a wineglass from the same servant. "Call me Sparks."

"Is that really your name?" Amon asked, flirting with suspicion.

Sparks sniffed but maintained his smile. "Is Amon really *your* name?"

Amon howled. "Amon likes that!"

"Mr. Sparks, a pleasure to meet you. You're one of Captain's?" Eli asked.

He wasn't supposed to be...

Watching the conversation unfold in front of Captain was like letting go of a balloon and watching it fly up, never to be able to catch it and get it back again. His mouth stayed shut even though he wanted to speak. His hands stayed at his sides even though he wanted to reach up and bust Sparks's nose.

Ripley joined the group, bowing slightly.

Ripley, where's Joan? The question scorched Captain's

tongue, but he stayed silent. He kept shaking, fighting to hold in lucid panic.

"I am," Sparks said. "I don't mean to brag, but it was my tall figure that won Captain over. He thought it might... boost morale."

Captain had never seen a tornado in real life, nor had he heard one. But he did learn from somewhere what it sounded like the closer it drew. The sound of a hundred train engines blaring at once, driving needles into nearby ears. That was what it felt like standing frozen listening to Sparks as he wooed Eli. Against his violent wishes, Captain had to pretend he and Sparks were on good terms. A lie that clawed away at his chest.

He faked a laugh, eager to play along. "He exaggerates! My standards are very..." An idea came to him. A bad one. "...Tall?"

Captain didn't have to hear anything from Trevor and Ripley to know they were cringing.

"Not funny," Amon remarked.

"It was *already* funny, Mr. Kostov, no need to add to it. Sparks here has a good sense of humor," Eli said.

Sparks lapped up the last drops of his drink. "More like a sense of humor *and* a sense of purpose," he corrected. "Two things a man needs to thrive in Glass. One is for making your name unforgettable, the other is needed to steal another man's wife." He stopped, stroking his chin in thought, his movements exaggerated as if he was in theater. "Wait...wasn't it the other way around?"

Eli and Amon both chortled. Even Trevor and Ripley couldn't help themselves this time.

This was supposed to be my night.

What was next? Was Sparks going to start throwing

shade at Captain? Was it Sparks's goal to elevate Captain or humiliate him?

"Amon thinks that's hysterical!" Amon cackled.

"*My* wife isn't my wife anymore, so go ahead and take her." Eli rubbed his forehead as if nursing a headache. "I think I'm done trying marriage vows. She was my fourth."

Sparks beamed. "Ah, *perfect* timing, I *just* left my second."

Eli turned to Captain and stuck his thumb at Sparks. "You were right to take him in, Mr. Kostov. I'm surprised *he's* not the captain of this crew."

The words were like a sack full of rocks falling on top of Captain's head from a great height.

This was Sparks's plan, wasn't it? To walk in like this and take all the attention. This was supposed to be my night. My victory. Suddenly, he's the favorite after a few jokes! And I'm nothing...Again...

Joan's words echoed in Captain's head: *Figure out what you're going to do with Sparks...before he figures it out for you.*

The longer Captain glared at Sparks, the more something about him looked...

Familiar.

Captain shook his head to banish the thought, but it retreated to the back of his mind, glued to it like honey.

Sparks's face changed. His eyes, which were shining when he first came in, darkened. "I'm not looking for a position of leadership. Even if Captain offered it, I would turn it down."

I'd never offer it to you in the first place, you idiot!

Eli turned solemn too. "Then what *do* you want?"

The dragon's head switched shoulders on Sparks, the

flames where its eyes were supposed to be stayed locked on Eli.

Sparks took another glass from a passing servant and exhaled a deep sigh. "My mother died when I was young. My father is in Glass's one nursing home with no voice. My uncle abandoned me, but not before teaching me how to survive in this...*place*, this City that lost its name. I did everything I could to survive on my own until I found Captain. *Now* look at me. I'm dressed in clothes I never thought I'd wear." Sparks held up his new wineglass. "And I'm drinking wine with men who had their fortunes handed to them on silver platters the second they were born...."

Never saw my *silver platter...*

"When I first met Captain, I looked...honestly, kind of pathetic. I was dragging a gift for Captain behind me—a bagful of guns—to win his approval, and now I'm here. Thanks to my sense of humor...and sense of purpose."

Captain regretted his next words instantly. "You're not *that* funny."

Sparks's eyes glittered again and his creepy smile returned. "You're right, Captain, I'm not. I'm *hilarious*," he said, his voice bone-dry.

Did I...piss him off?

Eli was speechless at first, his jaw bulging as if words tried to escape his mouth.

Sparks sipped from his glass. "Mm, anyway, enough about me and my dramatic story, maybe..."

Eli cut Sparks off. "Mr. Sparks, as hard as it might be at first for you to believe, *I* struggled while growing up too..."

Oh did *you now?!*

"My father was taking empty cans in for digital pennies so that I could get a semi-decent education. Everything I have, I *earned*. Some here *did* have their fortunes handed down to them," Eli side-glanced at Captain, then continued, "but others didn't have it easy at first. Not even here."

Sparks finished his glass, satisfaction beaming in his cheeks as if he'd won a stressful game of Odyssey. "If you and I work together, we can open doors for more people. There are people out there who need that hope. I've met *dozens* of them."

What's this 'you and I' crap? What is he talking about?

Eli swirled his glass around with a chuckle. "And *there's* the weak point. For all your talk of surviving and earning your way up, you don't seem to know who *really* calls the shots. Who *really* decides the fate of most people here. It's why I stay in here most days. It's safer than risking ruffling up feathers."

Sparks raised an eyebrow. "Whose feathers?"

Eli frowned. "If you're as smart as you seem, I think you know whose feathers."

Syl...

Sparks twitched. "Ah. Sylar Han's feathers."

Eli nodded. "Sylar Han's feathers."

It was like a nightmare hearing Sparks and Eli. Out of the corner of his eye, Captain saw that Amon was watching him closely, entertained by Captain's lack of control. Trevor and Ripley were no help either, never stepping in and offering their own two cents.

How can I get Sparks away from Eli?

"He's nothing more than a man," Sparks said. "And frankly, not as good-looking as me. The way you talk about him, you act like he's some kind of *god*."

"Even those who *think* they're gods are still dangerous," Eli said.

Sparks responded. "You're a wise and powerful man. But as long as you fear him, you'll stay huddled in here...

right where he'd like you to be. Down there, you can become unstoppable. You agreed to Captain's offer to meet him in Primitus, right?"

"I did," Eli answered slowly.

"Forgive me if I'm making a false assumption, but I suspect you would've changed your mind before morning. Right?" Sparks asked.

Eli glanced at Captain and Captain had to stifle a gasp. Sparks had ulterior motives, that was obvious, but to expose that weakness in Eli was nothing short of incredible.

"If it's any consolation, *I'll* be there too. You meet with Captain, then you and I can talk about how to get even further away from under Sylar's boot," Sparks proposed.

That's it, this has to end now.

Eli held out his hand for Sparks to take, bewildered and stunned. "I think...we have a deal, Mr. Sparks."

Sparks radiated a grin and accepted his hand. "Don't forget to bring your ex."

"I won't forget, Mr. Sparks. You'll see me there."

"Sparks, may I talk to you for a moment?" Captain asked, leaping in now that he had the opportunity.

Sparks's grin didn't fade. "Of course, Captain," he said without pulling his gaze away from Eli. "Excuse me a moment."

"Of course," Eli replied.

Sparks's grin was gone once Captain started leading him away. The sparkle in his eyes was gone. Even the dragon's head on his shoulder stared Captain down, wanting to burn him.

"What are you doing?" Captain asked once out of earshot.

"What do you mean?" Sparks asked innocently. "I'm helping you."

"You're *embarrassing* me. I already got through to Eli. I didn't need *your* help."

So Eli was on the fence. So much for loyalty...!

"Honestly, Captain, it seemed to me you did."

The dragon's head drifted closer to Captain, looking like it could open its jaw and snap his face clean off.

"What's this about messing with Sylar? You *don't screw* with Sylar."

Not true but I don't need Sparks to think so.

"*I* do," Sparks declared, dark and frigid.

Captain's next words vomited out before he could hold them back. "I should kill you tonight."

A roguish light glimmered in Sparks's eyes. "But you won't. You know people like Eli and Amon will wonder where I went, and what would you tell them *then?*"

Captain opened then shut his mouth, releasing only a pathetic whimper. Sparks's face twisted into an impatient sneer.

"That wasn't a rhetorical question...Daniel," he snarled.

Captain's body rumbled. His knees were melting. Like comets, dozens of evil visions of Sparks killing him in numerous different ways shot through Captain's mind.

My night...my victory...

Sparks sighed. "You didn't *have* to bring me into your family; but you did. So, whatever happens tomorrow...that's on *you.*"

Has he forgotten his dad's life is on the line?

It was as if Sparks knew what Captain was thinking. "Go ahead, kill my father. You'd be doing him a favor."

"Please...*please* just *tell* me what you want! Why are you *doing* all of this?" Captain whispered.

Sparks's eyes brightened and his cheery grin from before returned. The dragon's head reared back.

"Like I said, I'm trying to help you. So let me."

Sparks drifted back towards the energy of the party without waiting for Captain. Captain gripped his chest, heart hammering fast and hard against his sweaty palm.

What have I done?

Then finally, he saw her. Sitting at the bar counter with Benji was Joan.

WHEN JOAN ENTERED the party room, she saw *him*.

Her gaze veered away as if her husband was a ghastly sight. Instead, she turned towards the bar, clutching her third coffee in the last several hours. The flash of Captain's face was enough to paint a picture for Joan, every stroke and brush baring the agonizing truth about her husband.

The truth that hacked Joan up the most, however, was that he loved her. He *really* loved her, and Joan didn't reciprocate anymore.

She needed to talk to Sparks but she knew that that wasn't going to happen right away. She would have to watch him, catch him at a time when he wasn't close to Captain. Right now, he was close to *everyone* in the room. He had dressed to impress, disguising himself to steal everyone's attention and it was working.

Just my luck of course.

When Joan joined Benji at the bar, he was fixated on a knife in his hand. Joan's heart fluttered when she noticed the dried blood on the blade.

"Benji, what did you do?" Joan asked, afraid to reach

out. She wanted to comfort him, hold him close, assure him everything was going to be okay. How could she though when even *she* wasn't sure that that was true?

Benji set the knife on the counter, keeping his grip on it, then adjusted his earpieces. "Can you keep a secret?" He asked without looking at her.

No secrets.

"Sure. Why not?" Joan asked.

"Because I trust you," Benji replied.

"I didn't mean...never mind. What is it, Benji?"

"Before I joined Captain, I served Amon. Both my brother and I did. When my brother was killed, I became Amon's most important assassin. I wasn't just shadowing my brother one time and happened to meet Amon. I've known Amon for a long time, and I worked for him."

Joan was getting tired of secrets. *Tired* of learning that almost everyone around her were assholes. Ripley was different though. So was Benji. If anyone else deserved to get out, it was them. Unlike Captain's, Benji's lies were necessary to keep him from danger.

Way to go, Benji. You just won the prestigious award of 'not-being-an-asshole'.

Joan slurped from her coffee cup. "You don't work for him anymore, right?" Joan asked.

"No, but I know Amon wants me back," Benji replied.

"Captain has his problems," Joan said carefully, "but he made it pretty clear he doesn't want to give you away."

"I'm not so sure about that."

"Why not?"

"Because he told me today that he should've given me to Amon."

Joan's jaw fell and her shoulders wilted. "He told you what?"

"He told me he should've given me to Amon."

Any embers left in Joan that still loved Captain had now been stomped into oblivion.

Guess I don't need to be careful how I talk about Daniel to Benji anymore. Excellent.

"What are you gonna do about it then?" Joan asked.

Benji glanced at her, never locking eyes with her, of course. "I feel like I should leave. Captain doesn't like me, and Amon won't stop trying to get me back."

"You should do that," Joan said.

"I...I shouldn't go until after the meeting tomorrow morning. I don't want to upset him on his big day," Benji said.

"Whoa, no, hold up. Let me help you break this down step by step, okay?"

Benji raised an eyebrow but nodded. "Okay."

Joan raised a finger. "You want to leave Captain's group, right?"

"Yes."

Joan raised another finger. "Because Captain said he wished he gave you away, right?"

"Right."

Third finger. "And Amon won't give up on taking you back, right?"

"Right."

"Then why stay if Captain doesn't want you anymore, and your safety is at risk?" She sucked up the remainder of the cream at the bottom of her cup.

The gears were turning inside Benji's head, at war with millions of possible outcomes, but Joan's points were winning the night.

And it hurt.

Daniel's rain-drenched face as Joan drank Bathory for the first time, his smile penetrated by infatuation.

"*I love you.*"

He meant that. He also meant to kill Violet.

"I think I see your points," Benji said.

"No, you *know* you do," Joan argued, stroking his shoulder. "Go tonight while no one's looking. Don't tell Captain. He won't let you go if you do."

Benji bristled at the thought but he nodded in understanding. "I'll leave tonight."

"Awesome. I'm leaving too, Benji. It's not just you."

Benji vaguely grinned. "That's good to know."

"Remember, *don't. Tell. Captain.* Just go when you're ready, and do it before tomorrow."

Benji knew what he had to do, but it meant going back to square one, something Joan knew she was going to be familiar with again soon.

"You're one of the good ones, dude. Go be even better," Joan said softly.

Benji sniffed. "You too."

———

CAPTAIN

Joan didn't look at Captain when he joined her at the bar, but he couldn't take his eyes off *her*. The pale of her skin: like a divine ghost. The nape of her neck: perfect and breathtaking. Her emerald eyes...

Weirdly absent of that usual soul. The flesh around them too was red and raw as if she'd been crying.

Something's not right.

"You didn't have to do anything with the hair," Captain

said playfully, noticing the bob that was Joan's hair now. He softened his voice. "You look amazing though." He reached to ruffle her hair, but her head flinched away.

She still didn't look at Captain when she responded. "I look pretty amazing in the nude, so that's not much of a compliment."

So...something is wrong.

"I mean," Captain replied slowly with a bemused smile. "I wouldn't be opposed, but, uh, others here *might* be."

A joke like that usually made her laugh, or at least smile. Instead, Joan slapped her near empty coffee cup on the counter. Her expression was unfathomable to Captain.

"Isn't it...a little late for coffee?" Captain asked.

His heart soared up his chest when Joan's fist cracked the counter. The veins in her neck bulged, her skin turned sunburn-red, her nostrils flared, and her eyes were wet as she snapped her head aside and burned her gaze into Captain's.

"*That's* your *question*?!" She snarled.

Okay...less like a divine ghost, more like an angel of death.

Captain raised his hands. "Whoa, what's your problem? I just wanted you to wear a dress."

Tears snaked down Joan's cheeks, fracturing Captain's heart. "Is your head *that* far up your ass?" Her voice quivered.

I'd take pissed-off Joan over this any day...

Joan stood up and started to leave, but Captain stopped her with his hand. "Joan, wait. I can't help you if I don't know what's going on. Talk to me."

Joan glanced back at him, her face still crumpled like an empty soda can.

"Please," Captain tried.

Joan shook her head and shoved Captain's hand aside to leave.

"It's too late for that," she sneered, and stomped away.

Captain gripped one hand with the other as it started to tremble. The party around him lurched as if he was dizzy. The light of the dragon on Sparks's shoulder burned bright in his vision.

"Joan!" He cried. He saw his wife stop, watched her turn to face him. "Sparks is up to something. I screwed up!"

Joan grimly nodded, tears still rushing. "Yes, you did."

She kept going.

BANG!

An explosion of lights brightened the night sky, cloaking Ripley in rich colors. Another explosion followed, then another, and another. Glass was alive in an eternal party, sending its ecstasy up into the night sky in the form of fireworks.

Trevor stood at the balcony entrance, wanting to talk to Ripley but not sure if his brother wanted to. Part of Trevor regretted the way their last conversation went, but at the same time, finding Ripley talking to Saint bothered him.

When Trevor and Ripley's father died, Saint took them into her home, dressed them up in better clothes, fed them food she grew herself, and gave them makeshift beds to sleep on. She made them swear they'd never tell anybody on the streets everything she had. Ripley loved her for the attention and provisions she gave him.

Trevor, however, preferred it when Ripley relied on *him*. It was his purpose as the older brother to be there for Ripley and no one else's.

Banishing his worries, Trevor joined Ripley at the edge

of the balcony, watching the fireworks rise up and shatter into dozens of brilliant colors, lighting up his skin.

Trevor cleared his throat. "This is the first time we've seen them this close."

Ripley looked at him and nodded. "*Sí.*"

"They were still pretty cool in the Web, but," Trevor snorted, "you can't beat *this.*"

Ripley nodded again but his attention wasn't on Trevor.

Trevor pushed forward. "Do you remember what you used to call fireworks when our parents were still...here?"

A small, amused smile broke Ripley's defenses. "Banging colors."

Trevor laughed and punched Ripley in the shoulder, knocking the smile off of him. "That's right. *'Banging colors'.* It made our parents laugh every time."

As if on cue, another firework exploded closer to Ripley, painting him in blue, and Trevor saw a ten-year old boy wearing filthy clothes. Dirt was smeared across his face. His eyes were the same as they were now. Sleep-deprived and sad.

"Sorry I lashed out at you the other night," Trevor said.

Ripley glanced at him with a hint of gratitude. "*Está bien.*"

"It's not though. I was...jealous."

Ripley frowned. "Of what?"

"When Saint took us in, I was afraid that if *she* could take care of you, where would that leave *me*?"

A blast of colors in the sky radiated against Trevor, soaking him in red. Ripley slid along the balcony's edge to get closer to his brother.

"I think that was one of the reasons why I pushed so hard for us to go to Glass," Trevor continued. "That way *I* could take care of you again."

"*No estoy enojado contigo.* I'm glad you're telling me this," Ripley assured.

Trevor nodded and glanced away, feeling too awkward to look Ripley in the eye. Instead, he gazed out at the City.

Trevor's next words came out slowly and thoughtfully. "Have you thought about going back?"

The truth came out easier than Trevor expected. "*Sí.*"

Trevor peered down over the balcony's edge. "What if it's sooner rather than later?"

"Like, *how* soon?"

"How about 'tonight' soon?"

Ripley blinked at Trevor, his mind a whirlwind of questions.

"You were getting what you *needed* at the Web. I didn't think of that when I brought you here."

"You don't have to—."

Trevor cut Ripley off. "Forget about Captain. Forget about the Purpletells. I heard Captain tell Benji that he should've handed him over to Amon. I don't want you to follow a man who'd be willing to toss you away at a moment's notice. Most other people here would do the same."

Ripley fidgeted with his earring. "What if it was tomorrow instead?"

Trevor frowned. "Why?"

It hit him before Ripley could answer. "You're worried for Joan."

Ripley turned away, but he couldn't hide.

"She's with Captain!" Trevor exclaimed.

"It's not that, it's...I think she *hates* Captain. I saw the way she talked to him in there. You should've seen her when we were on our way here. I just want to make sure she'll be okay."

"If you wait to leave, it might get harder. Who knows what happens after tomorrow?"

"If I leave *now*, I'll risk never forgiving myself."

Trevor heaved a sigh that ended with a chuckle. "You and I couldn't be more different."

Ripley smirked. "That a bad thing?"

"Well, it's annoying."

Ripley glanced back at his brother. "Would you go back to the Web *with* me?"

Ah, here we go.

Trevor shook his head. "No. If I go back, I'll fall back into old habits. I know *you* won't. You're stronger than me."

"Don't..."

"This is what *you* want, so I'm going to help you get there. You can see Saint again and figure out where you want to go from there. This is the last time I decide what's best for you."

Ripley nodded, tear tracks on his cheeks. Then, to Trevor's surprise, Ripley threw his arms around him in a hug. Trevor returned the gesture, resting his head on Ripley's shoulder.

"You know I love you, right?" Trevor asked, bracing himself.

"I know. *Yo también te amo*," Ripley replied.

Trevor hesitated before speaking again. "Have you told Joan your *real* name?"

Ripley frowned. The two of them had been hiding their real names ever since they got to Glass to avoid being recognized as rats from the Web. They didn't want to take any chances.

"No. Are you saying I should?" Ripley asked.

"I'm saying you do whatever you want." Trevor answered.

The two pulled away, but Trevor kept his hands locked on Ripley's arms. A smile he couldn't control crept across his face.

"You have papa's smile," he said.

"And you have mama's *eyes*. Always so angry."

They laughed and stayed where they were, fixed in their embrace under the fireworks.

"MR. SPARKS, care to do the honors of leading this dance?" Joan asked, offering her hand to Sparks.

The sharp ache in Joan's head was hacking away whatever threads of sanity she had left. Her hands shook. Her heart was out of control, fighting for life against her chest. Her breathing was uneven and her face was slick with sweat. It felt like a bug was stuck in her stomach. Alarm bells shredded her temple.

Everything hurts, everything sucks. Still have to do this. Find a way.

Sparks raised an eyebrow at first, then beamed and took Joan's hand. "As you wish."

Joan gulped when Sparks guided her towards the dance floor. Once there, he raised the hand that was still hooked through Joan's, and moved his other hand around her and settled on her upper back. Joan used her free hand to rest on Sparks's back, and the two struck up a rhythm.

"You look incredible tonight, Ms. Joan. It's no wonder you caught Captain's eyes," Sparks complimented.

"Drop your little act, you don't have to pretend with me," Joan said, breathless.

Sparks frowned. "My 'little act'?"

"I know when a guy is faking, okay? I used to call my dad out on the same crap."

Sparks's smile stayed but his movements signaled he was more guarded now. The two continued their rhythm.

"What's the *real* reason why you joined Captain?" Joan asked.

"I thought I already told you."

"I've spent enough time in the Web to know the difference between truth and bullshit."

"I don't know what..."

Joan leaned in and lowered her voice, hissing her first three words. "Daniel...*killed*...*Violet*. Sylar Han told me..."

"Sylar?" Sparks interrupted, eyebrows raised.

"He told me Daniel killed Violet."

The two continued swaying, a torturous silence shared.

He knows more than he lets on.

"I underestimated you," he finally said.

"About damn time you noticed. Now start telling me... why you're here." Breathing became more and more of a chore for Joan, and Sparks was taking notice. "Daniel wants to kill you tomorrow, so you might as well start being honest with me."

"And how do I know Captain isn't using you to get to me?" Sparks asked.

"I stopped drinking Bathory earlier today. Daniel doesn't know."

Sparks's eyes widened and his grin finally slipped.

"That explains some things."

"Like *what*?"

"You don't look very good."

"*Which is why* you need to help me. Whatever you're doing, I want in so that I can..."

A flash of sharp pain in Joan's temple slowed her words.

"...So that I can go back home to the Web."

Sparks's eyes darted back and forth, as if there were spies listening in on them.

He held on to Joan's hand while walking back until they were a fair distance from each other. Then Sparks pulled her towards him, and she took the cue and spun her way across his arm and into his embrace. He dipped her and his smile was back.

"You can't help me. Especially if you feel and look like *that*."

He pulled Joan back up and they resumed their rhythm.

"There has to be *something* I can do," Joan begged.

Sparks halted and the dance froze. He spoke quickly as if he was on a countdown. "There isn't, and maybe for you that's for the best. If you don't care about Captain's life anymore, tomorrow will be a lot easier for you."

Joan's head was on fire now. Her heart raced and it hurt to breathe. "You're going to kill him?"

Sparks's eyes flashed as if offended she asked that question. "I will do whatever I have to. This dance is over."

As Joan walked off the dance floor, she wanted to cry but her body was too weak to make tears. She couldn't bring herself to look at Captain anymore.

He was already dead and she was one of the only people who knew it.

———

RIPLEY

As Ripley walked back into the party, his steps were lighter and his shoulders felt less heavy. For the first time, he felt like he had control over his life.

The party was slipping into a lull now. His eyes searched for Joan, hoping he could talk to her.

He saw her, and was immediately worried. Her walk was sloppy and dazed, her skin ghost-white pale, and she appeared to be close to vomiting. Perturbed, Ripley rushed to Joan.

"Hey, are you okay?" He asked.

Joan looked up at Ripley, tears brimming in her eyes. "No, I'm not," she cracked.

"What's wrong?"

Joan lurched forward and Ripley caught her before she could hit the floor.

"My head..."

"What happened to you?" Ripley asked.

"Sparks plans to...tomorrow, he might...k-kill Daniel."

What?

Joan whimpered, fighting to say something else but failing. Her head slumped, hanging there seemingly lifeless.

"Joan? Joan!"

Joan didn't hear him.

Not too far from them, the digital flames of the dragon on Sparks's shoulder howled up in the air, dissipating in a glorious plume of smoke followed by obnoxious cheering and clapping.

What do I do?

70

BEFORE

JOAN

JOAN SUCKED in a breath and was startled by how cool and fresh the air felt. How *real* it felt. A gentle wind rustled her pink hair, which had a black flower pin in it. She stood atop a large circular platform that resembled a clock in the middle of an ocean. Clock hands ticked under a layer of glass. At the bottom middle of the clock where the six was, a staircase diverted from the circle and descended into the water. Standing on the platform were Trevor, Ripley, Carmilla, Damien, and Violet, with Captain standing opposite to Joan, holding her hands.

She heard the sound of the rushing water beneath them...

Felt the wind caress her...

Smelled the salt in the water...

Tasted that salt on her tongue...

Joan wore a white knee-length skirt covered in ruffles and a black shimmery tank top over a black leather studded jacket and, to finish it off, black boots on her feet. For

Captain: a snowy white buttoned up collared shirt underneath a shadier white wool jacket. His eyes affectionately peered at Joan underneath a fedora that matched the collared shirt.

"Joan?" Captain asked.

Joan snapped to attention. "Hmm?"

Captain chuckled. "I said, are you ready?"

"Hell, yeah. I'm ready."

Joan heard Captain's throat catch when he started guiding her to the stairs.

He's happy too.

"Come on, let's clap!" Joan heard Damien cry.

The guests clapped and hooted, encouraging them all the way. Violet was the only one who didn't holler. Captain and Joan slowly walked down the silver steps, Joan's heart racing faster with each step. Captain looked at her once they reached the bottom step.

"Hey, it's okay. Just one more," he said.

Joan glanced from him to the water, then back to him. With a sigh, she took one last step and her foot stayed above water. Captain stepped with her, and his foot didn't drown either. They both left the stairs and kept walking.

Will I fall?

When she looked down, her boots were missing, the water licking her bare feet. Unable to resist, she laughed.

"Feels weird, doesn't it?" Captain asked.

"Yeah," Joan breathed.

They both stopped. The wind was picking up a bit more and shoving Joan's hair into her eyes. She and Captain both turned so they were facing each other, and her fear faded to nothing.

Captain took a deep breath, his eyes ready to spill tears.

He reached over and swept some of the loose hair from Joan's eyes.

"You and I...we're gods," he declared gently, barely above a whisper.

Joan tried to think of something snarky to say, but nothing came. Instead, Captain took off his fedora and let the wind take it so he could lean forward and kiss Joan. The two of them locked lips and held each other. A tear slid down Joan's cheek.

I wish you were here, dad.

They reached up and clicked the pieces attached to their ears that created this virtual reality and whisked them off so they could hold each other in the real world. They resumed kissing and Joan couldn't remember when they stopped.

71

CAPTAIN

NO ONE WAS outside in Primitus when Captain returned. Joan was sprawled across the backseat of the car, her face pale, her breathing shallow. Trevor said something but his words came through like static to Captain. The moment the car stopped, Captain got out, threw open the passenger door, yanked Joan out, and carried her toward their house. Footsteps followed. Out of the corner of his eye, he saw Ripley.

"Leave us alone," Captain growled, not slowing.

"Will Joan—."

Captain spun. "I said *leave us alone*." The strain in his arms sent sharp aches through his shoulders. Ripley froze, afraid to argue. He stayed put when Captain turned back and ran inside the house.

He laid Joan on the couch in the living room. Her eyes fluttered open, unfocused. She mumbled something Captain couldn't make out. Captain reached into his breast pocket and pulled out a flask of Bathory.

"Drink," he urged kneeling beside her.

Joan gazed at the flask, her eyes flaring with something hotter than pain. She shoved it away.

"I stopped drinking that," she hissed.

What?

Joan's breath hitched, and for a moment, she just stared at Captain, disbelief trembling in her jaw. Then: "How could you?"

Captain blinked. "How could I what?"

Joan heaved and heaved until she was finally able to spit the words out. "You *killed* Violet!"

The room seemed to tilt. Captain's grip on the flask faltered. He set it down on the table behind him.

"How do you know that?" He asked, voice quivering.

"It doesn't matter! What happened to 'no secrets'?" Joan cried, her voice brittle and raw.

Captain swallowed, his eyes narrowing. "Maybe I should ask the same question. You stopped drinking Bathory and didn't tell me."

Joan flinched. "At least I didn't kill an innocent woman."

Captain sat down on the edge of the table, rubbing his hands over his knees, trying to steady his breath.

Innocent...Innocent...

"You knew what you were marrying, Joan. Killing Violet wasn't a secret. I told you from the beginning what my father did and I thought I made it pretty clear that I do the same. I thought you understood. I thought you accepted me anyway."

He crouched beside Joan again and took her hand. Her fingers were cold and stiff.

"We can move on from this, right?" Captain's voice softened, almost breaking.

Joan's lips parted, but only fractured sounds escaped. A broken woman fighting to reconcile.

"I can't," she whispered.

Joan's fingers were icy. That warm, tender love Captain missed so much was hidden, possibly extinguished. There was a chance he'd never see it again, hear it again, *feel* it again. He slowly rose to his feet, frightened like a child lost in the dark. His shadow spilled over her like smoke.

Still, no regrets. Violet deserved it. Damien is gone because of her.

He exhaled. "Fine."

Joan tried to push herself up, but her strength gave out. She sank back into the cushions.

Pathetic.

"We were gods together," Captain murmured.

Joan didn't respond. Her breathing came heavy and haggard and her jaw stayed open. A silent suffering that Captain would've once leaped to save her from.

Captain stood over her, watching her trembling form.

She can't leave. She'll stay here. There's still plenty of time for her to change her mind about me.

Captain glanced at the flask on the table, the deep red inside calling to him. He picked it up, popped it open, and sipped from it. The Bathory didn't burn his throat like it used to. The taste was flat and dull, even.

Yet he still felt the aches dissipate and his body regain strength. His fingers tightened around the flask until the metal squeaked. He took another sip, the blood red liquid cooling his chest. Finally, he set it back down.

"You still have a chance. Take what's left, and save your life," Captain said.

Joan didn't move. Every exhale sounded paper against

stone. The couch looked too big for her, as if it were swallowing her up.

Disgusted, Captain turned away and left the room.

If she comes to the right conclusion, we can salvage this. If not...

Well...Chase and Violet proved what I'm capable of.

RIPLEY FOUND SPARKS—STILL in his party attire minus the dragon hologram— sitting by the fountain with an earpiece. The young Webster trained his gun at the man's head.

"What are you planning to do with Captain?" Ripley asked.

Sparks tapped the earpiece and stared daggers at him, not devoid of some sympathy.

"Why should I tell you?" He asked.

That might as well be a confession.

"Because I'm trying to get out, and I don't want your business screwing up mine," Ripley said.

"You don't want to just leave. You would've already done it."

Ripley stiffened. His grip on the gun tightened, his finger a hair's breadth away from pulling the trigger.

"It's because of Joan, isn't it?" Sparks asked.

Ripley's heart thundered in his ears and cold sweat trickled down the bridge of his scarred nose. Before he could answer, Sparks stood up. He was a looming, dark shadow. Far beyond the skinny, pathetic man that dragged a bagful of guns into Captain's office.

Ripley lowered his gun, but only a little bit. Sparks wasn't trying to intimidate him, but he was succeeding anyway.

"Listen," Sparks whispered.

"What?" Ripley asked.

"*Listen*," Sparks repeated, touching his ear.

Ripley listened. He also surveyed the block. He took in the buildings and the sidewalks and then discovered what he was listening for.

Nothing.

Primitus looked abandoned. There were no lights in the windows. None of the shops were open. Even *The Glass House* was shuttered. There was no one outside like there usually was, even that late at night. It was like a ghost town.

"I can help you get away, *and* Joan. But in order to do that, *you* need to help *me*," Sparks said.

"What do I need to do?" Ripley asked.

Sparks reached into his tunic and took something out. Ripley squinted at it, confused at first. Then, his eyes lit up.

"Do you know what this is?" Sparks asked.

"Yes," Ripley breathed. "You managed to get *that*?"

"It's not hard when Captain isn't around. Now I'll tell you *your* part. If you're still in, of course."

There was a countdown, set by Sparks. As if Ripley could hear it ticking, he knew he had no choice. He had to help Sparks.

Consequences be damned.

A HOLOGRAM of one of the border cops in Glass materialized atop Sylar's desk where the elite sat lazily, squeezing a stress ball. Sae was sitting on his desk too, swinging his legs out.

"Yes?" Sylar asked in a long hiss.

"We may have a problem," the cop replied. "We've got a massive turnout of people crossing the border to Central. I recognize some of them from Primitus."

Sylar raised his eyebrows and his hand holding the ball stopped squeezing.

"I see," he replied coldly.

"Wouldn't this be cause for concern?"

"Um, *yes*. An *entire* section of Glass up and left. *I'd* say that's cause for concern."

"What do you want us to do?"

Sylar resumed squeezing his stress ball. "Have some men watch Primitus *closely*, and report back to me anything weird they see. *Anything at all.* Captain is there with his people and plan on meeting with major crime families. We need to see where this goes."

Sylar glanced over at Sae, who smiled and waved back at him. Sylar's frown unrolled into a grin.

"And find out what motivated these people to leave."

PART FOUR

CAPTAIN

"V, OPEN MY CLOSET."

"As you wish, Daniel," chimed his home computer.

Captain's closet door slid open and the white light inside switched on, spotlighting his long, luxurious line of suits and outfits, most of which he'd never worn.

"V..."

"Yes, Daniel?"

Captain was still for a moment. The quiet was somber. Normally at this time, Captain would hear Joan cooking in the other room or remarking about his clothes.

"Call me Captain," he said.

"As you wish, Captain."

Captain ran his hand through the suits until he stopped at one he liked. One that felt fitting for the day and the occasion. A dark gray suit with matching pants and a black button-up shirt underneath. Forever, he had strutted around wearing white. Today was a different day. He peered in the mirror hung up on the wall beside the closet, smoothing his hands down the suit and tilting his head side to side to unwind his neck muscles. He took a thin flask full of

Bathory from the table beside the bed and slipped it into the breast pocket of his suit. Next, he browsed his lineup of pistols until he came across one of the guns that Sparks gave him when he first showed up in his office. A PSA Rock 59 spray painted in red and white.

Feels fitting to finish Sparks off with it.

He slipped the gun in his holster, sheathed a knife in his belt, and made for the door.

This is it.

————

Captain passed by Joan who was asleep on the couch, the Bathory flask he had left on the table still untouched. He emerged outside, the morning sky brush-stroked by orange veins threatened by incoming clouds. Standing near the fountain waiting for Captain were Trevor, Ripley, Sparks...

Where's Benji?

"Where's Benji?" Captain asked as he caught up.

The three of them glanced at each other, their faces grim.

"We don't know. We tried checking his room, but he wasn't there," Trevor explained.

"Well, what about one of the restaurants? Maybe he..."

"Captain, everything is closed," Ripley said.

Captain jerked his head around, a creeping uneasiness chewing away at him. He looked for people. He looked for an open business. He looked for *anything* moving.

There was nothing. Only silence cooled by the early morning wind. Captain's hair blew in his face.

"Where's Joan?" Ripley asked.

Captain didn't face him. Instead, he kept searching for someone with answers.

"She's sick," he said.

"Sick how?"

Captain spun around to glare at his associate. "I said she's sick! Don't worry about it!"

He stomped up to Sparks and his hand went for his throat, pulling the scrawny man inches from his face.

"*What did you do?*" He growled.

Sparks stared at him without speaking.

Captain shook him, as if answers would tumble out of him. "Where's everyone else? What happened here?" He shrieked.

"Captain..." Trevor started.

"Hold on!" Captain barked at Trevor, then turned back to Sparks. "So, what did you do, Sparks? Tell me or you're done," Captain said.

"Captain! It's the Purpletells," Trevor said.

Captain saw them, led by Leon, coming out of an electric limo parked right by the fountain. The driver stayed inside.

"Sweet! Looks like we're the first to show up!" Leon crowed.

Captain let go of Sparks, who smirked and whispered. "I'm not done *yet*."

"Yo, why does it look so *empty* around here? I thought *some* losers still lived here," Leon said.

"I don't know," Captain replied before he could think of a lie.

Leon frowned. "You really have no idea?"

Captain's next words were blasted out by a horn shearing through the wind as another limo pulled up close to Leon's. This time, the Jacks filed out.

With them was Chase.

No, not Chase. Wild.

"Sup, bitches!" Royal exclaimed with his arms outspread, cocooned in a furry pink coat.

"Well, well," Ace said, snapping his cane down on the ground when he stopped. "Check it out, boys. It's the Purpletells." He turned to Captain. "What did you promise *them*?"

"I—uh—," Captain stuttered.

"We just want space to store our product, ya think that was too much to ask?" Leon asked Ace.

"That depends on if *we* get this street," Ace said.

Leon faced Captain. "What did you offer them?"

"*Stop* for a second! I need to figure something out!" Captain motioned to Trevor. "Hold them back for me, will you *please*?"

Trevor, along with a reluctant Ripley, stood between the gangs and Captain, and Captain stepped away to speed dial Benji's number. The first ring didn't even finish before a disembodied voice came on.

"The person you are trying to reach has your number on a blocked list. Goodbye."

Benji!

The insults and the arguing between the Purpletells and the Jacks grew louder behind Captain as he stood dumbfounded and listless.

Amon was at the party. What if...what if...?

Next to show up was Eli, accompanied by a set of armed bodyguards wearing masks with spray painted skulls and cracked hearts.

"Hello, Mr. Sparks. Good to see you again so soon," Eli said, adjusting his tie.

Sparks slightly bowed. "Likewise," he said, his tone warm.

Captain took Trevor's shoulder and lifted his face up to his ear. "What am I supposed to do when Amon shows up?"

"He won't get what he *really* wants then. I see that as a win," Trevor whispered.

"And if he was the one responsible for Benji's disappearance?" Captain asked.

Trevor frowned but didn't say more as a fleet of motorcycles roared up to the fountain, led by Elsa, the leader of another budding group, the Poker's Many Faces. Captain had never negotiated with her; never even *thought* to talk to her. The group wasn't even assembled as well as the Purpletells yet.

"Wow," Elsa removed the shades she had on. "This place looks deader than usual," she remarked as she slid off her bike.

"Elsa Routerman?" Captain exclaimed.

"Oh, hi! Yeah, I didn't give a heads-up I was coming. Honestly, I thought Royal was gonna do that *for* me," Elsa said.

"Right, because I was *totally* going to roll out the red carpet for *you*," Royal said.

Captain wasn't engaged anymore the second after he said Elsa's name. He pushed his feet up, trying to see past everyone to catch sight of Amon once he arrived. Still no sign of him. Instead, the Delanos arrived, with Alex leading his pack. He was young, handsome, wore his studded green jacket with pride, but at the base of his neck was a scar where the speaking chip would be. Ace had told Captain about it before he visited the Garks. Seeing it in person, however, was doubly disturbing.

"Captain. It is good to finally. Meet you..." Alex droned.

"Yeah, yeah, don't strain yourself. It could overheat on you," Captain warned. He had heard less-than-pleasant stories of people attempting to use their own versions of speaking chips with sometimes graphic results.

"Amon is here!"

Amon's voice struck lightning through Captain's heart. He and a group of his men were standing by the fountain, no car in sight. Amon had a cigarette planted between his teeth, his eyes teasing and his lips twisted in a deceptive grin.

"How did you...get here?" Captain asked.

"Amon finds his ways."

"Like you find ways to break promises?"

A symphony of *oohs* spread through the gangs. A few people standing closest to Amon backed up.

Amon forced a half-hearted guffaw. "What do you mean?"

"You were there at the party last night, and so was Benji. What did you do to Benji?" Captain demanded, voice low.

"Amon did nothing! Amon never broke promises!"

His face changed when something dawned on him.

"Wait a minute. Where *is Chi no Akuma?*"

His eyes weren't lying. He really didn't know.

"That's what I was asking *you!*" Captain cried.

"Maybe the party last night was too much for the little man," Eli said.

If it wasn't Amon...if it wasn't Sparks...then WHAT...

Captain's last words to Benji were...

Oh...

A dark pain spasmed through his chest as something squeezed his heart and didn't let go.

"No deal then," Amon said.

"Excuse me?"

"Amon said *no deal*. If you can't even keep track of your

men, how can Amon trust you to manage Amon's territories? It's not worth it. Not even for Primitus."

No no NO.

"Wait! Maybe I can find Benji. We can...!"

"Name your price, darlin', and I'll *double* it and take Primitus off your hands," Elsa said, stepping forward.

"Why do you want this place so badly?" Ace said.

Elsa rolled her eyes. "Oh gee, I don't know, ex! Maybe it's because we want to have some of what *you* have too! Sharing a little bit of the pie won't hurt you, I promise!"

"Enough!" Captain roared, stomping his foot.

Captain spotted Eli from the corner of his eye looking around as if worried people were hiding somewhere and were going to shoot them all down.

"I will name my price. But Elsa has squandered her chance already," Captain said.

She's barely a gang anyway, and she has nothing to offer except money that probably won't be enough.

"*What?*" Elsa exclaimed.

"Wait. Hold on," Alex stuttered. He drew closer, squinting. Captain followed his gaze. It ended at Sparks.

"I know. Him," Alex said.

Wait, what...?

"You know *him?*" Captain gasped, his heart blasting out his ears.

"He was on our. Security camera. Footage! He. Stole. Weapons from. Us!" Alex bleated.

The guns. The gift...

No!

Captain threw himself at Sparks and forced him to his knees with his grip on the back of his neck. He trained his gun on his head.

"You set me up! Is this what you were talking about last night? Is this what your plan was?"

"Hey, that gun is *mine!*" One of Alex's associates pointed at Captain. "That's *my* paint job!"

"Captain! Are you. Blaming. Your associate?" Alex huffed.

"Alex, careful! Your chip!"

Alex's associate was right. The skin around his scar was turning a bright red.

"I didn't have him do it! He did it *before* he was part of my crew!" Captain pleaded.

This isn't happening...this isn't happening!

"Seriously, bro?" Leon questioned.

"So. Let me get this straight. You had our guns. Stolen. And now you want to negotiate. With me?" Alex whimpered. Tears filled his eyes. "All I. Wanted. Was something better. For my voice. I would rather. Deal with. This chip's limits. Then buy from you."

"No! This is for our future!" Captain cried, driving the barrel of the gun further in Sparks's head. Sparks himself stayed silent, head bowed.

Captain knew he looked insane, and all it took was one move by Sparks. How many more moves had he made? How many more did he have left?

"That's not all," Ripley spoke up.

Captain turned and saw Ripley remove something from his pocket and hold it up.

Is that...? Is that...?!

Dangling from Ripley's hand was Chase's black and white pearl necklace.

Ripley's voice rattled as he dropped the truth. "Captain killed Chase."

———

WILD

The rain. The alley. The body.

It all came rushing back to Wild and smacking him like a wave in a virtual beach. He heard his own screams again when he wept over his brother's body.

Wild, along with the rest of the Jacks, stepped back as if the necklace was a crucifix and they were vampires.

Ace managed to find his voice. "How do we know that *you* didn't kill him and are using that to frame your leader?"

"If I killed him, I would've never given this to you," Ripley answered, and he tossed the necklace towards Wild, who reached up and caught it midair. Tears were already spilling from his eyes as he held the necklace close with both hands.

Holy shit. Sparks was right.

CAPTAIN FOUGHT to stay on his feet. His mind was reeling, pulling dozens of memories from the past couple of days, all interconnected, entangled, and damning. Almost nothing that had happened in the last couple days would've happened if he hadn't let Sparks in in the first place.

He wanted to shoot Sparks in the head. He wanted to get to the nursing home and kill Sparks's father, finishing what he started.

The problem was that no one was mad at Sparks. They were mad at *him*. His own *team* was against him, including Joan.

With an inhuman cry, Wild unholstered his own gun and pointed it at Captain, but Ace and one of the other Jacks shot their arms up and held him back.

"Let me kill him! *Let me kill him!*"

"Well, hey, now that the Jacks hate you and obviously won't negotiate, maybe reconsider your decision from earlier?" Elsa said.

Captain wanted to say so much but nothing came.

Ace pointed at Elsa. "I'll take this place by force if I

have to! Captain doesn't deserve this place and neither do *you*."

Elsa reached for the twin pistols underneath her fur coat. "Your move, babe."

"Not what Amon expected," Amon whistled.

"I can't in good conscience do business with you, Mr. Kostov," Eli bemoaned. "I thought I was finally seeing some of your father's strength in you. But this," Eli gestured to Captain and Sparks. "This isn't strength."

Captain's hands shook, his ears burned, and his teeth were ground together so hard they hurt. Enraged tears gushed. He switched the safety off on his gun.

"You're *wrong*."

Louder than he intended. Not that he cared at this point.

"I'm *better* than my father. I *have* to be! We *all* have to be! If we can't get along and work together, then Sylar will *always* have his boot on our necks, and it'll be like that *forever* unless *we* do *something* to change it!"

"You killed Chase, how is that 'working together'?" Leon asked.

Through stinging tears, Captain's answer spilled out, having been locked up for a long time.

"Because *destroying* something is the only way to climb to the top! The *only* way to *win*! Building something is a joke as long as men like Sylar exist to break it! So I'll *break* the rules over and over again to change this city piece by piece if I have to, and I'll *rip* apart the old to make something new—something *better*—to create a brighter future! For *all* of us! Whether you're with me or not!"

Captain looked down at Sparks, his gun still pressed against his head.

"Next, I kill *him*," Captain glanced at Eli. "*That's* strength."

One...two...

"Wait," Sparks grunted. He looked up, the green of his eyes glitching to reveal dark brown.

"My real name is Arbor Ira. My uncle is Sylar Han."

———

A shockwave shredded through the crowd, as everyone stared aghast at Sparks. They were all gathered around Captain, his gun trained on a man who was family to the most powerful person in the world, out in the open. Hovering nearby out of sight of everyone was a drone, capturing everything.

———

CAPTAIN

"Mr. Kostov, put the gun down. Now," Eli quietly urged, raising his hand at Captain.

Captain wanted to insist that Sparks was lying, but even he knew the truth. It was no wonder to him now why Sparks looked familiar. He saw the resemblance now. Those dark almond-shaped eyes that Sylar had.

Captain's first thought was to do as Eli said, but then he noticed a drone floating close by, and his next thought gave him peace.

"We're all dead at this point anyway," he said, and he tightened his grip on his gun again.

"*No!*" Alex and Eli both cried.

Then the air was ripped apart by gunfire.

76
SYLAR

IN THE DRONE footage captured over Primitus, Captain was standing over a man on his knees with a gun drilled into the back of his head. Surrounding Captain was his own gang and almost every other major gang in Glass, even a few new ones.

"Computer, zoom in on the image," Sylar requested, stroking his chin.

The image crept up closer to Captain and the man on his knees. Sylar leaned forward and blinked.

Oh, that's...Arbor.

Standing beside him watching the image too was Ratchet, his fingers drumming the hilt of his katana.

"I thought you killed him," he said.

"So did I," Sylar replied through a smile.

He keyed in a number on his desk panel, and the image was replaced by a hologram of a police captain waiting for orders.

"Sir," he said.

"Sightseeing is over. Take every man you can and break

up what's happening. Shoot anyone who tries to resist you," Sylar ordered.

"Anyone?"

"Anyone. *Now.*"

"Yes, sir."

The hologram vanished and Sylar was forced to wait.

"Sylar, look," Ratchet said, pointing out the window behind Sylar's desk. Sylar stood up and followed Ratchet's gaze, where Primitus was supposed to be.

There was smoke.

What's happening down there? Is this Captain's fault? Arbor's?

Sylar considered himself someone who always had his ducks in a row. Someone who always knew what to do and how to make plans within plans. He had spent hundreds of years learning how to do this.

This was different. He didn't see this coming, and he wasn't sure how he was going to handle it in a way that wouldn't put a crack in Glass. Family had always been a difficult situation to resolve.

His earpiece chimed. "We're entering Primitus now, sir," said the voice on the other end.

"Crush them. By any means necessary."

WHEN THE SHOOTING STARTED, Ripley was too shocked to react at first. Something flashed in front of him and his chest was soaked in what he imagined was blood. Hopefully not his. Looking down, he saw the bloodstains on his shirt. He braced himself for the pain that would follow after getting shot.

Except it never came. The blood wasn't his.

Then he saw Trevor. He saw his brother lying on the ground with a bullet wound in his stomach.

The shooting around him didn't matter. He sank to the ground and snatched Trevor's hand.

"No," he wept.

Trevor squeezed Ripley's hand and forced his voice through wet coughs.

"I did suggest you leave before this," he wheezed.

"I can't leave you," Ripley replied, his cheeks burning.

"I wasn't going to go with you anyway. At least...I got to protect you. Now go or I failed," Trevor begged.

"Trevor—."

"Go!" Trevor cried, shoving Ripley away.

Ripley scrambled up, and he noticed that most of the shooting had already stopped. Gangsters were still standing around with their guns out, looking lost, wondering what to do. He recognized some of the people dead on the ground, like Leon and Alex. The flesh on Alex's neck where the scar used to be was opened up, revealing a blackened, smoldering chip. He didn't see Amon or Elsa or Eli. Captain and Sparks were gone. None of the Jacks were among the dead.

People started shooting again, screaming and shouting this time, some of them outraged over the death of their leaders. Ripley glanced back at Trevor one last time, whose eyes were gazing up at the sky unseeing.

On his face, a permanent smile.

Lips quivering, eyes watering, Ripley turned and ran, thinking at first to get out of Primitus as quickly as possible. He could get on a train and head back to the Web, never to set foot in Glass ever again. He'll get what he wanted, thanks to Trevor.

Joan.

Ripley didn't want to just leave her.

I have to get Joan out of here too.

CAPTAIN

WHERE'S SPARKS?

Captain had managed to crawl away just before the shooting stopped. He had no idea who was dead or alive. What he *did* notice was that Sparks was missing from the fray. Behind him, the gunfire died down, reduced to occasional shots and anguished cries. A car's engine blared to life, followed by a gunshot and shattering glass.

Where's Sparks?

Captain thrusted Bathory down his throat. Red, glowing liquid dribbled down his chin as he smacked his mouth to collect as much as possible. The bleeding in his shoulder, thanks to a bullet when the shootout started, receded and the pain numbed. He was able to sprint easier now, moving in a beeline towards his house.

I can grab Joan and get out of here! Don't look for Sparks! Don't do another stupid thing. Don't...

Captain stopped when he noticed his front door was open.

His hands quaked as he raised his gun, taking a cautious step through the doorway and into the living room.

Joan.

Ripley was at the couch, trying to help Joan up. She looked better than before but still too weak to stand on her own.

What's this?

"That's far enough, Ripley," Captain announced, targeting Ripley's head.

Ripley turned to face him, surprised. When Joan peered at him, all that was there was fear and scorn.

"Daniel, just let us go," she said.

Needles pricked the back of Captain's throat and he shook his head. "I can't do that." He redirected his attention back to Ripley.

"You betrayed me. You took that necklace from my room," he whispered, tears pooling in his eyes.

Ripley straightened. "*I* wasn't the one who took it."

Captain's heart cratered. "You helped Sparks?"

Ripley turned grim but determined. He didn't say anything. Captain kept his aim on the young man but looked at Joan.

"And you. I suppose *you* buddied up with Sparks too. I saw you two dancing last night. Did you know he was going to do this?"

Joan's chin sunk, her answer obvious like Ripley's. Captain didn't know if it was possible he could feel more pain and heartache. What more could possibly happen now that could break him any further?

"Let them go, Captain."

Captain already knew who was behind him. Turning around, he saw Sparks standing in the doorway, a silent dark statue blocking his way to freedom.

"You..."

The rage couldn't be contained anymore. A bullet from

Captain's gun sailed towards Sparks. He shot his arm up to catch it. It smacked against the back of his hand with a loud *twang* and bounced off, rolling in a half circle on the floor before stopping.

Bewildered, Captain stumbled back.

"How?" He breathed.

The skin of Sparks's hand deteriorated away like a fading hologram, revealing dark metal and skinny android fingers.

"Get out of here," Sparks told Ripley and Joan.

"No!"

Captain's protests didn't make a difference. He reached out attempting to grab Joan's arm as she and Ripley ran past him, but Ripley was able to shove him back, and the two made it out the doorway and around the corner. Captain twisted his head around to face his enemy.

"You took *everything* from me!"

Captain moved towards Sparks and fired several more rounds at him, which Sparks blocked with his arm. One bullet caught Sparks's suit, the impact enough to force him back, but the sound it made tipped Captain off to what he needed to know.

Of course he's wearing a bulletproof vest. He knew something might go down.

Captain's gun was empty, but he seized the opportunity he had to retrieve his Bathory flask from his suit pocket and take a swig. Renewed strength radiated through him, and he didn't waste a second. He lunged towards the man, and shot his arm forward to deliver a hard gut punch. Sparks folded and was launched backwards by inhuman strength against the wall with a pained gasp.

Captain was too quick though for Sparks to recover and counter his next attack. He ran after him and lifted Sparks off his feet with his brief Bathory-given strength using one hand. He dragged Sparks along the wall and, with a cry, raised his body with both hands and slammed him down on the floor. Shaking the impact off with alarming speed, Sparks rolled back onto his feet and delivered a kick to Captain's chin. He felt his feet leave the floor and his head struck the ground. White exploded in front of his vision and his ears rang. When he lifted his head to see Sparks, there was no one there.

Time to finish this.

THE FIRST SHOT that kicked off the shootout belonged to Wild.

He was able to wrench his hand out of Ace's grip, but his hand slipped, the gun went up, and his finger pulled the trigger. The bullet launched and didn't hit anyone, but the next bullet—fired by Amon—hit Captain's shoulder.

Wild was crouched behind the fountain with his friends nearby huddled together.

Of all the people who'd give me answers...someone from Sylar's family...

"Wild, let's go!" Ace cried.

"You guys go on ahead!" Wild replied.

Ace reached out to pull him over, but Wild recoiled and shook his head. "I'm staying."

There was the loud sound of an engine. Through the smoke, Wild saw the outlines of what he, as well as everyone else, feared most.

Large black trucks came barreling into Primitus and swerved around with the side doors facing everyone. They slid open, revealing dozens of police dressed in riot gear that glowed red and blue patterns. An orchestra of boots hit the ground running and the red and blue lit up the street and created an invasive swarm.

The last man to step off the truck was the captain, wearing a tactical jacket that reached below the waist. The emblem of Glass' law enforcement agency glowed on his chest. On his head was a helmet with a built-in HUD that flashed holograms in his view to assess the situation.

"Take them!" He barked.

In compliance, the riot police lifted their shields and moved in sync with each other to form a crude circle around the showdown, making sure to block all the cars. One officer fired through a car window to stop a Delano bodyguard from escaping.

Wild looked to Ace again. "Don't worry about me!"

Ace hesitated at first, but grimly nodded.

"Good luck!" He cried and rejoined the others.

Wild could see the other Jacks shouting at him, but he couldn't hear them over the gunfire and screams.

"I'll survive," Wild thought aloud. He scrambled to his feet and took off.

Hopefully Captain hasn't wandered off too far.

CAPTAIN

CAPTAIN SLID a new mag into his gun and stood ready as the door to the garage attached to the house slid open. The garage itself was a masterpiece only his father and his people were capable of building. Pale white light that matched the floor covered the entire ceiling and reflected off of the sleek, stainless steel of the rows of cars, all of which belonged to Captain's father once upon a time. Each car was the product of a different era, but was made out of the same steel and intended to look authentic, ranging from steam powered cars to the first electric vehicles and beyond.

Captain slowly entered, startled at first by the movement of hover drones that were floating from car to car doing the routine checkups they were programmed to do. His father had never shut them down, so they slaved away in an eternal cycle. Despite the hissing sounds they made as they cleaned and checked the insides of the vehicles, the room was still dangerously quiet. Captain remembered when it used to bustle with activity. He'd visit it with his father once in a while, back when dozens of people were inside wielding tools and playing with welding torches. It was a safe haven for the cars of criminals on good terms with Lazarus. Holographic schematics and diagnostic read-outs floating in midair being manipulated by people's finger-tips were also common at that time.

Now it was like a museum with no owner.

Captain wanted to say something, seeing if it might make Sparks move and give away his position. Every step he took triggered a soft echo.

Then he heard a bullet flying, suppressed by a silencer. Captain saw the headlight of a car directly to his right erupt. With a heart in danger of rupturing out of his chest, Captain returned fire twice in the direction that the bullet came from and backed up to toss himself behind the car. With his cover, he checked his mag and counted the number of bullets left.

Eight.

"I wasn't sure at first, but I think you and I would've made a good team," Sparks's voice echoed.

Captain clicked the mag back in and stayed put, listening closely for any sounds that might tip off what Sparks was doing.

"After everything you've done to me?" Captain called back.

"*You* did a lot of that. Not me."

Captain lowered himself with his belly on the floor to peer under the car. He saw part of Sparks's back behind the car across from him. Slowly, he lined his sight up with his target and fired.

He missed. The bullet just barely grazed Sparks's jacket. With a grunt, Sparks yanked himself up. Captain leaped up too, saw Sparks, and fired again. Another miss, and he ducked just in time to hear Sparks's gun go off too.

BANG.

His opponent's bullet missed him and cracked the glass of the car door behind Captain. At that point, Captain was on the move again, creeping alongside his car and jumping up to surprise Sparks with two shots this time. He ducked before he could see where his shots landed and heard two bullets explode and whiz overhead.

Then he heard clicking.

He's out!

Captain double checked his mag, counting the last four he had, then recounted.

I'm going to beat him.

He set his sights on the car directly across from him on the opposite side of the garage.

Need a better angle.

He sucked in three rapid breaths, then sprinted for the car, craning his neck to get a good look at Sparks. He opened fire at Sparks's car. Two shots rang through the air. One struck glass, the other kissed flesh.

Captain ducked behind the car he had run for and chuckled when he heard Sparks grunt in pain.

Hit! I hit him!

"Come on, Sparks. You've won. You've taken everything from me. Take the win and die with honor," Captain chided.

"I haven't won yet," was the reply.

Captain heard broken glass crunching and the whirring of the hover drones. Sparks was on the move. The next time Sparks spoke, his voice boomed through the room.

"I don't win until Sylar is dead."

Captain heard a sound like metal buckling and he felt the car he was using for cover jerk back.

He scrambled up and his eyes bulged when he saw the car getting yanked along by a cable extended from Sparks's metal arm. The cable whirled as it detached from the car and a scarlet laser exploded from Sparks's artificial wrist. With a cry, Captain pitched himself out of the path of the laser and frantically crawled behind the cover of another car, though he knew now it did him little good. He needed to stop the laser somehow.

An idea came. "V, activate the sprinkler system!"

"Activating sprinkler systems," V's disembodied voice answered.

There was a hiss as the sprinklers in the ceiling came on and showered the room. Water drenched Captain from head to toe but he was giddy now that he knew Sparks couldn't use his laser without risking his own life.

Only two bullets left.

"Why do you want Sylar dead?" Captain asked, deciding to make time as he assessed his next move.

"Killing him will destroy this system we're all under."

Captain couldn't tell where Sparks was. His voice seemed to bounce everywhere. He checked both sides of him and began inching his way along the car to get a view around the other side.

Cripple the criminal underworld and you force Sylar's hand, making him a more vulnerable target. Not gonna lie, that's smart.

"Why destroy *my* empire to get to him?" Captain asked.

"Because your 'empire' wasn't an empire yet. It was easier for me to blend in with you than it would've been with an empire that's stronger and has been around longer," Sparks confessed. "So many others are loyal to Sylar. You clearly are not."

Captain edged closer to the headlight of the car and peered around the corner. He didn't see Sparks. His heart began quickening.

I need to get him talking again.

"And you think *you're* the one who can kill Sylar?" Captain called.

"I think so," Sparks replied. Captain strained to hear where the voice was coming from, frustrated he couldn't pinpoint the source.

Dammit, Sparks, where are you?

Captain almost said something again to get Sparks talking more, but Sparks did that for him.

"I feel somewhat responsible for the way you turned out."

Captain's pulse accelerated when he heard tires swishing and the creaking of metal.

He's trying to escape!

Captain shot up to get a better look...

And screamed when he saw a car flying straight towards him.

He ducked and rolled out of the way, water splashing his face and singeing his eyes. The sound of shattering glass and twisted metal grated against his ears. One disadvantage to activating the sprinklers was that there was no way at this point that he would be able to mask where he was going. Water spattered as he crawled to another car.

Did he just...throw that?!

Sparks's prosthetic arm was his best weapon. Captain needed to disable it somehow.

Wait, are those footsteps?

Sure enough, there were wet, swift footsteps thundering closer and closer.

Captain leaped up and fired in the direction of the steps. The bullet thwacked against metal and ricocheted to the floor. Sparks had his artificial arm crossed in front of his chest already just in case.

Sparks caught up to Captain just as he was running around the car to escape. He swung his steel fist in an arc towards Captain's face.

Captain dipped out of the arm's path and came back up with his dagger in hand, grateful he was wearing it. He slashed away at Sparks's chest, managing to shear off a thin layer of flesh.

Adrenaline exploded through Captain and he lunged at his enemy again and Sparks parried it with his arm this time. Captain kept the blade up against the arm, forcing them both across the flooded floor. With another idea, Captain skimmed his dagger across Sparks's arm and snatched it with his other hand, pulling himself forward so he could smash his elbow into Sparks's face. Sparks barely seemed phased, but Captain kept his grip on the arm and delivered two more elbow shots to Sparks's throat, then used his other hand to retrieve his gun and aim it at Sparks's face. Sparks used his free hand to grab Captain's wrist and force it up at the ceiling. The weapon exploded, and Captain's final bullet pierced the ceiling.

Oh no.

Captain struggled and struggled but even his grip on Sparks's arm had released. He tried desperately to regain control of the fight, but Sparks's face turned wildly triumphant. He still gripped Captain's wrist with the gun pointed up.

His metallic arm swung up. Captain's breath caught as red-hot pain detonated through his entire body. His feet were up in the air dangling helplessly. He looked down.

There it was. A long blade from Sparks's metal arm deep in his stomach. Tears of pain streamed down Captain's face and he fought to say something, but nothing except gurgling and sputtering came. Sparks retracted the blade, meaning another wave of pain through Captain's body. The syndicate leader collapsed in the water and blood, wheezing and gasping for breath.

Sparks, the victor, towered over him.

"*I* was the one who killed Angel. *I'm* the one who inspired you. I regret that," he said. "You, on the other hand, don't regret. That's why we wouldn't work together. You're just like Sylar."

Captain's mouth was filled with blood, preventing him from being able to get a final word in to his foe. He stared up at Sparks, his hate burning brighter than the pain that was slowly killing him. When he blinked, Sparks was gone, for the final time.

The flask...I still have the flask...

Captain's hand drifted to his suit pocket, his fingers shaking so hard it was nearly impossible to get to the flask. He unscrewed the lid and allowed the liquid to splash over his face and open mouth, brightening his face in red. The water from the sprinklers washed the red away. Already, Captain could feel the Bathory working slowly but effectively in his system, fixing what needed to be fixed. It wasn't perfect, but he was already feeling better than he did a moment ago.

A renewed confidence welled up in him, but hopelessness gripped him too.

He couldn't shake the thought of Joan's face when he saw her last, devoid of the love and affection she used to have for him.

He remembered the shock of finding out Benji had abandoned him.

Even if he got up, nothing would be the same.

I can fix this. I can recover. I'll find Sparks, I'll kill him, and Joan will understand. She'll forgive me.

Captain blinked again, and a new face appeared. Wild.

Seeing him, a low chuckle squeaked from Captain's mouth. It turned into a giggle, then an amused laugh, and then swerved into uncontrollable, bubbling laughter. It was getting hard to breathe.

Wild stared down at Captain, sickened by him. Then, to Captain's surprise, he too started laughing along with him. The two stayed there for a minute, laughing at each other, two minds fracturing together alone. Sprinkler water like rain continued pelting the ground. The drones were even on the ground now, fizzing out.

Finally, Wild raised his gun, pulled the trigger, and darkness dragged Captain under forever.

———

WILD

Wild wasn't laughing anymore. He wanted to crash to his knees and scream. Wanted to drown himself in the water on the floor and join Captain.

He gripped the black and white necklace that was around his neck now, feeling the beads along his thumb.

"No matter what humans achieve to stave off death, no one is safe from it forever."

You weren't, and neither am I. So I'll live as though I don't have eternity.

CAPTAIN'S OFFICE door slid open for Sparks. The fake water on the floor still roiled and swayed. The TV on the wall was still broken.

The white desk was empty. Everyone Sparks had met in the room were never going to be in it again.

He crossed the office to sit at Captain's old desk. He leaned forward once he was in the seat, feeling his hands on the desk as if he couldn't believe it was there. What else he felt was guilt.

On the desk was a laptop Captain left behind. He pulled it towards him and booted it up. It instantly opened a login screen. Sparks was able to get in after one try with the password.

Joan.

Obvious. Predictable. Sylar would've been able to guess it right away. He would've had a thing or two to say about it.

Finding what Sparks was looking for wasn't easy through the dozens of disorienting tabs Captain had left open and the extra security attached to certain files. Finally, Sparks found the blueprints for the SpeakWare chip.

Hang on, dad. I've almost got it.

Then the desk chimed, signaling that someone was trying to call via hologram. Sparks stared at the blinking blue light for a long minute before answering. At this point, most people knew he was alive. He didn't have to hide anymore.

A tall hologram of Sae sprouted up, his arms folded and his face stone-cold.

"I thought you might be here," he said.

Sparks blinked up at Sae. "Thank you for keeping quiet for me."

Sae shook his head. "Honestly, I don't know why I did that. Maybe I was feeling a little nostalgic. Don't know if I would help you again now."

"I understand," Sparks said, his voice aching.

"You're declaring war against Sylar, aren't you?" Sae asked.

Sparks nodded. "Yes."

Sae uncrossed his arms and sighed. "Remember when we used to read *Moby Dick* together?"

Sparks winced. "Yeah..."

"It's gotten me thinking. Maybe you're not the whale, like you think you are. Maybe you're Ahab. And you remember what happened to him?"

"That won't be me."

"I think it will. Don't ask me for any more favors. Sylar is family. Nothing will change that."

Sae's hologram winked out before Sparks could argue. He sat staring at the spot where the shimmering image used to be. A tear fell from the corner of his eye. An aching pain constricted his throat.

Trevor.

Damien.

Captain.

Violet.

Helping Ripley and Joan escape was the one thing over the last week he felt good about.

Sparks turned the chair around to face the window behind him and stare out at the City. Koa was on his way, and from there, they'd plan the next step.

Guilt can happen later.

Let's get to work.

The problem with the guilt was that there was a lot of it.

JOAN DIDN'T HEAR the announcement over the speaker when the next subway train pulled up. The news segment she had seen not even an hour ago was replaying in her ears, over and over again.

"Among the passed are Trevor Aguilar, Alex Delano, Leon Purpletell, Daniel Kostov..."

Daniel.

Though she tried reaching for some of that fondness she used to feel for him, it was impossible now to find it.

And yet...and yet...

Memories were forever. The wild ambition and unrelenting pursuit of meaning scratched and clawed at Captain's face all the time, preventing him from being there for Joan in the way that she wanted him to be. *Needed* him to be.

Sometimes though; sometimes he was there for her in ways no one else had been.

Ripley, standing beside her, glanced at her and gestured with his head towards the train doors. Joan nodded, and followed him onto the train. The doors whistled shut and they sat down, colliding their heads against the wall and staring up at the dingy ceiling, its purple neon lights coating them. As the train started moving, Joan expected at first to feel regret. She expected something to whisper in her ear, scolding her for leaving and incentivizing her somehow to stay.

Instead, there was nothing. She released a content sigh.

As the train took Ripley and Joan further away from Glass and carried them home, their scarred hands intertwined but they stayed staring ahead.

"I'm glad you're with me, Ripley," Joan said.

"My name isn't Ripley," was the reply.

Joan frowned at her friend, expecting an explanation. Ripley looked back, and told her his real name.

No secrets.

PRIMITUS WAS nothing more now than an empty shell.

A relic of past lives, past experiences, and forgotten history.

Once a community that held on even as Glass was raised around it—now spoiled by the bodies and the broken glass littering the street around its fountain. The whole street was blocked off by faceless police, and a train of armored men and women carried out everything from *The Time Capsule* while Sylar Han watched with pride, accompanied by Sae and Ratchet. Sae was excited to see if he could get his hands on any of the stuff being taken out of the shop, wondering if Sylar was going to add any of it to his library. On the other hand, he wondered where Sparks was now, what he was planning, and if there was any way he could stop him from killing the only man that took care of him.

The only man he could *remember* taking care of him anyway.

Ratchet was keen on hunting down Sparks and killing him as soon as Sylar allowed him to. As long as he was out there, he was a threat to his master. And to the Children of Glass.

To Sylar, the fall of Primitus and the deaths of many within the underworld wasn't a defeat dealt to him. It was hardly even an inconvenience. It was an opportunity. The kind he'd been hoping to have for a very long time. The coming weeks were ripe with potential.

Most valuables were taken out of Primitus that day. There was, however, one thing that remained. On the balcony of Captain's Primitus home, ignored by all, there was a green, untainted plant growing from one of Joan's pots.

ACKNOWLEDGMENTS

Of all the books I've envisioned, attempted to write, and never finished, this is somehow the one that made it. This book was made possible by pulling concepts from several unfinished projects and combining them, taking three years and six or seven drafts to complete it. That being said, there are a couple of people I must thank for making this possible. This book would not be what it is without them.

I'd like to thank Grandma Dana, Skyler F, Lauryn Gindl, and Cate Smotz for their amazing proofreading skills and their harsh truths. Sometimes those truths killed dialogue I thought was great or scenes I thought were dope. Little did I know at the time, cutting them was essential, even though it hurt.

I'd like to thank my father Lee for using his own experience in writing and publishing to help me along the way and lay out everything I need to do to put a book out in the world in a way I can understand and follow.

I'd like to thank Daniel Smotz and Blade Peterson for their support, belief in the story, and—from Dan—a killer book cover I ultimately didn't get to use but still deeply appreciate the gesture!

And finally, I'd like to thank my wife Kayleigh for reading every draft (which included reading multiple scenes over and over again), the ideas she contributed, the passion she had for Glass, and the ways she helped me make it so that the plot didn't burst into flames and die a horrible death. For her patience, her superpower to say 'no' when I needed to be told 'no', and for rushing to my aid when I thought one of my later drafts had been lost forever. I love you, adore you, and am honored that you are the near-future mother of my child. Oh, and Sylar and Sae exist because of you.

ABOUT THE AUTHOR

Forrest grew up here, there, everywhere, never seeming to stay in one place for too long. He is the host of *The Pancake King: Life and Marriage On the Spectrum*, a podcast and YouTube video series about his experiences on the autism spectrum. He spends his days working his 9-5, writing more books, watching *Star Wars*, and making content with his wife on their collaborative YouTube channel *VanZot Mediums*. He lives with his wife and incoming son.

Visit his blog at thepancakeking.substack.com

X x.com/TheZotteMan

instagram.com/thepancakeking95

youtube.com/@thepancakeking8065

tiktok.com/@thepancakeking1995